# RED BOX

# RED BOX

## HUNTING THE DRUG TRAFFICKERS

### WILL STRANG

Copyright © 2024 Will Strang
The moral right of the author has been asserted.

Apart from any fair dealing for the purposes of research or private study, or criticism or review, as permitted under the Copyright, Designs and Patents Act 1988, this publication may only be reproduced, stored or transmitted, in any form or by any means, with the prior permission in writing of the publishers, or in the case of reprographic reproduction in accordance with the terms of licences issued by the Copyright Licensing Agency. Enquiries concerning reproduction outside those terms should be sent to the publishers.

This is a work of fiction. Names, characters, businesses, places, events and incidents are either the products of the author's imagination or used in a fictitious manner. Any resemblance to actual persons, living or dead, or actual events is purely coincidental.

Troubador Publishing Ltd
Unit E2 Airfield Business Park,
Harrison Road, Market Harborough,
Leicestershire. LE16 7UL
Tel: 0116 2792299
Email: books@troubador.co.uk
Web: www.troubador.co.uk

ISBN 978 1805142 751

British Library Cataloguing in Publication Data.
A catalogue record for this book is available from the British Library.

Printed and bound in Great Britain by CMP UK
Typeset in 10.5pt Adobe Garamond Pro by Troubador Publishing Ltd, Leicester, UK

To everyone who has assisted me in my quest, particularly Emily, Carol, Sue, Paul and all at Troubador Publishing. Not forgetting Alfred, who, when I started the project, lay patiently at my feet and took me for walks when I needed a pause and time to think.

# 1

# CREATURES OF HABIT

The wind squalled against the window, gently rattling the sash in its frame. Outside was dark; the meek lights draped an orange cloak over the street and immediate buildings, and highlighted the dark corners, black crevices and sharp angular building-lines.

No-one moved – no walkers, no cyclists, no cars. It was late, nearing eleven o'clock midweek, and most sensible people were at home tucked up in their beds or watching late-night television. In the distance, however, the constant whir of the traffic on the main road, like a drowsy air con system, was occasionally interrupted by a loud motorcycle or a hurrying siren.

Richard Kenny peered out of the window and watched a thin, feral-looking cat pass silently along the line of parked cars, slide underneath the nearest one and leopard-crawl to a prime position beneath the still-warm engine to carefully observe the outside world. There it remained, silently looking, always alert but feeling warm and secure, very aware that any activity in the vehicle would provide plenty of notice to move to another warm and yet protected position.

The traffic lights covering the crossroads outside the window like sentinels monotonously changed their colours: red, amber, green and back again. Still no traffic. The bricks on the building opposite blossomed, the road brightened, and a small, dark car gently came into view towards the junction below the window. The lights were red. The car slowed and then stopped. Kenny leaned forwards slightly to watch more closely; he could see the car clearly now from above – dark roof, clean, apparently just the driver inside, no music.

The lights changed and the car shuffled on, out of view. Silence returned under the hue of the lights outside.

His mind wandered. *Where was the car going? What was the driver like? What would they have said if they'd known that their every movement for that brief twenty-second period was being carefully monitored? What would they have thought if they had known that a man had been looking out of the window above them for the past six and a half hours?* As the car moved out of view, he carefully leaned forward and looked up and down the road. No cars, no people. He then leant back in the chair and carefully scanned the house across the road; no signs of movement, no lights, no sounds – all was quiet. He could relax a little and allow his mind to wander. A cup of tea. He bent down to the side of the chair, picked up the metal Thermos, unscrewed the cup and the stopper, and poured himself a cup, then replaced the stopper and placed the sleek metal tube back in the same place. He savoured the cup of warming liquid; steam rose and he blew gently across the top before taking the first tentative sip. It was a sweet elixir. He glanced out of the window; still no activity. His mind wandered. A ciggy would go nicely. He dove his hand into his coat pocket, pulled out a tab and carefully lit it, ensuring that the light from the lighter and the glowing cigarette were obscured from the window. His anonymity and that of his lofty perch were vital.

After several cursory forays to the window, he sat back and contemplated his surroundings. The room was cold and dark, for which he was thankful. Warm rooms stupefied the brain, brought on a lack of alertness and hence sleep. Light, bright rooms highlighted any movement and shadows became instantly noticeable; dark, dreary rooms didn't attract attention and the contents became uninteresting. They had removed any possible light sources when they had moved in, unscrewing light bulbs, taping over switches to ensure they couldn't be used, and masking the windows that had no tactical importance.

The room was bare. It was about ten by five metres, on the first level of a two-storey house and therefore above street level, and strategically located at a minor yet busy crossroads. It had probably been a bedroom but hadn't been decorated for many years; some of the wall and ceiling plaster had fallen away from the lath onto the bare floorboards and the black outline around the edges, now exposed, showed where the carpet had originally been laid, positioned squarely in the middle of the room. There was no heating and it smelt damp, musty, unaired, dusty and – above all – dirty. It was, however, perfect.

There were three medium-sized Victorian sash windows that overlooked the street outside. The two nearest the outside corner of the house, and furthest from Kenny, were at right angles to each other. One overlooked the traffic lights and junction, whilst the other gave a view of the straight road beyond the junction towards the town centre. They had matt black paper taped to the frames. In the centre of the blackout sheets on each window, about a metre up from the floor, they had cut hinged square slots, which were temporarily taped closed. This would enable them to view the junction, if required, by opening the small slits and to close them when they were finished, ensuring the integrity of the observation point.

The third window, the same size and slightly up from the junction, was the one currently being used by Kenny. The top three-quarters of it had been blocked out to reduce the glare of the streetlights at night. The bottom quarter was clear glass and gave a good view of the house opposite and the street below. The paper had been carefully folded up to enable anyone using the room to drop the blackout completely and cover the remaining quarter of the window, thereby plunging the room back into complete darkness and protecting it from outside interference.

The room was empty of furniture apart from two wooden chairs, both eminently uncomfortable. The one used by Kenny was about one and a half metres back from the window and the other they had moved out of the way and up against the inside wall,

Kenny became aware of some movement outside. He leaned forward slightly and saw a middle-aged man walking stiffly, past the house, on the other side of the road. He reached a parking limit post and held on grimly, embracing it with both arms before looking up, assessing the distance to his next safe refuge – a lamppost – before launching himself towards it, grasping it, steadying himself and going through the same routine again. *Another pisshead,* Kenny thought. *He'll be in shit-street when he gets home.* He chuckled knowingly.

He looked up. All quiet in the house. All good. Another thirty minutes and they could call it a day. He took a sip of his tea – sugary, now a little tepid – and took a long drag of his cigarette, being careful to shield the glow from the window.

He looked around again and paused over the equipment: camera on a tripod, fixed on the front door of the house; a pair of binoculars – *All the better to see you with,* he thought; a log sheet with the day's movements, in duplicate, of course; odds and sods – extra batteries for the camera, extra batteries for the radio, more log sheets, extra tape and extra clothing – all stashed in a bag in the corner; and the bottles in case someone wanted a piss, always in the corner and removed after every day. Hygiene.

In the half light, a dark mound in the middle of the room stirred.

A strained and muffled, "You alright?" came from that direction, in a deep and yet contented voice, as if the person was speaking out of the corner of his mouth.

"Yep, all quiet," he hissed in response.

The lump moved to one side. Tom Franks, the other person in the room, normally tall and stocky, was lying uncomfortably on the floorboards, half in a sleeping bag and half out. In his right ear was an earpiece that connected to a radio that enabled him to monitor comms in the outside world.

"Your end?" Kenny whispered.

"No, nothing – usual shit. Coming up for a changeover." was the response, Kenny looked at his watch. It was eleven o'clock; shifts would be changing over, teams would be returning, others would be briefing. There would be fewer people on the street – less risk to the baddies.

He leant down and glanced at the house across the street; still no movement.

It was an elegant brick-and-slate, three-storey, late-Victorian terrace. To one side was a large blue wooden front door, reached by a flight of steps that ran up from the street to a large square granite doorstep. A small separate gate at pavement level gave access to some more steps that curved around and down, beneath the main steps, to a basement door that was below ground level. To the left of the main door was a large window, and a further two windows on each of the floors above. Three similar houses ran off to the right towards the junction, and to the left, they continued up the street. Kenny knew that at the rear of the house, there was a small, high-walled evergreen but overgrown garden, and a rear gate that gave access to an alley that ran behind all the houses in the block. The rear gate was covered in ivy and had not been used for many years. In their initial recce, he had established that the only access to the house was indeed the door that he could see.

As if on cue, the front door opened slightly and a young man peered out through the gap before poking his head through more fully to look up and down the street.

"Standby," Kenny said in a voice loud enough for Franks to hear but quiet, low-key and authoritative.

He pushed the camera button and it whirred off four or five shots of the front door and the man with his head poking out. Franks was up and moving towards Kenny, discarding his bag as he went. He picked up the log and pen:

22:59hrs. Subject known as WARDEN to front door. Door opened slightly. Subject looked out left and right and then returned inside - 5 seconds. 4 shots.

"OK, got it," he confirmed. "I wasn't asleep, you know, just daydreaming." He wiped his eyes and signed off the entry in the log by the light from the streetlamps outside.

Again, all was quiet. The drunk had long since gone, and had, apparently, arrived home safely.

"Oops, here we go," Kenny whispered. "Door open, subject Warden looking out again, up and down the street, and then out onto the doorstep, closing door quietly, looking up and down. Dark clothing, hoodie, dark trainers, moving down steps to the pavement." Kenny spoke as he saw; he knew that his mate would be writing his very words onto the log.

"He's hovering." He watched as Warden stood, quietly scanning the immediate area.

"Down the steps, onto pavement, looking up and down street and left, left towards junction. Constantly looking around. To the junction, straight over, now jogging on nearside of road, away from the house, down the main road, towards town."

Kenny moved across the room to the far window overlooking the junction so that he could see the street beyond. He peeled back the small eyehole they had inserted in the blackout.

"No deviation, subject left, left, left into alleyway on the other side of the small car dealers and out of sight. Time now 23:02 hours. He's all about himself," he added.

"Little shit," said Franks. "He knows no-one's about – difficult to follow. How long's he going to be, do you think?"

"Don't know, five mins, tops," replied Kenny.

Franks moved to the seat vacated by Kenny, leaving him to keep an eye on the entrance to the alleyway.

A couple of vehicles silently moved through the junction. When the second one had gone through and passed the alleyway to its left, Warden re-emerged into the street, looked around and headed back up the street, towards his house.

"23:08 hours. Subject out of alley, right, right towards HA, to the junction and across, same clothing. Towards house, out of view." Franks picked it up.

"To the stairs and up to door." He was looking through binoculars. "Two sharp taps on door followed by one short one, door open, quick look around and in. Time now 23:09 hours. What do you reckon?"

"Stash," Kenny said with a sigh. "He's waited until nightshift changeover – less chance of a tug. How long was he away?"

Franks looked at the log.

"Seven minutes. So he goes out, stashes his gear or money or both, comes back clean, no problem. Interesting, two taps then one tap on the door, he doesn't take keys with him – even less risk. Little fucker."

"OK, let's give it another half an hour and call it a day," said Kenny.

"I'm dying for a pint," replied Franks.

"Me too." This irritated Kenny a little, but only because he wanted a pint as well, before closing time, but knew it would be impossible, and it concentrated his mind on wanting to piss that he had been resisting for the past thirty minutes.

When no toilet was available they always used a sealable container, any container.

They persevered on into the night. All was quiet; a few people meandered past, cars moved almost silently through the lights. This was the boring time, and the period of highest risk. Tony Warden had packed up shop; having placed his 'stash', he would probably be putting off people who phoned him and wouldn't take any callers. Business was closed. But it was important for the two detectives to know when Warden had shut down for the night, to establish a system, his method of working, that was important evidentially, but also to enable them to adjust their hours according to his activities and negate the need to cover the period immediately after he had been to his 'stash'. Any future observation could be terminated after he had stashed his gear: nothing to see – no evidence – no proof – no conviction.

They had been watching Tony Warden – known as 'The Warden' to his friends – for a couple of weeks, establishing his habits and methods and profiling his business. He was a minor criminal who had been propped up as a substantial crack dealer; in fact, probably the main crack dealer in town and the only one who was serving from his house. The others worked the streets, going to where the business was rather than the business coming to them. Both had benefits and drawbacks. Those who served on the street, from a bike, a car, or simply on foot, had a greater risk of being robbed of their gear or money; they were more exposed, more vulnerable, and dealt with a more transient and therefore riskier customer. On the other hand, serving from home provided security, four walls and a front door that could be strengthened and fortified, and guaranteed a more reliable customer base; but it was static, immovable, less flexible, and it was more difficult to hide drugs, money and evidence of dealing that would lead to incarceration. Hence the nocturnal activities of the Warden that were now being carefully monitored and interpreted by the two detectives.

"OK, let's call it a day." Kenny leaned over to his companion. Everything was packed away, equipment quietly placed in a dark holdall; nothing must be left to record their presence in that room. Cups, cling film and sweet wrappers, even the bottles of pee, had to be taken away – all in darkness and complete silence. A quick scan around to confirm nothing was left, a final check on the front door of the house, and the log was completed and signed off. The window slots were closed and taped down and then, in a hushed voice, Kenny whispered, "Ready?"

Franks gave a thumbs-up and they moved to the door, floorboards creaking as they opened it. It led out to a disused and unfurnished corridor. Kenny moved into the corridor and stopped, waiting for Franks to follow. As he did so he closed the door and nodded to Kenny, and they both moved towards the stairs at the end of the passage that led down to a small hall at ground level, which had two adjacent doors. The front door faced them.

The ground floor was occupied by the owner, an elderly lady, wonderfully called Patience. She had apparently lived on her own for a couple of decades since her husband had passed over to the other side. Beautifully spoken, she was the epitome of gentler, quieter times, and had been an ideal candidate for an initial approach.

As soon as Kenny had learnt of Warden's activities, one of his first jobs was to recce his house: assess the location, access and position relative to the other buildings, occupants, and – most importantly – find a secure OP which would give them the ability to watch the subject's house and the comings and goings securely from a vantage point, without interference, for a prolonged period and with the agreement of the owner. Which is where Patience came in.

It was very simple really. An undeveloped house with wooden windows and doors and a dual-colour paint scheme – cream and green, and slightly run down, it had quickly been identified as a property with potential. Very usefully, because it was on a corner, and the main door – which provided access – was out of view of Warden's house, movement in and out was easier and presented less risk to the watchers or the owner. When Patience was approached one sunny afternoon, she had no hesitation in agreeing, happy to have the security, albeit temporarily, of two men in the house. She provided a key and didn't ask any questions: "I don't want to know what you're doing… just let me know when you've finished." And that was it!

Kenny opened the door very slightly, looking left and right, ensuring that the immediate area was clear of prying eyes. They moved quickly and stealthily out of the door, Franks closing it very carefully and quietly before joining his mate at the bottom of the short flight of steps that led onto the street. No conversation, no looking back, no undue haste – just a steady pace away from the OP to where they had parked the car a few streets away.

Once they had reached the vehicle, a silver non-descript Japanese car, they loaded their kit in the back, gently closed the boot with a reassuring click, got in, closed the doors quietly, started the engine and were away. Once again, no fuss, no noise. Entering and leaving an OP was always a period of high risk and they wanted to move away without attracting any attention. No headlights for a hundred yards – they could wake the neighbours and some nosey parker or sharp-eyed villain could clock the number of the car – another complication.

They turned the corner and could start to relax.

"Good job," Kenny said, with an underlying sense of relief that the observations had confirmed the intelligence that Warden was an active dealer and, importantly, that they had managed to achieve this without being noticed themselves.

# 2

# SPLENDID ISOLATION

The sea tumbled into the bay as it had done for thousands of years, the lines of surf climaxing onto each other as they rolled onto the rocky shoreline. It was only about two to three hundred metres across and nestled between huge granite outcrops, like the paws of a gigantic lion that poked out into the sea protecting the low-lying softer core between them from the worst excesses of wind, sea and rain.

Some of the waves were taller than a standing man and the steady, deep, resonating hum that surged inland was only interrupted by the occasional thump as a wave slapped against a resistant rock, causing water and foam to surge up into an ever-changing flute of intolerance and annoyance.

The day was clear yet a little overcast beyond the waves. Brumber Tompkins could see the horizon clearly, its dark straight edge separating cloud from sea as it wrapped itself around the cove in perfect stillness. As he scanned it, the only other land visible was a distant headland dribbling out beyond the rocky outcrop to his left, layered shades of grey, darker than the sky yet lighter than the sea. He knew that there was no other habitation on this promontory, or roads, for in all the years he had lived there he had never seen any artificial light on this desolate landscape. Indeed, the only lights he saw other than his own were those of small fishing vessels plying their way left or right across the ocean, but these were usually no closer than a mile distant.

The tide was just turning and he moved down the rocky beach to where it merged into a flat sandy plateau interspersed with low ribbons of rock running out to the water and at right angles to it. He moved through the rocks looking for flotsam, jetsam, anything that might com e in useful to supplement his existence and to save the hassle of carting items from Poundscombe, the nearest habitation. Normally this consisted of bits of wood, always useful once dried out for building or simply for firewood. This habit was now almost routine and one he enjoyed; finding other people's discarded objects and putting them to good use was comforting, and, of course, free.

After about half an hour and having collected all the wood he could carry, he re-traced his steps up to the cottage that sat defiantly, yet snugly, in the womb of the cove. It was perched a little higher than the high-tide mark and, therefore, beyond the reach of the sea. It had been a fisherman's cottage, small windows were embedded in its metre-thick granite walls and a solid wooden door with a small porch protected it from inclement weather. A semi-circular low wall made of stones that had been recovered from the beach and packed out with earth, grit and pebbles, which had long since become infested with grass, moss and lichen, arced between the water's edge and the front of the building. Alongside, ran a small stream; a trickle in the summer, it changed into a deluge in winter as precipitation increased, but it sustained life and Tompkins nurtured it. He repaired its banks, cleaned it of weeds and ensured its uncluttered entrance to the sea.

The narrow coastal path passed between the cottage and the cove and this was often used by walkers. A second footpath wound its way past the cottage and up the valley in which it sat, eventually reaching a small sunken road at its head that ran parallel to the coast and was firmly embedded in the patchwork of small fields that surrounded it.

He reached the front door and after allowing George – a proud orange roan cocker spaniel, his dog and sole companion – to enter, he went to the outhouse to store the wood with all the other bits of rope and assorted oddments that had been liberated from the beach over the years, joining jerry cans of diesel and petrol that he didn't want in the house. Brumber stood back and admired the storeroom for its diversity and its ability to sustain life in such a remote spot on the north Cornish coast. After placing the wood in the shed, he closed the door securely, returned outside and, hesitating before entering the house, he turned to look at the sea and scan his domain, which had steadily increased as he had bought adjoining fields from local farmers. Apart from the house, that he thought was about two hundred years old, and gardens, he owned about four acres surrounding it, which included two fields and a small stone hut – now engulfed by brambles – halfway up the side of the valley, overlooking the bay and the cottage. Originally used to store fishing and boat equipment, he now used it to store larger items such as nets, large timbers, buoys and bits of metal.

He turned and entered the cottage. It consisted of a large living room, a kitchen, a bathroom and two small bedrooms set into the loft space, with dormer windows – later additions. Water was pumped in from a well above the house and heating was provided by an open fire and a wood-burning stove in the kitchen. Power, when it was needed, mainly in winter, came from a diesel generator kept in the outhouse. A recent addition, he thought it to be a wise investment to ensure light and power when it was needed.

He had bought the cottage at Southcott Mouth and the land surrounding it following an acrimonious divorce from his wife, Gloria. They had no children but she was keen to fleece him of all the money he had garnered from working in the City for twenty years, a desire that she very nearly achieved. It was, Brumber thought, an intervention by the judge during the proceedings that altered the possible outcome when he asked her what she had contributed to the marriage. She had had a significant inheritance from her late parents, never worked, hadn't contributed financially to the marriage and, strangely, had never opened her own bank account. Not expecting the question, she had blustered; her usually confident aura slipped and she thrashed around, striving to provide a plausible answer. She did not succeed. As a consequence, the judge ordered that their estate be divided into two equal shares. This, he felt, was fair, but it left him with a singularly large pot of money, with which he bought the cottage and some adjoining land and set about renovating it to a standard fit for habitation. He left his job as a portfolio consultant, took what pension was offered, and invested the rest in a range of equities.

He had decided to leave the real world behind – for the time being, anyway. He was fed up to the back teeth with the challenges of competition, material wealth, personal insincerities and the drudgery of endless and pointless meetings, emails and the ever-present requirement to conform to other people's opinions and philosophy. He wanted, for the first time in his life, to work outside the box, to live where he wanted and in the manner that he wished, without the constraints of society and the laws imposed by unpopular governments.

As a consequence, he had limited contact with the outside world. One of the first steps he had taken was to dispose of his mobile phone; he wanted to control with whom he had contact and how that contact was to be established. He had no internet access at the cottage or anywhere in the area of the cove and therefore relied on postal deliveries. He wanted to live, as far as possible, off-grid.

Poundscombe was about two miles to the east and reached by foot along the coastal path, by boat around the headland or by the road running along the top of his valley. In the other direction, a five-mile hike would bring him to the larger village of Moorworthy. Brumber had only been there once.

He had only four compromises to this self-imposed isolation: two boats, a radio and a car. The first boat, a small, rigid-hulled inflatable boat, was generally pulled up from the beach in front of the cottage, and he kept the outboard in the outhouse. The RHIB was light enough to lift, tug and tow out of the water with the help of a winch that Brumber had embedded in the semi-circular wall surrounding the cottage. Once at the top, by removing the small outboard he could manoeuvre the vessel into shelter. It was small and flexible enough to overcome small waves and with a shallow draught could be launched relatively easily. The second vessel, a small fishing smack with inboard engine, was moored in the middle of the harbour at Poundscombe. The harbour itself was deep, gouged out by the sea from the underlying rocks. A fairly substantial sea-wall protected the various boats and the village itself from inclement weather. The car, an old blue Polo, was parked in the corner of the village car park; rarely used, it sat under a car cover, protected and anonymous. He had taken the precaution of disconnecting the battery heads to deter would-be thieves, but it was always there, always started and was forever reliable. Finally, the radio: an old transistor capable of receiving BBC Radio stations 3 and 4, and vital for weather reports, especially when launching the RHIB.

He visited Poundscombe, generally by boat, twice, or maybe three times, a week and this fulfilled all his immediate needs: to pick up food and groceries at the local shop, check for mail at the post office and cast a wary eye over the entombed Polo. He had reached an agreement with the Post Mistress that the local branch, embedded in the grocery store, would receive and hold all his mail, and there seemed to be an increasing amount, mostly from the bank – he held an account in the county town – and his stockbroker, who had to meet legal requirements and receive signatures and required certain authorities. If the weather was bad and thick lines of white surf pounded the cove, he would walk around the headland, known as 'Bullhead Point', to the village. This took about twenty minutes and he quite enjoyed the experience, sucking in the views and benefitting from the change of scenery.

This morning he had decided to walk to the village; he had supplies to collect and probably post to recover, and the sea was a little too rough to launch the RHIB. Anyway, he thought, he would probably have been soaked by the time he arrived and would have remained damp for much of the day before returning later, and that wasn't a particularly attractive proposition.

He went out to the hut on the side of the slope overlooking the cottage. Unlocking the door, he saw that the small wedge of brown cardboard he'd jammed between the door and the bottom of the frame when he locked up on the last occasion fall to the floor, which told him that no-one had entered the building since his last visit. He clambered over the odd bits of wood to the rear and palmed away some dry soil to reveal a square piece of plywood the size of a laptop. He lifted this carefully. Reassuringly, the plain top plate of the ground safe was revealed, embedded in concrete, with a circular brass escutcheon in the centre surrounding a keyhole. He knelt down and moved his hand over the soil beyond and behind the safe until his fingers settled on something round, about three inches below the surface. He tugged at the lid of the object, a small jam-jar, placed it between his knees, unscrewed the lid and removed a key, which had been in a polythene bag inside the jar. He then opened the safe. It was about a cubic foot in size and contained a large amount of money, assorted packages and other miscellaneous items that he didn't want anyone to find. He didn't really know how much money was there but thought that it was in the region of a hundred thousand pounds. He took a hundred quid and re-secured the safe, being particularly careful to cover it and the jar with a substantial layer of soil and then place odd items of timber, boxes and netting to conceal its presence. He placed the money in his jacket pocket and made his way to the door, where he paused, looked back and checked that everything was as it was when he had first entered and, more importantly, would be unchanged when he returned later. He closed and locked the door and re-inserted the small cardboard plug before returning to the house. The wind blustered against his face, buffeting his ears, and he felt slightly self-conscious and a little vulnerable with a hundred pounds stuffed in his coat pocket as he walked back to the cottage.

He thought about the safe. It had been a good investment and a sensible way of looking after his money. He had bought it when he purchased the house, then found a suitable location that would be accessible, dry and reasonably well hidden, dug a hole, mixed some concrete and then embedded it in the ground. If the shed were destroyed by a gale, or worse still, burnt to the ground, he surmised the safe would still survive. He always tried to think ahead. What if he was robbed or even arrested and the key to the safe was found and there was no lock for it to open? This would lead to awkward questions, and he had decided to stash it separately and close by.

With his background in the financial world and knowledge of money laundering, he knew that cash was the answer. His accountant paid the tax on his pension, dividends and so on by credit transfer from funds available, but he preferred to use cash wherever possible; it was difficult to trace and made life, he thought, just a little easier. Transactions other than cash left a paper trail that could be traced: bank accounts, tax returns, stockbroker statements, locations, dates, amounts, even what the money was spent on. No, he had decided a long time ago to reveal the tip of the iceberg, not the iceberg itself.

He made ready. The weather was going to be dry but windy, hence the choppy water. He allowed George out and then closed and locked the door. Sometimes he wondered why he bothered – there was nothing worth stealing apart from the contents of the safe and any would-be robbers would need a day to find it, two days to winkle it out from its concrete sarcophagus, and a good day to heave it onto a beached boat; carrying it along the footpath was just not feasible. He returned the key to his pocket and turned towards the village.

George bounded up the path ahead of him, young and agile with limitless energy, stopping occasionally to savour a scent, whilst Brumber trudged behind with the large empty rucksack on his back through ankle-deep waves of damp heather and grass. When he reached the top of 'Bullhead Point', he stopped and looked behind him. This was his domain and he loved the freedom, his cottage snuggled in the hollow of the slope, the valley, and the headland facing him on the other side of the cove, known locally as the 'Devil's Head', clinging onto the side of which was his small store, barely visible beneath the undergrowth. This was, he decided, an idyllic life, and long may it continue

There was no-one in sight, not even walkers, to see line upon line of waves relentlessly rolling into the little cove to dissipate their energy on the huge slabs of rock. He turned and continued walking along the old coastal path, up to the high point of 'Bullhead Point' where the cliffs, hard vertical strips of granite, dropped steeply before becoming flatter and more eroded until they disappeared forever, out to sea, beneath the frothing mass of water. The searching wind was strong and gusting but it made the walk invigorating with George, who occasionally stopped to examine a rabbit hole or pick-up an interesting smell. After about ten minutes, he had rounded the point and the path dropped down to meander along the side of another cove, but one that was far deeper and wider than Southcott Mouth and from where he could see the village of Poundscombe backed up onto the high ground with the harbour wall protecting the boats and houses from the worst excesses of the weather. He remembered seeing a photograph of the harbour wall taken from the village at the time of a particularly vicious storm. A wave had just slammed into the wall and sheets of white spittle had launched themselves into the air above, perhaps ten or twenty metres high, before presumably landing, like a sudden heavy rainstorm, on the boats sheltered within. The photograph reminded him of the power of nature but the ability of man to protect himself from the elements. His little boat would be safe.

George trotted down in front of him as they closed on the village itself. He hadn't seen anyone on the path but this didn't surprise him, most people wandered along in mid-summer when the weather was warmer and the breeze gentler and more forgiving. At last he reached the randomly cobbled lane that took the path into the village and around the small harbour. The tide was nearly out but there was sufficient water to allow the boats to gently bob around in the haven, safely tied to buoys and protected by the powerful dark rounded granite wall thrown up about two hundred years before from weathered and sea-sculpted stones that had been retrieved from the beach.

He made his way through a side street away from the harbour and climbed up between tight cheek-by-jowl houses until he reached the municipal car park set above and behind the village. He was reassured to see his jacketed car where he had left it. He threw the cover away from the driver's door, lifted the bonnet and checked the oil, re-connected the battery terminals and started the engine. It fired into life and he let it idle gently for about ten minutes whilst he circled the vehicle, kicking the tyres and looked at the body work. He found the process immensely satisfying – reliability and dependability were very undervalued assets. He turned the engine off, locked it up, replaced the cover and walked down to the quayside, passing the old parish church on the way.

The village was small and pretty but did not become overburdened by tourists, particularly in the winter. The narrow roads, lack of parking and absence of any sandy beach made it less attractive to visitors than other, more well-known places along the coast. Village life centred around The Anchor, the local pub, and the post office/convenience store that were both positioned centrally. The pub was busy in the summer but gratingly quiet out of season. It was popular with the locals, who tended to occupy the rear bar – it was less attractive than the front bar, used by outsiders – where there was a dart board, snooker table and the results of all the locally inspired competitions and events; incomprehensible to visitors, interesting to locals, but very exclusive to the community and almost intimidating by its very existence. The back bar of The Anchor was, Brumber thought, one of those places where a stranger could saunter in at lunchtime out of season, with the locals already huddled in their well-worn seats around the polished bar, and as they entered, the conversation would stop and everyone would turn around to look or glance over to peruse. No conversation, no pleasantries, but the locals, naturally inquisitive and interested, would like to know who the person was and the reason for their visit.

The Anchor was run by Reg and Peggy, an older couple, he in his buttoned cardigan and she in her flower-patterned apron. They chugged along with the trade they had developed without being inspired to launch into expensive improvements or new initiatives. They knew everyone and everyone knew them, and they ran it as they liked, with a few rooms to let on the side, Brumber occasionally visited but found them a little too inquisitive, which made him feel uncomfortable.

On this occasion he walked past the pub and the café, which was seasonally closed. There were a couple of other small trinket shops selling clotted cream, crab lines and copies of Daphne Du Maurier's books, but these were owned by outsiders, staffed by seasonal staff, and only remained open for a few months of the year. He reached his destination, Poundscombe Stores – a short distance from the pub and set back slightly from the quayside. He tethered George outside, walked up the small flight of steps and opened the door. As he did so the top of the door triggered a small mechanical bell that lightly dinged and warned the owner of the presence of a new customer. He closed the glass door, which was covered in advertisements and local notices, behind him and wiped his feet on the mat. They were always expecting people with muddy feet.

It was the smell that confirmed what his eyes and ears had already told him – a complex mixture of aromas. He briefly closed his eyes and breathed in, gently savouring the experience, and somehow his brain merged fresh fruit, fabric conditioner, soap and newspapers together and identified them as 'The Corner Shop'. The shelves were jammed with all the essentials of daily life, yet they still managed to squeeze in a freezer section, some fresh meat and veg, and stationery items ranging from brightly coloured paperclips to envelopes and letter-pads. He moved through the shop to the slightly shaded rear.

"Hello, Mr Tompkins, how are you?!" a very deliberate female voice exclaimed from behind the post office counter at the rear.

"Fine, thank you," said Brumber.

This was Nancy, the elderly owner, hair pulled back into a bun, horn-rimmed specs, wearing a workman-like pinny and a pale blue cardigan. Brumber often wondered how she survived on local trade out of season – presumably by having low overheads and high summer turnover. She popped up from where she had been bending down.

"Oh, the weather's been wicked," she said as if she was describing an errant schoolboy.

"How's it been round at Southcott? Bit rough I imagine?" Decades of experience were embedded in these questions.

"OK," replied Brumber, "a bit blustery, you know."

"Very quiet here, just locals" she said. "The odd walker but not the right time of year – hardy souls. A couple came in yesterday soaked to the skin, staying at The Anchor, I think."

Brumber knew that Reg and Peggy provided accommodation, but it wasn't general knowledge and they didn't go out of their way to attract guests.

"Not worth the effort," Reg had once said, "keeping rooms up to standard, tidying up, meals, all the questions and queries."

"Now then, let's see. Oh yes, I've got some mail for you." Nancy stooped down to her left and, after a few seconds of rummaging beneath the counter, emerged with a small bundle of envelopes secured by two elastic bands. She removed the bands and flicked them onto her wrist in one smooth operation and, adjusting her glasses, went through every envelope to ensure that Brumber's name was on each one.

Whilst he waited, Brumber cast his eye over the organised chaos that was the post office counter – a selection of envelopes, bags, receipts, shelving with forms and Post Office reference books – and he once again breathed in the unmistakable smell. Once she had finished sorting out his mail, she re-attached the elastic bands, lifted the guillotine window and passed them through to him.

"There we are, nothing that you don't know about, I'm sure – all the usual stuff. Will you be wanting anything from the shop?"

"A couple of things," Brumber replied.

"OK, well you carry on and let me know when you're done. I've got a few things to sort out here."

Brumber grabbed a basket from the pile by the counter and began scanning the groaning shelves. He gathered together some long life milk, a few vegetables and fruit, a couple of loaves of bread and a range of tinned food – tomatoes, beans, soups, etc., and loaded them into the basket. He glanced at the newspapers; nothing unusual there – murder, mayhem, exposé and the inevitable politician lying about something. When he had finished he moved back to the counter. Nancy wasn't in view so he said, in a slightly louder tone than normal. "That's it I think, Nancy, can't think of anything else."

"OK, dear, just give me a minute," came the response from the back room.

Brumber looked outside and could see George standing guard, looking around, waiting patiently. Nancy joined him at the till. She was smaller than he'd imagined and he realised that he didn't normally see her bottom half; she was usually behind the post office counter, which was slightly raised, or the till shelf, at one end. He noticed she was wearing blue slacks. Nancy sensed this.

"It's a bit chilly, dear."

He placed the items on the counter whilst she passed them through the till, he then placed everything in his backpack: tins first, bread last and the post on top. When he had finished, he secured the tie-top and straightened himself up to pay.

"Twenty-six pounds and thirty pence, dear. Thank you."

He handed her thirty pounds and she gave him the change. The odd bits of shrapnel, in this case seventy pence, made a little plonk as it hit the rest of the loose change sitting at the bottom of the Lifeboat Box. Brumber didn't bother with coins.

"About time you emptied that, Nancy."

"I know but I have to wait for them to come around. They'll be here next week I expect."

"Could I leave my pack here for about half an hour, Nancy? I'll be back shortly."

"Course you can, dear!"

Brumber manhandled it around to the other side of the till cubicle so it was out of the way. "Back soon!"

"OK, see you in a tick," said Nancy as she disappeared again to the post office counter and all its envelopes, forms and papers.

He left the shop and the bell tinkled once again as he closed the door. Nancy looked up and Brumber glanced back, sorry to have disturbed her once more. They waved to each other. He untethered George and strode off, up the street. He had one more task to complete. He looked at his watch.

Brumber walked up through the village to the outskirts, where an unused and now nearly derelict Baptist chapel was located high above the road on a grass bank. Opposite, where the pavement ran, was one of only two telephone boxes in the village. The other one was on the quayside close to the pub; that was far too public for Brumber's liking – too many people passing, staring in, or worse still and very inconsiderately, using it.

He looked around. The box was not overlooked and it

wasn't on the main thoroughfare. He put his gloves on, pulled the door open and entered. George scuttled in. He was used to the confined space, but not entirely comfortable with it; nevertheless, he sat obediently in one small corner. Brumber glanced at his watch again – eleven fifty-eight a.m. *How time flies,* he thought. He lifted the receiver, confirmed the dialling tone, replaced it on the cradle and waited, all the time passing his eyes along the road in either direction and across onto the high embankment. All was quiet.

If the telephone rang, he would answer it, have a short conversation with the caller and replace the hand-set.

If, as was usually the case, it was silent, he would walk away and return another day at the same time.

Five minutes later he left the box, patted George on the back and then strode off in the direction of the parish church. He entered by the lychgate and walked across to the right-hand side, where a wall formed the boundary between the graveyard and a small area of open pasture. No-one else was there and he zig-zagged across the damp grass, through the maze of graves to a small granite headstone at the end of a hollow grassed rectangle, itself bordered in granite. He stood looking at it:

*LILLIAN PITCAIRN – DIED 1953.*

Reassuringly untended, it had all the signs of the family having died out or moved on: no dead flowers, no trampled grass and no apparent attempts to tidy it. The headstone backed onto the wall, but left a small two-inch cavity behind it, running along its width. He moved to the rear of the grave, looked around, glanced down at the gap and then moved away, walking purposefully towards the gate. He closed it behind him and then returned via the harbour to the shop.

He lingered at the head of the harbour to look at his boat,

hanging around with its neighbours in the tranquil water whilst the hum and roar of the surf continued in the world beyond the wall.

"Still there, then?"

Brumber was slightly startled but looked around to see who was asking. It was Reg, the pub landlord, sucking on a half-finished cigarette.

"Yep." He was going to cut this short; he didn't like other people prying into his business and asking questions.

"If you ever want to sell her, I've got people interested!"

"No, I'm fine thanks," said Brumber.

"Don't get much use," Reg persisted.

"Enough," said Brumber, "you'd be surprised."

"OK, but don't forget what I said."

"I won't. Thanks."

With that short and sharp conversation, Reg returned to the warmth and bonhomie of his pub, leaving Brumber to contemplate what had been said and the likely consequences for him. Reg knew him, knew he was connected to the boat moored in the harbour and that it didn't get used a great deal. This could naturally follow on to further questions and comments such as, 'Why is he keeping that boat?' 'Hardly worth it.' 'He pays his mooring fees on time. What does he actually do?' and then, more incisively, 'Where is he from?' 'Does he have any visitors?' He returned to the shop, tethered George and entered. The doorbell rang and Nancy looked up. He raised his hand in salute and Nancy returned the acknowledgement and said in a muffled voice, "See you soon, Brumber, safe journey home."

He picked up his now fully laden bag and left the shop, collected George en-route and then walked around the harbour and onto the footpath towards the headland to go home. Once free of habitation he let George off the lead and noticed that the waves had become a lot angrier, long white manes of spray following the surf as the waves flung themselves onto the rocks below. It had become quite squally; hard tips of rain, like small pebbles, began tapping his waterproof and hitting his face. Brumber increased his pace to reduce the time it would take to reach the cottage. He thought, as he walked, that it was a little strange… it was the first time Nancy had used his Christian name since he moved to the area. He didn't know she even knew it, she must have seen it on an envelope or something. Strange though.

# 3

# THICKENING PLOT

Kenny and Franks agreed to meet in the office after lunch the following day. This would give them enough time to check and sign off the logs from the night before and submit the memory sticks with all the photos for printing. New technology, they agreed, was great; it made life a lot easier, with no hassle with times, dates and sequences of events. It was just that, at the end of the day, whatever the type of operation, hard copies of photographs were needed to identify suspects, intel logs and, eventually, a file of evidence. Memory sticks don't tell you what they contain – you need a computer or viewer, at the very least, to look at them.

They were keen to get out on the ground in daylight, to have a look at the place where Warden had wandered off to the previous night, with a view to plotting it up that evening so that they could find out what he had been doing. Both men had dark clothing but Kenny had brought with him a dark balaclava, gloves and an old green army poncho. Once they had finished their boring admin tasks, they collected their kit: bins, cameras, radio, batteries, flask of tea, food, pee bottle, warm clothing, log sheets and new memory sticks.

When they had finished packing, they put on their covert radios, tested the earpieces and night vision scope, and once reassured, went down to their vehicle to drive out through the daylight traffic to the spot where their suspect had slipped down to the canal from the road. There was a line of parked cars opposite the alleyway but they managed to slide their vehicle between two so that they were as unobtrusive as possible. Both men were very conscious of being no more than a stone's throw away from Warden's house and aware that visitors would be coming and going, and perhaps walking past the car, but they also knew that going to the OP would be too risky in daylight.

Kenny got out and quickly walked across the road towards the alleyway. Once there, in a more secluded location, he could slow down a little and test his radio: "56A, 56, permission."

"Yes, yes, R9," replied Franks. "You likewise."

He walked down the alleyway. It was about one hundred yards long and bordered by long grass, stinging nettles and the usual detritus. Each side was lined by the two-storey gable end walls of terraced houses.

"56A, be aware, an old bloke on a push bike has entered the alleyway behind you."

"Yes, yes," whispered Kenny.

He could hear the *squeak, squeak* behind him as the wheels turned. As they became louder and a little closer he moved to one side. The man on the bike passed and on reaching the towpath at the end of the alleyway he turned left.

"56 subject continued nearside onto the towpath. No-one else in view."

"56A yes, yes."

Kenny stopped at the water's edge. He hadn't visited the canal before and didn't know much about its reason for being, but it was tired and stagnant, a reminder of the area's industrial past. He was standing on the outside edge of a long bend and smelt the dampness in the air; the ground was unpleasantly muddy underfoot and a chill went through him. To his left came the faint hum of traffic as it passed over the road bridge that spanned the water about two hundred yards away, and to his right, a footbridge, equidistant, but smaller in size. On his side of the canal, the gardens of the terraced houses backed onto the towpath. The space between was overgrown with brambles and nettles that rolled out in both directions, towards both bridges, and beyond in a great arc. Facing him on the other side of the canal was another towpath, and behind that, a gentle two-metre-high embankment, again smothered in weeds and topped by a chain link fence. This enclosed what appeared to be a grey and unremarkable light industrial unit or warehouse, much of which was hidden by the overgrown embankment. He noted that there didn't appear to be any lights apart from those above the road bridge and, more importantly, an absence of cameras, which was probably why Warden was attracted to the location in the first place.

He turned right and walked along the path to the footbridge. The putrid smell of stagnation, rotting food and sewage filled his nostrils and he remembered that there had been some publicity about rejuvenating the area, repairing the locks and bringing some life back to the waterway. Presumably this had all petered out. The towpath on this side was narrow, muddy and overgrown, and the banks of the canal were undefined and purposeless. Reaching the footbridge, he climbed the slope and crossed, pausing briefly at the top to take in the view. He walked down to the other side and re-traced his steps towards the road bridge. The footpath on this side was more unkempt and the embankment more overgrown.

"56A." His earpiece crackled into life. Kenny fumbled for

his voice switch in his pocket and pressed the button three times.

"Three clicks received. Welfare check? Everything OK?"

Kenny clicked his transmitter three times. "Three clicks received."

It was always comforting to know that someone was looking after you, had your interests at heart and was concerned for your welfare. Tom Franks was a good man. He continued down to the road bridge, a far larger brick structure but with no pedestrian access from the canal to road level. He lingered a little and then turned back. A quick look around confirmed there was no-one about. He had settled on finding a convenient spot on the embankment from where he could see the point where the alleyway reached the towpath on the other side of the canal but also be able to cover its entire length from the footbridge to the road bridge. It would need to be sufficiently set back from the towpath on that side of the waterway so as not to attract attention, particularly from dogs, and be reasonably high, sufficient to provide a good vantage point, but low enough to prevent being silhouetted against the chain link fence.

As he had done before on many occasions, he'd approach the problem as if he was the suspect: avoid the road bridge (too many lights and pedestrians who would have a good view of the canal as they passed over); avoid crossing the footbridge (too exposed and limiting). He reckoned Warden would have remained on his side of the canal and, because of the amount of time they knew he'd taken, he would probably not have reached the footbridge.

Kenny passed the entrance to the alley to his right on the other side of the canal and reached a point midway along the embankment. As he did so, he contacted Franks. "56."

"Yes, yes."

"Coast clear on your side?"

"Yes, yes."

"Let me know if anyone comes down the alley."

"Yes, yes."

He did a final check of the canal sides and the rear of the houses on the other side of the water – all clear. He knew he could be seen from the first-floor rooms at the rear of the terraced houses facing the canal, but he had considered this and accepted the risk as it only really applied to this one occasion when the site was being recced in daylight, during the night his movements would be cloaked in darkness. Anyway, he had already thought of a cover story – his child had lost her front door key in the dark the day before.

He waded through the undergrowth and halfway up the embankment until he reached a spot covered on four sides by brambles; dark, impenetrable and seemingly ideal, in a slightly elevated position. He stooped down and looked towards the alleyway and canal. Perfect. He marked the spot with an old upright petrol can, and then returned to the towpath and marked the point of access with two broken bricks sitting on the side of the small path. Finally, he glanced up, swept the windows of the terraced houses for movement and/or faces, orientated the position in relation to the alleyway and the footbridge, and then walked towards the footbridge. As he did so, he said, "56A," and gave three clicks.

"Female pedestrian with dog in the alleyway to you. Dark clothing, woollen hat, small dog."

He hesitated; he didn't want to confront her on the footpath, or worse still, on the bridge if she wanted to pass over it. He slowed his pace and glanced over to his right, just as the woman emerged.

"56, I have her, right, right, right, my direction."

The woman was walking fairly fast, tugged along by the

eager dog, and quickly reached the footbridge, where she hesitated whilst the dog sniffed a small sapling and pissed against its base. She continued under the bridge away from the alleyway.

"No deviation, under bridge, away from alley."

"56 yes, yes."

"Am returning to you, keep me posted on the alley."

"Yes, yes."

Kenny crossed the bridge and re-joined the towpath. "Fifty metres… all clear… still clear." He turned into the alleyway and re-joined Franks. As soon as the car door was closed they drove away.

"And?" Franks enquired.

"Yep," replied Kenny. "Doable. I've got a spot on the far side of the canal where I can see the alleyway and both towpaths. I'll go there this evening after we've settled in the OP. You'll have to cover the house on your own for a short while – hopefully he won't hang around."

They went to get some grub at the local Sainsbury's and, as darkness fell, went to the observation point in Patience's house. They opened the side door and drifted upstairs. The room was as they had left it: dark, draughty and uninviting. The blackouts were still covering the windows.

After they had set up their kit, Kenny carefully lifted the bottom part of the blackout of the window that overlooked Warden's house and looked out. It was as they had left it. He spoke quietly to Franks. "You ready?"

"Yep."

"Time now, 19:05 hours, lights on 0/1 and 0/2 and 1/1 and 1/2. Doors closed. Following cars parked outside – so far…"

A small pause as Franks caught up. "Yep."

"Left to right, red Peugeot, black Nissan, blue VW and a

dark-coloured car, no make. No numbers, too tight."

Kenny knew that if the cars became relevant, they could clock the numbers as they drove off. He clicked off four frames of the house and the cars outside.

"Four piccys of outside view."

As the night rolled on, a constant flow of visitors came and went, all of whom stayed for less than three or, perhaps, four minutes, long enough to score and then away, all on foot; none of them arrived in a car, probably because of the proximity to the traffic lights and the tight parking. Photos were important to ID the punters. Most of them were very paranoid, very aware, looking around constantly. Handily, having climbed the steps to the house and tapped on the door, they would wait for ten or twenty seconds and take the opportunity to turn around and scan the area to assess any immediate risk before entering, providing a good full-frontal facial image.

The door contained a peephole and presumably this was used to clear the visitor before the door was opened about three or four inches, and then opened fully to allow the person into the house.

During this time Kenny and Franks had swapped places a couple of times to relieve the pressure and stress of watching.

"How many visitors then?"

Kenny paused to count. "Thirty-one over two and a half hours. Busy chap – bet the neighbours are a bit pissed off."

"They probably don't want to get involved."

"It's 21:00 hours. I'll make a move down to the canal."

Kenny moved across to get his backpack, which contained everything he needed, signed off and handed the log to Franks, and then struggled into his radio harness and planted his earpiece in his ear.

"Give me a test call," he whispered.

"Testing 1, 2, 3, 4, 5," came into his ear.

"56A, 56 testing 1,2,3," he said in response in his microphone.

"Yep, all good."

"Give me an all-clear at the door."

"Yep."

He moved to the door, opened it and went into the corridor, closing the door after him. He went down the stairs and whispered, "56, 56A, I'm at the door."

"You're clear."

He opened the door and went out into the neat world. A chilly breeze caught him. He turned right to take the long route around and come towards the alley from the other direction. This took a few minutes longer but was safer.

As he approached the alleyway, "56, 56A, permission."

"Yes, yes, 56A."

"Approaching the alleyway."

"You're clear."

Kenny turned into the alley; it was in darkness. At the canal he turned right and then over the footbridge to the other side and walked slowly to where he had marked the footpath. There were no lights, only the road bridge glowed brightly – and something that he hadn't noticed during his daylight recce: some dim lights lit up the warehouse and yard on the other side of the embankment, which made the embankment appear darker.

*Very, very good*, he thought.

He found the two bricks and once again swept his eyes over the two towpaths and the rear of the terraced houses. All clear.

He moved as quietly as he could into the undergrowth. The initial set-up and exit stages were always the trickiest; noise and movement, being unfamiliar with the terrain, eyesight unadjusted to the light, and unusual movement – getting kit out of his bag, unwrapping the poncho, uncapping the bins. He had done this procedure many times and some golden rules applied: get it done quickly, don't faff around, keep all the kit in the bag so you don't lose it in the dark, and then find the right place, settle down and get as comfortable as possible – do not fidget.

He put on his balaclava, being careful not to dislodge his earpiece. He drew the poncho over himself and spread it out so it covered his entire body, stuck his head out through the hole in the top and put the hood over his head. He then sat down, making sure that he could see what he needed to see through the undergrowth in front of him that screened his bulk, and that he was below the level of the bank and therefore not profiled against the lights that were behind him. His bag was to his right side, up against his body, with everything to hand.

He looked ahead of him; everything was quiet, there was no movement from the rear bedrooms of the terraced houses, four first-floor lights were on out of probably sixteen houses along the line of buildings.

The traffic on the road bridge was steady. The only sources of light were from the first floor of the houses opposite, the lights on the road bridge, the occasional car headlight, and the ambient light from the factory estate behind his position.

"56, 56A, permission."

"Yes, yes."

"In position, all quiet."

"Yes, yes, five further visitors, time now 21:20."

He settled down. It could be a long wait and it would take time for his eyes to adjust to the darkness.

From watching people on similar operations it had confirmed his theory that everyone had certain habits and routines, which generally didn't change. From the manner in which they brushed their teeth to the way they tied their shoelaces, to the clothes they wore, their morning routine and evening rituals. These processes brought comfort and structure to their lives and he was confident that Warden was no different.

It was damp and he could taste the smell of the crushed vegetation and the deep earthy aroma. He slowly adapted to his new environment; he could see more clearly now. He became more aware of the sounds of birds on the water and the gentle rustling within the bramble bushes. It was very quiet, with little sound and even less human activity. He began to focus on the interior of the terraced houses he could see. He was too far away to make out individuals, but the occasional movement would catch his eye as someone crossed an un-curtained room.

After about fifteen minutes, he heard, "56A, 56."

Kenny sent three clicks in response.

"Welfare check."

Three further clicks.

"Three clicks received. Yes, yes, quieter at subject house."

Three clicks.

His mind wandered. He remembered the time, not so long ago, when he was doing exactly the same thing at the back of a bloke's house. It had been snowing heavily and the poncho was white with flakes; it had been so cold that the fabric had stiffened around him so that in effect he was sitting in a small conical self-standing tent. The bloke came out of the back door and walked over to where he was sitting. He thought he had been seen and prepared himself for confrontation when the man stopped a metre in front of him, unzipped his flies and pissed on the ground, the steam rising between them. He was probably a bit drunk and couldn't be bothered to find a toilet. This little session seemed to go on and on until he abruptly halted, zipped up again and went inside.

His daydreaming was interrupted by the sound of someone walking along the far towpath from the footbridge to the alley.

He settled his breathing and followed the subject with his eyes, resisting the urge to move his head. This was a good test and would show him how much he was able to discern. He produced a mental picture: male, dark hair, medium build, dark clothing, light trainers. The man turned left into the alleyway.

"56, 56A, permission," he whispered.

"Yes, yes."

"Male, IC1, dark clothing, light trousers, into the alley from the canal on foot to you."

"Yes, yes."

A pause.

"I have him, right, right, right, general direction of subject's house, as described."

Kenny found the last bit particularly satisfying.

"On same side as subject house, approaching house, no deviation, no deviation, past subject's house and away from OP."

Three clicks.

*Not connected,* he thought.

Ten minutes elapsed, then, suddenly, "Standby, standby, subject to front door, looking up and down. Door closed. Time now 22:12 hours."

*Man of habit!* he thought.

Two or three minutes later, "Standby, standby, subject out of front door, door closed and held. Wearing a dark hat and dark clothing, white trainers, down steps to the road. Off, off, off and left, left, left into street to the junction and across. Subject looking around. Temporary loss, eyeball needs to re-position."

He knew that Franks would have to move from the window facing the house to the window that looked down the street. There was a ten-second pause.

"Eyeball regained, still walking down the street towards alley… thirty… ten and left, left, left into alley and loss of eyeball; to you, 56A."

Kenny had a quick look around. There was no-one else in the vicinity, nothing else that could possibly disturb Warden's routine. Ten seconds, twenty seconds. A dark figure emerged at the end of the alleyway. Kenny transmitted a series of clicks.

"Series of clicks received. You have control. Do you have eyeball on the subject?"

Kenny transmitted three clicks.

"Three clicks received."

Warden had paused at the end of the alleyway, his bright white trainers resplendent against the dark background. He wasn't moving. Perhaps he was spooked.

*Has he forgotten something?* Kenny thought.

He then heard a distinct click and a bright light illuminated the subject's head for a split second, followed by a pinhead-like glow as he drew on a cigarette. Kenny followed the glow down as Warden dropped his hand by his side and then brought it up again to his mouth, sucking in; the light glowed brighter. He did this a number of times without moving; he was stock still at the end of the alley.

"Do you still have eyeball?"

Kenny transmitted three clicks.

"Three clicks received, yes, yes."

After what felt like an eon, Warden discarded the cigarette; the glow continued on the ground for a short while. The white shoes then moved right towards the footbridge to a point almost exactly opposite Kenny's position, and then stopped.

*No-one around. Go on, do it!* he thought.

The figure stooped and there was the sound of disturbed water, a slight rippling, dripping, scraping. Warden was now crouching on the footpath, almost lying flat. After a short while he stood up and stared at Kenny's position in the brambles.

*He can't see me – not possible,* Kenny thought.

His pulse racing, he glanced left and right to see if anyone else was going to disturb the unfolding saga. He noted Warden's rough position by counting the number of chimney stacks in from the alleyway that was in line with his OP. Five.

"56A, permission."

Kenny sent two clicks, indicating that it was too risky to transmit.

"Two clicks received."

After about thirty seconds, Warden moved back towards the alley and turned left towards the main road. Kenny updated the OP with his movement and direction.

"56A, 56, I have the eyeball. Right, right, right, direction of HA across the junction, right, right, right towards front door. Knocking on door... door opened and in, in, in. Time now 22:29."

"56, 56A, permission."

"Yes, yes."

"For the log, when you're ready." Pause.

"Yes, yes."

"Subject waited at end of alley, cigarette, white trainers distinctive in light. Moved to the offside approximately thirty metres and stopped, fiddling with something in water, on canal bank. Scraping, water sound, then to the alley and then temporary loss."

"Yes, yes."

"Will hold here for fifteen minutes and then join you at vehicle, so far."

"Yes, yes."

He was acutely aware that Franks was trying to do a number of things at the same time – camera, logs, observe, radio – and he needed time to complete each task properly.

Kenny waited a full ten minutes. Slowly the orange lights at the back of the terraced houses were extinguished and curtains were drawn, leaving a black hue where it had been and two vertical lines of brightness poking around the closed drapes. No-one else passed and he began to prepare for a rapid exit.

A final call. "56, 56A, permission."

"Yes, yes."

"Leaving plot."

"Yes, yes, all quiet."

Kenny rapidly wrapped up his poncho and stuffed it in his bag, made sure his position remained marked by the upturned can and two bricks, and re-joined the towpath. He walked quickly and reached the bridge, crossed over and made his way to the alleyway.

"56, 56A, permission."

"Alley clear?" Slight delay.

"Yes, yes."

Kenny transmitted three clicks as he turned left.

"Three clicks received, yes, yes."

He moved through the darkness and entered the brightness of the road, crossing straight over, away from Warden's house, back to the car. Franks was already there. He put his kit in the boot and got in the passenger seat.

"OK?" his opening gambit.

"Yep, usual visitors, very busy. You?"

"Yeah, good. Looks like he's stashing in the water, somehow."

"Fucker!" said Franks.

He fired up the engine and moved off. There was no need to expose themselves unnecessarily in the area.

# 4

# HELP IS AT HAND

Bertram was in his office, wading through the reams of paper that layered his desk. He had been there since first thing in the morning, keen to shift what he could before the rest of the team arrived and the world awoke. It was seven a.m.

To his right, he had a reviving cup of sugary tea on the desk, ready for his hand to seek, clutch and bring to his mouth when he needed a few seconds to think, to contemplate his next move. The office was small and somehow they had squeezed four desks into the limited space, together with a couple of filing cabinets and chairs. The décor was seventies, but it was functional. The door was closed and locked; the only method of entry was by key and each member of the team had one. The window next to Louis' desk was open and faced a small, flat roof and beyond that, a small alleyway and yard. He was smoking – strictly forbidden, but in a small secure office, who was to know? He sucked on the cigarette he was holding in his left hand, squinted his eyes to protect them from the fumes and smoke, looked carefully at the documents in front of him and then lent back, exhaling through the open window. He had no idea how effective this was, but it made him feel better and thought that it may help to dissipate the smell of cigarette smoke when the others arrived.

He flicked through his Day Book, a small hard-backed book in which he recorded his daily activities whilst at work – timed telephone calls, to whom he had spoken, any meetings he had had during that day and, of course, authorisations. Most importantly, he recorded payments made: when, where, to whom and why. As he completed the administrative task of formally recording all his work, he ticked it off and ensured that any money expended tallied with accounts. This was work he didn't enjoy, slow, painstaking, boring and very repetitive, but he knew it was important and that he could be held to account for any errors or discrepancies.

Louis looked around at the other desks, the emptiness of them, trying to summon up the energy and endeavour to carry on before returning to inscribing his daily working life on numerous documents and computer records.

He gathered some papers together and then slid the computer keyboard in front of him, typing from the documents onto the screen. He was starting to lose the will to live. But this was his life: a small, tight team dedicated to obtaining information or intelligence from human sources (HUMINT), duplicated across the country in hundreds of similarly small but discreet offices, normally called SMUs – Source Management Units. It was the way the 'job' had of getting in amongst it, finding out what was happening in the dark, grimy world of criminality and managing that process. Who was doing what with whom, when, where and how, and to be on top of it, constantly, twenty-four hours a day.

His mobile phone rang, startling him. He rummaged around and retrieved it from the sea of papers and looked at the screen. He didn't recognise the number, a mobile, but he answered it and flicked through his book to the next fresh page. A male voice on the other end spoke, deep, throaty, slow.

"Hello."

Louis said nothing.

"Mr Bertram?"

"Who's calling?"

"It's Pete. Pete Trinket!"

Louis remembered the name but couldn't place the face; he tapped the name onto his screen. He had access to a closed system of informants and this would provide a profile.

"How can I help?"

"It's been a long time, Mr Bertram. Sorry to call you first thing but I've got something for you, something you might be interested in."

Louis knew the system.

"Let me call you back in about ten minutes, if that's OK?"

"OK. Don't delay, I can't hang about!"

"OK."

The short call finished. Louis had Trinket up on the screen now and memories became firmer, more established. *OK... what have we got?* he said to himself. *Ah, that's it.* Pete Trinket, source 259, real name Ned McAffrey, source off and on for ten years, money lender, receiver, small dealer, known as 'Spond' or the 'Moneyman'. Lost contact three years ago, fell in love and left the area, or so he said. Good information. Motivation: financial, revenge, removal of competition. But reliable, as far as Louis could tell. The authority had lapsed, which would need to be renewed before any meeting. He ran a quick check on his record; Trinket had been arrested a couple of times – wrong place, wrong time – but had no convictions since last contact and apparently was not on bail.

Louis recorded the contact in his book and timed it, marking the call duration. He then called his Controller, told him of the contact, provided an outline of the individual and sought authority from him to make a telephone call to 259 and, if necessary, arrange a meet. Authority was given, and Louis recorded the exact time in his book. The only provision was that a 'third eye', a second officer, needed to be provided at any meeting, as it had been about three years since the last contact. After a brief conversation, Louis sought and was provided with authority to contact a number of other more regular sources during the course of the day – and these were, as was 259, timed and recorded.

About ten minutes later, Louis phoned 259.

"Yeah."

"It's me. You around today?"

"Yeah."

"OK, can we meet later, say after lunch?"

"Yeah."

"You got a car?"

"Yeah, a red Nissan. How about the Park and Ride?"

Louis knew the Park and Ride and it would be OK for a regular customer, but it was quite exposed and difficult to monitor properly. The difficulty was that it was a large, flat area with perhaps two thousand cars – too many angles, too many viewpoints and therefore risky. And anyway, he wanted to control the meet.

"Can we make it the café at Brown's Garden Centre?"

"Yep, say at three?"

"Make it two." Again, he wanted to control the time to disrupt any counter activity, bring it forward rather than push it back to disrupt any arrangements and thereby reduce the risk.

"OK, two at Brown's. I think it'll be worth your while."

"See you later." The conversation finished. Louis logged it, lit another cigarette and continued the endless task of chasing his paperwork around the desk.

By nine o'clock everyone was in the office, bustling around, making tea and calls, and generally altering the dynamics and disturbing the karma of a once-tranquil environment.

Louis arranged a third eye and comms were checked.

The third eye would be a new addition to the team, Carol. She was a keen and methodical worker and knew what would be required. She was shown a photograph of 259 and given an outline description, and was to arrive at the meeting place twenty to thirty minutes before the arranged time, keep an eye on the plot and the meeting place, observe people entering and leaving and in the immediate vicinity, and most importantly, watch the back of the officer conducting the meeting.

Louis arrived alone at the garden centre and moved through the car park to see if he recognised any cars, or whether anyone was carelessly sitting alone for no particular reason. Having satisfied himself that it was clear, and that, as far as he could make out, he wasn't being watched, he parked the car and waited. He could see Carol's car so knew she was already on plot. He called her and she confirmed everything was good – five people in the café, all middle aged, shop quiet – and she had positioned herself inside, on the right-hand side, where she could see the café and vehicles entering the car park.

Louis left his car, locked it and went in. A large, open-plan area, he saw his cover as he entered. She was reading a magazine and having a cup of something; there was no acknowledgement. He went straight to the counter and ordered a tea, then sat down on the left-hand side of the eating area, furthest from Carol and facing the car park. He leafed through a dog-eared copy of *The Guardian* as he waited. The time, he noted, was 1:50pm. He made no eye contact with Carol but checked the car park as cars arrived.

Fifteen minutes later, the phone rang.

"Your man's here." It was Carol. "Dark trousers, grey hoody, on his own, driving a red Nissan."

"That's him. Once he's settled could you get the number?"

"Already done." The phone call terminated as 259 entered the café, ordered a coffee at the counter and joined Louis at his table.

"You OK?" asked Louis.

"Yeah, you?"

"Fine. How's business?"

"Trying to keep out of trouble... started buying and selling a few second-hand motors, you know, but not a lot of money in it."

"Still with the missus?"

"No, we split a couple of years back."

"What can I do for you?"

"It's what I can do for you, Mr Bertram." (259 liked to use people's surnames; it all seemed so much more business-like somehow.) "How much is it worth?"

"It depends what you've got, and how useful it is. I can't tell you how much until you tell me what you know. Chicken and egg, really. But you know the score – you'll be paid; you know the system." And quickly, he added, "Oh, before I forget, in case anyone comes over that knows one of us, my name's Richard, you're Ned, and I'm interested in buying a blue Ford Fiesta from you – one thousand pounds tops, OK?" *Always pays to be prepared,* he thought. He did not like to be surprised.

"I know, Mr Bertram, but like, it is pretty specific and not many people know what I know, know what I mean?"

"Yep. OK, look... why don't we start by you telling me what you know and we'll go from there?"

"OK."

Louis' phone rang. He looked at the screen; it was Carol. He picked it up and pressed the answer key.

"Two likely boys, parking up and static in the car; I have the number, I'll come back to you."

"Listen, Pete. Stay here. Drink your tea. I'm just moving away for a minute. Two geezers in the car park."

259 looked slightly alarmed, but he was facing away from the car park and was unsighted.

Louis moved several tables away to read his paper. He could see Carol on the phone, writing down some details. He glanced across at 259, who was looking at him, and Louis moved his flat hand down on the table and then moved it up and down several times, slowly, as a sign to stay. *Stay calm. Stay where you are.*

Louis' phone rang; he answered it.

"No trace on the vehicle or owner. They've just exited the vehicle and are making for the entrance."

Louis looked up.

"OK, I can see them." He terminated the call.

He phoned 259, who was sitting about four yards away. "Yes?"

"Two blokes about to enter the café; don't look around now, but when I say." Pause. "OK."

He could see 259 wheel round and clock the two newcomers. "Don't know them. Should I?"

"Just checking. They're sitting down. I'll come over to you."

"OK."

Louis phoned Carol.

"OK, in the clear. Thanks."

The two men bought coffee and as they moved across to the far side, nearer to Carol, with their backs to Louis, he returned to his original position, opposite 259.

259 leaned closer and, in a hushed tone, said, "Thanks, Mr Bertram, can never be too careful." It had pleased him to know that Louis had been watching his back; it was professional and

reassuring. But he knew he had to tell him what he knew. It was a little risky and he was getting nervous.

"OK, bloke called the 'Warden', first name Tony. Good dealer, very switched on; lives up Barnet Street by the traffic lights. Smart cookie, difficult to catch. He gets all his gear from London, goes up once a week, maybe twice. Doesn't drive or doesn't have a licence, not sure. Goes on Thursdays during the day, uses a driver called 'Shanks'; don't know much else about him, but he drives a black Renault Clio, lives up on the Duchy Estate. They go to Ealing – don't know the address but he's sourced his gear there for two or three years."

"How do you know?"

259 looked Louis in the eye and raised his eyebrows.

"I used to drive him there. Haven't done for a year or so but I know he goes to the same area. I've been there four or five times. I park up and he says, 'I'll be about an hour.' Off he trots and comes back, happy as Larry. When he carries he keeps it around his bollocks or in his socks. Oh, and he's that cute he walks along the other side of the road past me, and then doubles back on himself, and then gets in. Threw me at first, I thought, *What the fuck are you doing?* I thought he'd missed me. I was going to turn the car around and pick him up, you know. But then I thought, *Well, if he's lost, he'll phone.*"

"Where did you used to pick him up?"

"Depends. Sometimes he'd phone and I'd pick him up in Sainsbury's car park; another time it was down at the swimming pool. He's all about himself, but he never carries."

"What do you mean?"

"Knives or nothing. He says it's not worth it, shivving someone, just not worth the bird."

"What do you know about the geezer in Ealing?"

"Not much – he's loaded, got his own gaff, think he's quite heavy. Warden phones him when we're close so he knows when he's due. I think he calls him 'Patch', but can't be sure. I don't think he goes to his house; I think they meet somewhere, don't know where."

"Where do you drop him?"

"Anywhere. As we got close he'd say go left, go right or whatever, never the same. Cute, see!"

"And how much did he pick up each time?"

"Don't know. Must be a fair quantity, mind – he'd bung me two hundred for my trouble, like. I suppose four or five grand's worth."

"Of what?"

"Crack normally, sometimes smoke, but he didn't tell me every time."

"Where do you drop him when you get back?"

"He asked me to get close to where he lives; I suppose he doesn't want to get caught carrying." 259 was getting nervous. The arrival of the two blokes earlier had unnerved him, and he began looking around.

"One other thing!"

"What?"

"This 'Patch' bloke, he looks very normal but he carries; he's got a shooter and I know Warden is shit-scared of him."

"OK, anything else?"

"No, that's about it. Anything else, I'll let you know."

"Thanks, Pete, I'll be in touch, OK?"

"Yep." 259 stood up and moved towards the exit, straight out of the door.

Louis' phone rang; it was Carol.

"Straight in his car and off. You going to hang around for a bit?"

"Yeah, just make up the notes – make sure we're clear."

"OK, do you still want me here?"

"Yep, ten minutes, then I'll meet you in the office. Oh, and thanks for earlier; I know it was nothing but you were on the ball. I appreciate that."

"No probs."

The call finished and Louis began writing down the conversation he'd had with 259 in his book, before his memory faded.

Ten minutes later he was making his way back to the office, independently of Carol, and they met twenty minutes later. He transcribed the contents of the meeting, submitted it and phoned the Controller to update him with the situation. The intelligence report was submitted to the intelligence cell:

*Subject Tony Warden, aka the Warden. Travels to Ealing, London in car driven by U/K driver 'Shanks'. Black Renault Clio. Usually Thursday. Purchase of crack cocaine and other. Warden significant dealer. U/K distributor in London, can carry firearms and/or weapons – nickname possibly 'Patch'.*

The next day Louis had a call from his Controller, who had read the contact report, worrying that 259 had implicated himself in the commission of a crime, and to be cautious of his continued involvement. Louis was already aware of the implications, but the Controller had covered his ass by putting it in writing as an addendum to the contact report.

# 5

# BORING STUFF

A few days later, Kenny arrived in the office. Their intention had been to continue the operation against Warden and carry-on with the obs, but it was becoming a little repetitive – same people, same place, same times, very routine and they had reached the stage where they needed to plan his arrest and scoop-up the street dealers that relied on his supply. Kenny began thinking about the various options to make the arrest whilst, at the same time, securing the best evidence. Warden appeared to be using one stash and, although it wasn't clear exactly where it was located, he was confident they could take him out successfully, secure the evidence and remove him from the area discreetly and, importantly, in isolation, to enable them to continue with the operation against the rest of the group. He thought that they should hit him one evening when he went to the canal where they could lift him quietly, take him away and then mop up afterwards. The most important part, and the vital link, of course, was that he needed to be lifted with gear and money on his person and this would rely on timing, speed and surprise.

But something occurred that would change this course of events, there was a knock on the door and one of the intelligence team leaned in and handed Kenny an envelope with the note:

*Thought this might be of interest.*

He opened it and read the intelligence report that had been submitted by Bertram a few days earlier. Of course, he knew that the report had been sanitised to protect the Handler and the Source and there was nothing in it that could lead to their identification, particularly the Source. But, what was in the body of the report provided them with another perspective, a different angle, and confirmed some information that they had already gleaned from Warden's phone records that might enable them to go one step further with the investigation. One that had eluded them thus far.

They were in receipt of Warden's mobile phone records and although he changed his phone occasionally, he was not overly diligent and they were generally able to keep reasonably abreast of any changes. Kenny found this really quite surprising, bearing in mind the precautions that he had taken in relation to his business and the stash. Nevertheless, the records showed that over the last four months he had contacted a different mobile number on Thursday afternoons, a number that appeared on those days only and never repeated on the records before or after the contact had been made. In addition, on several occasions he called a number of different London telephone numbers on the same afternoons. Those had been checked by the intelligence cell, which showed that they were telephone boxes, six in total. When these were plotted on a map it showed that they were in and around the Ealing area, within about a half-mile radius of Ealing Broadway Underground Station.

It was now Wednesday. Only one day left if they wanted to progress the investigation in that direction. Crack dealer Warden, working and serving from home, stashes away from house, which is probably fortified. Indications are that his regular distributer, from whom he collects, is based in London, probably West London, maybe Ealing.

There was a list of things to do: identify Shanks, but in the knowledge that he may no longer be providing the wheels; see if the surveillance team were available to drop onto Warden on Thursday, to see where he was going and who he was meeting; obtain detailed analysis of Warden's phone calls; and finally, get things moving quickly before they lost control of the situation.

Kenny gazed into the distance, thinking about the options. Ideally, it would be nice to take everyone out at the same time or to co-ordinate it so that everything fell into place simultaneously. But where would it take them?

The door opened and Franks wandered in.

"You OK?" he said.

"Yep."

Kenny updated him with the latest developments whilst Franks made coffee for them both; he placed a mug in front of Kenny and sat down. They were both in agreement and quietly excited. If they could at least get to the man 'Patch' in London that would be great, but they had to obtain the backing of the boss to continue the operation and put some more resources into the investigation.

"Leave him to me," said Franks.

He had known their boss for many years; they had served together as DCs. A good man, but pressured from above to obtain results with the minimum of resources or financial outlay.

"You crack on with finding stuff out, I'll go and see the old man."

They went their separate ways and met again in the office midway through the afternoon. Franks had managed to persuade their DI to run with the new information, but he wanted updating; the surveillance team were available and willing to help. In the meantime, Kenny had identified Shanks, one Steven Pritchard, thirty, living with his common law on the Duchy Estate. Bit of a villain, not much form, van delivery driver, mostly in the evening. Drove a Renault Clio. Kenny knew him as an associate of someone he had dealt with on a previous occasion. A cold fish, not very outgoing, a minor user; bit of an idiot really. There was an up-to-date photo from last year.

Franks had jacked up a meeting with the surveillance team that afternoon in their office. A couple of hours to gather photos and throw together an op order (operational order) so that everyone knew who was doing what, how they were doing it and what they were trying to achieve. The actual tactics would be left to the surveillance team. By the time of the meeting they were prepared, including maps of the immediate area; they knew the area well but the team were outsiders and although they knew the town, the one-way system and traffic light sequence could cause them problems.

They came into the office on time – a DI and one of the DSs. They were handed the op order, photos and maps, considered them carefully and were offered and accepted hot drinks – a black coffee and a tea, no sugar.

The DI took the lead as he flicked through the paperwork.

"How long have you been running this op?"

"Two weeks," Kenny responded.

"Operation…" he flicked through the papers, "Tundra, that right?"

"Yep," said Franks.

"You're certain about Patch?"

"No, but we'll run with what we have. We know Warden's been phoning a different mobile number each Thursday, always changing, and we also know that he sometimes phones a TK when he's there – in the Ealing area."

"What do you want?"

"To sit on Warden this Thursday, go with him to London and then switch subjects after the London connection so we can identify and house his contact."

"So, let Warden run?"

"Yep, we know where he's going back to and the OP will be in place to let us know."

"Why not sit on Shanks?"

"Because we don't know for certain it is him. Information is that it's been him, but don't know the current sit-rep."

*Sounds like Any Questions?,* thought Franks.

"OK." He looked at Kenny. "You come with us – do the log, ID anyone, take piccys. It tidies up the evidential chain and adds continuity,"added the DI. The DI looked at Kenny.

Kenny looked at Franks, who shrugged his shoulders,

"Yeah, that's fine." But secretly he thought, *Boring bits, the bits they don't want to fucking do.* But it made sense.

After some further deliberation the DI said, "OK, that's fine. We'll do the recce this afternoon and plot it up tomorrow. What time do you want to start?"

Kenny and Franks looked at each other. They hadn't considered that. They wanted it early enough to catch him when he left, but late enough to reduce the overtime footprint. They knew he wouldn't move before ten.

"Nine thirty in the office, on plot at ten… seem OK?"

"Yeah, good." He looked across to his DS, who had said nothing to that point.

"If you can plot the house, bearing in mind the traffic lights, OP has good control so we should have a good off. Meet at the services at eight. I'll come here; you go straight to plot."

"OK, boss."

*Suitably deferential,* Kenny thought.

The DI added, "Anything else?"

"No," said Kenny, then remembered, "information is that the London man carries either guns or knives and he may be dry-cleaning our man – not certain, but the use of TKs makes it a possibility. It may be that he's running him through open spaces or locations to make sure we're not there."

The DI and the DS looked at each other.

The DI raised his eyebrows.

"We'll bear that in mind."

He looked at his DS again. "Remind the guys not to get too close; we don't want either of them spooked and we certainly don't want the London man feeling trapped."

The meeting concluded and everyone left. Kenny tidied the mugs and papers. As he was doing so, he looked at Franks.

"You'll need someone in the OP with you – too much for one person on their own. I'll see if Fred's about… he might want a change of scene. And you'll need to get in there before the surveillance team get here in the morning, just in case the little shit moves a little early."

"Suits me. I hope they're fucking careful. It really sounds as if this London bloke is ultra-cautious and is willing to protect his corner."

"I think we'll knock it on the head tonight. I'll phone Patience and let her know we won't be in tonight but that we'll be with her tomorrow morning."

"Give us a chance to catch up on the crap," added Kenny.

That afternoon and into the early evening, they worked in the office, tidying up the logs, photos and subject profiles.

# 6

# INTO THE UNKNOWN

The weather was good the next day: blue sky, high clouds, dry, no wind. They met in the car park below the nick and then walked up the bare concrete stairwell to the first floor and their office. Unlocking the door, Franks made straight for the kettle to make a coffee and Kenny dumped his bag and checked the answer machine for messages. It was seven in the morning and the nick was stirring; prisoners to be processed, remand files to be completed, crime figures to be compiled and paperwork to be submitted. Clipboards, meetings and targets.

Fred Coaker, known to those that knew him as 'Fred the Bed', walked into the office. He wasn't late, but later than the others would have preferred.

"Sorry I'm a little late." He fumbled for a coffee.

"We'll be off in five, Fred!" Franks reminded him and minutes later he and Fred had left the office and were headed for the OP.

The DI from the surveillance team walked into the office

shortly afterwards, was offered and accepted a cup of black coffee, and sat down.

"Everything's good. Difficult plot because the house is at the junction and there aren't many places to park up. We'll be relying a lot on the OP to give us a good heads-up and direction, so they'll need to be on the ball. If everything goes to plan and we swap subjects, it will be handy to know when Warden arrives back at home, you're with me, the others are double crewed. I'm the only single."

He made sure he had enough logs and that he had spare batteries, collected his bag, trundled to the door, let the DI out, closed and locked the door and then followed him to his vehicle, a silver-coloured, non-descript and very boring Japanese saloon car. He loaded his kit into the boot and settled into the front seat. He checked that his covert set and earpiece were turned off and in the box that he kept safely in his pocket. He had brought with him log sheets and pinned them onto a clipboard, which he kept in the footwell.

The car felt personalised; little things seemed to reflect the personality of the user – wires attached to the cigarette lighter, UK Atlas and London A–Z in the door pocket, a small packet of tissues in the control console and two or three changes of jacket on the rear seat. All the unnecessary clobber was in the boot. The DI leaned across and dropped down the glovebox lid on the passenger side; it was jammed with two radios and mics, spare batteries and various leads. He then bent down to a small switch that was in the central console, hidden by a lifting armrest. He switched it on and the lights on the radio sets were instantly illuminated.

"That's the remote switch for both radios – handy if someone walks past or if you're in a car park or something. We're on Channel Three. This is the mic." He handed Kenny a small mic, about the size of a memory stick, with a small button on the top.

"We'll dispense with the main radio unless we need to speak to control. Five of us on plot." He handed him a hand-drawn map of everyone's position.

Kenny could see that the position of Warden's house had made plotting the units quite awkward. His house at the junction enabled him to go off in two different directions in a vehicle, or four different directions by foot. *But the OP,* he thought, *should give ample warning and good direction.* He moved the knurled knob on the radio tucked under his right armpit three times clockwise to what should be channel three and then pressed his own mic three times, and a corresponding three clicks came over the car speaker.

They moved off, leaving the underground car park and joining the morning traffic. Kenny could hear other units arriving on plot and Franks telling them that he was in the OP and that there had been no movement at the house.

They manoeuvred into a supermarket car park about five hundred yards from the address, on the correct side of the one-way system in the event that he took off in a car.

"We're 55. You're 55A," said the DI.

"OK," replied Kenny.

Kenny turned his earpiece on, checked the volume and placed it in his ear; again, three clicks on the microphone corresponded with what he received in his earpiece. He took it out, turned it off and replaced it in the box, which he then put in his pocket. He turned off his covert set to preserve the batteries.

He turned to the radio. "55, permission."

"Yes, yes, 55," Franks pronounced.

"55 on plot."

"Yes, yes, 55. All units on plot, OP has control. No movement. Lights on at one, no cars in vicinity. 51?"

"51, yes, yes."

Kenny and the DI settled into their new environment,

wedged in the middle of a line of cars that were parked up against a long, high brick wall. The car park was medium-sized, with perhaps one hundred and fifty cars spread out in the neat lines. They had backed into a slot and were facing out directly opposite the exit/entrance that flowed onto the main road, a one-way street from left to right

It was nine-fifty and Kenny started the log; he would maintain it, or the DI would if he was absent for any reason, throughout the day. He had brought a number of props – changes of upper body clothing and hats to change his appearance. He knew that people generally remember a person's upper body clothing rather than trousers or shoes and that, when in a crowd, this is all you could probably see.

The car park was busy with elderly couples trudging up to some sliding doors, grimly holding onto their shopping trolleys for support, urgent young mums with toddlers wedged into the fold-away seats, and women, generally gossiping and exchanging titbits. Occasionally, a young man – a supermarket employee – breezed through the parked cars waving his trolley cord, collecting the trolleys as he went, and then earnestly pushing a long snake-like line back towards the trolley corralling point at one side of the entrance.

"OP. No change, no change. No sign of Subject. 52."

"52, yes, yes."

The DI whipped into the shop for a paper and returned, and life drifted on. There was some movement at the house but nothing excessive – a few visitors but the subject, Warden, was yet to be seen.

Kenny reclined his seat. They were well away from the plot and any movement would be picked by the OP and then the units closest to the junction. He could relax a little whilst the radio blurted away. He drifted off.

Suddenly, the OP came up. Kenny woke with a start. He

had been asleep; he wasn't sure for how long but he glanced at his watch. It was eleven thirty. Eleven thirty-two, to be exact.

"Standby, standby. Subject 1 at the door looking up and down the road, light coloured top, blue jeans and brown boots. And in, in, in. Doors closed, 52."

"52, yes, yes."

"Looks as if he's looking to go out, or waiting for someone," said Kenny."

"OP, Subject 1 at first-floor window, looking down on road."

The DI started the engine and began looking at the exit but Franks in the OP had control of Subject 1 and they were all waiting for a commentary.

"OP. Front door open. Subject 1 out, out, out, same clothing but with dark jacket, carrying small blue holdall over right shoulder. Door closed behind him, down steps to gate, looking nearside and offside. And, off, off, off. Left, left, left on foot towards traffic lights. Still looking around. Held at junction, traffic. For the log, 11:35. 53?"

"53, yes, yes."

"Across the junction, no deviation. Towards RA and you, 52."

"OP still has eyeball. Walking nearside Barnet Street towards RA. Stop, stop, stop! Subject 1 standing on kerb about one hundred metres RA side of traffic lights."

"Lighting cigarette looking up at the oncoming traffic."

"52, OP."

"52, yes, yes."

"Be aware that if it is a pick-up, he will come to you."

"52, yes, yes."

"No change, no change."

Kenny sensed a fresh intensity. Everyone was alert, ready to move in anticipation that Warden was going to be picked up and that there would be a very short lapse of time between the subject being static and then moving at speed. The beginning of any surveillance was the most critical. Kenny was thankful that Franks knew what he was doing. There was no sign of tension in his voice, no indication of stress, just calm control with no hint of the excitement of the moment.

*Good man,* he thought. *He could be landing a fucking 747 at Heathrow.*

Several 'no changes' were given by the OP, indicating that Warden had not moved. No-one else spoke; it was vital that the eyeball had complete control otherwise information or movement could be lost.

Then, "OP. Standby, standby. Black Renault Clio pulling up. Passenger door opened, repeat, black Renault Clio. Unable to see driver. Rear nearside brake light not working. Subject 1 in, in, in. Door closed. Front passenger seat. Cannot see any other occupants. Time now 11:42, 52."

"52, yes, yes."*Good, rear light not working – easier to ID at night,* Kenny thought.

"OP, no change, no change." They were obviously chatting. Then suddenly, "Standby, standby, offside indicator. Driver has dark hair. Manoeuvring and off, off, off towards RA and you, 52, in lane 2 of 3. OP still has the eyeball. Subject will be held in 2 at red signal. Still held. Still held. Light changing and onto the RA and loss of eyeball. 11:44."

There was complete silence; Kenny could visualise what Franks had seen and how far he could see down the road, but why hadn't 52 picked him up? The DI had moved out of the car park and turned right towards Warden's house, and then been held by traffic lights behind a line of three vehicles.

The seconds ticked by and then, from 52, "Contact, contact, contact. 52 has the eyeball, three – no, four – for cover, third exit towards the motorway and will be held at red ATS."

"53, your backup."

"Lights changing, subject is through, eyeball is through. Let me know when you're through."

"53 through."

"54 through."

"51 held."

Kenny added, "55 held."

"No deviation, straight on in 2, speed – twenty-five, traffic moderate. McDonald's nearside."

Kenny knew that although this stretch of road was relatively straight, with just one set of lights, he wouldn't be able to put his foot down.

"No deviation, towards motorway."

"51 through ATS."

"55 through ATS."

"52, yes, yes, still four for cover in 2, twenty. Convoy check."

"53 backup."

"54 at 1."

"51 at 2."

"55 tail end," Kenny added.

"Convoy complete. No deviation in 2, 20."

Kenny was relieved that everything had clunked into place; the team was now embedded in the local lunchtime traffic and the initial scramble to latch onto the vehicle had now passed.

"No deviation in 2, twenty, steady traffic, college to nearside, approaching green PDX, subject is through." There was a pause. "Eyeball is through. Tail end, let me know."

"55, yes, yes."

Kenny had forgotten how useful this was. When he popped up to say he was through the PDX, everyone would know the relative time and distance between the front and back of the convoy. About twenty seconds later they passed the crossing.

"Tail end through PDX."

"Yes, yes, convoy complete, no deviation, in 2, fifteen, heavy traffic, cemetery offside."

The convoy continued. Kenny could not see the subject vehicle; the whole convoy was relying on the eyes and commentary of the eyeball to tell them what was happening.

"Advance warning RA."

"53 in position."

"Yes, yes, 53. At the RA, two for cover."

"Yes, yes."

"Held at RA, two from pole, one from pole. Subject on RA, eyeball on RA. Not one, not one, not two, not two, third exit, third exit, A329 towards London. To you, 53."

"Yes, yes, 53 has the eyeball. Up slip road."

"54, your backup."

Kenny moved towards the roundabout and as he entered he saw a vehicle holding back at the junction – presumably 52. They entered and increased speed, moving around the roundabout and up to the slip road.

Having seen all units through, "52 now tail end, convoy complete."

"Yes, yes, 52. In 2, three for cover, my speed 70."

Kenny knew that as speed increased on the motorway, the convoy would stretch out, causing difficulties if the subject took it upon himself to visit services or leave the motorway, and making communication between the various units more intermittent, and therefore less reliable.

"In 2, my speed 75, traffic moderate, advance warning sign, Junction 1, one mile."

This was handy because it enabled everyone to judge their distance from the subject and adapt their speed accordingly.

"No deviation, no deviation, advance warning Junction 2 M4 East one mile." Then, "Quarter of a mile," and finally,

"Countdown markers, nearside indicator onto slip road, and committed left, left, left, M4 towards London."

*So he was going towards London,* thought Kenny.

He telephoned Franks to let him know. Franks told him it was all quiet at the house. The surveillance settled down, the convoy was comfortably systematic, and it turned out that the driver, believed to be Shanks, was steady – between seventy and seventy-five miles per hour, no rash moves. This presumably suited Warden, who didn't want anything too flash and definitely didn't want to draw attention to himself.

The vehicles following him had inevitably stretched out for about a mile, when, after about thirty minutes, "Nearside indication in 1, my speed fifty, ten for cover."

"Advance warning, services half a mile." The units at the rear of the convoy would have to accelerate hard to close the gap with the front runners without overtaking the closest vehicles.

"Countdown markers three, two, one, nearside indicator, left, left, left, towards services, two for cover, committed, Heston Services. Convoy hold back, manoeuvring in car park. Backup come through."

"Stop, stop, stop. Subject vehicle stationary, nearside car park, about three rows from the entrance. Both subjects still in vehicle. Convoy come through. Backup cover the exit to the motorway. 53 will retain eyeball."

*Fuck it,* thought Kenny. *He may be meeting him here... not ideal.*

"Subject 1 on phone, Subject 2 out of vehicle – can confirm identity of Subject 2. Subject 1 out of vehicle and moving towards services entrance. Subject 1 still on phone – no holdall, no holdall. Alphas?"

The Alphas were deployed on foot if the subject was on walkabout, and were generally the observers in a two-crewed vehicle.

"54A out."

"51A out, ahead of subject in main building."

*Nice anticipation,* Kenny thought.

"53 still has control. Subject 2, dark clothing and dark baseball hat. Both subjects towards entrance, calm, relaxed, talking to each other. At the entrance and in, in, in to services and loss of eyeball." This was followed by one of those pauses that makes you want to fill the gap with a radio transmission. Ten, maybe fifteen, seconds later came.

"51A has eyeball, moving though the services to men's toilets, both in, in, in, men's toilets, temporary loss. 51A to toilets. 54A cover exit."

"54A, yes, yes."

Silence. No-one spoke; they knew 51A was in a confined space and even with a covert earpiece, noise travels in a bare toilet.

The silence lasted for about three or four minutes.

"Contact, contact, contact. 54A has the eyeball. Into main thoroughfare and into café. In the queue for drink."

"51A, permission."

"Yes, yes."

"No meet in toilet, I repeat, no meet in toilet."

"Both subjects ordering, still in queue."

"No change, no change."

"Picked up coffee, cash paid, in seated area and now sitting together talking. 51A, cover the exit."

"51A, yes, yes."

"55, permission to plot." Kenny took control.

"Yes, yes."

"55 is rear."

"51 rear offside."

"52 rear offside."

"53 eyeball on vehicle."

"54 ahead exit to motorway. 52, relieve 54 at exit."
"Yes, yes."
"54 rear nearside, position to pick up Alphas."
"Yes, yes."
"All units plotted, back to you, eyeball."
"Yes, yes."

Kenny knew they were doing a simple cross system, one vertical line crossed by a horizontal line with the subject car in the middle where the two lines crossed. The units could then be plotted ahead, behind, left or right, or whatever, in order that all eventual routes were covered. Kenny marked his log and sat back. He leaned across to the DI.

"I want to have a gander at the car whilst we have the opportunity."

"Go for it," said the DI and then added, as an afterthought. "Be quick."

"55, permission."

"Yes, yes."

"Want to deploy 55A to check vehicle. Do the two subjects have subject vehicle in view from their present position?"

"No, no."

Kenny put in his earpiece and checked reception. "55A moving now."

"No change, no change."

He opened the door and walked towards the vehicle, which was parked about seventy five yards ahead. The car park was packed with vehicles, people moving about, dogs being walked, but Warden's vehicle was nicely parked with no-one in the immediate vicinity, in a complete line of vehicles obscured from the café by a small box van. He knew it was important not to look suspicious, not to dawdle, to look meaningful. He approached it from the rear and slowed, walking along the left-hand side, looking in as he passed. He could see the holdall in the footwell of the front passenger seat. All doors appeared locked, buttons down. He walked around the front and back down the other side to the rear, which was tight up against the front of the car in the next row.

"No change, no change," chanted his earpiece.

He had time. He touched the boot button and it pinged open. Nothing of note. Clean, empty, spare wheel. He closed it again.

"Standby, standby." *Fuck it,* thought Kenny, and he made his way back to his vehicle. By the time he reached his car, both subjects were moving and he dipped into his seat just as they exited the services' entrance.

"OK?" enquired the DI.

"Yep. Holdall in front passenger footwell, zipped up. Piece of paper on the front passenger seat with writing, couldn't read." He updated the log and had completed it as Warden and Pritchard reached the car.

The transmissions continued. "55, permission."

"Yes, yes."

"Any meeting?"

"No, no."

"For info, bag front passenger footwell."

"Yes, yes."

The Alphas returned to their vehicles and 53 took control.

"Engine started, manoeuvring and off, off, off, towards exit and motorway. 52, 12:55."

"52, yes, yes."

"53 has the eyeball – no vehicle cover, now picked up two for cover, towards motorway."

"52 can take."

"Yes, yes."

"52 with eyeball, slip-road towards motorway, onto motorway in 1."

"53 backup."

"54, Alphas picked up." Kenny counted all the units onto the slip road.

"55 tail end. Convoy complete."

The DI accelerated hard onto the motorway and the engine strained. He knew how much ground he had to make up if he was to stay in contact. The commentary continued whilst Kenny made up the log and the DI sought to reduce time and distance.

The subject continued along the M4 and up onto the Chiswick flyover, running above the old A4. The distance between the eyeball and Kenny, as tail-end Charlie, reduced as they passed the Lucozade building. Then, without warning, "Left, left, left onto slip-road. I have five for cover, convoy hold back."

There had been no warning, no indication, and as the subject vehicle and the eyeball disappeared down the slip road, the remaining convoy caused a small traffic jam in the left-hand lane of the flyover.

"Onto A4 towards London, convoy come through. Approaching green ATS, subject is through, eyeball through, in 2, 30."

"53 backup."

"At the RA, 53."

Kenny followed the remaining vehicles as they hurtled snake-like down the slip road and onto the main road. As they did so, the lights changed at the bottom, close to the slip road, ensnaring the vehicles in traffic.

"55 – remaining convoy baulked at lights."

"Yes, yes," a calm voice responded.

Subject 2 continued on his journey, oblivious of the turmoil he was causing behind him.

"Approaching the RA, no indication."

"3 for cover."

Still the lights remained unchanged, provoking oaths and increasing the levels of stress.

"Left, left, left before RA towards North Circular and left, left, left onto North Circular. Convoy make ground, 53 when ready."

"Yes, yes."

The lights changed. Kenny sensed that tensions were rising in the three cars that had been stranded at the junction. The three vehicles at the head of the queue, those that had blocked the remaining members of the team, moved off almost in slow motion and when a gap emerged, the first of the follow team took the opportunity to accelerate through, weaving between the other cars and on towards the North Circular. The second car followed, and on its tail, Kenny in the last vehicle.

"55, all units through ATS."

"Yes, yes, 55. No deviation, still North Circular, general direction Wembley."

Kenny followed the other cars as they accelerated along the A4 and took the slip road onto the North Circular.

"Subject held in 2 at red ATS Junction B4491, lights green, subject moving forward and through; eyeball through, 53 come through."

"53 has the eyeball, no deviation, North Circular, general direction Wembley."

Kenny and the remaining cars accelerated towards the ATS, aware that once the convoy had become fractured, disconnected, it could be a struggle to re-connect, to re-establish the necessary rhythm. They all wanted to get through before they changed and avoid being held again. The vehicles moved lanes to take advantage of the gaps that developed. He could see the lights ahead, still green, still green…

"Hold, you bastards, hold," he mumbled whilst staring at the green lights.

One through, second through and finally, Kenny swept through beneath them just as they were changing.

"Fuck me, that was tight!" declared the DI.

"55 through the ATS, tail end and convoy complete."

"Yes, yes, no deviation, heavy traffic, over railway bridge, four for cover, 20."

"Ealing Riding Stables nearside." Once again Kenny was able to orientate himself and had dug out the A to Z to see what lay ahead.

"Parkland nearside and offside in 1, advance warning junction ahead, close up."

"Ealing Common, 51 come through as backup."

"Red ATS, subject will be held in 1, four for cover. Convoy check?"

"51 backup."

"52 at 1."

"54 at 2."

"55 tail end." Kenny knew they were about ten to fifteen vehicles behind the subject with no lorries or buses between them.

"Green ATS, no deviation," then, "left, left, left, A4020, two for cover, next natural 51."

"51, yes, yes."

All the cars ahead of Kenny turned left onto the Uxbridge Road, followed by Kenny.

"Tail end through."

"Yes, yes, no deviation. Uxbridge Road, general direction Ealing Green. PDX, Church to offside. To you, 51."

"51 has the eyeball, no deviation, two for cover."

"52 is your backup."

"Yes, yes, no deviation."

As Kenny passed the PDX he could see that 53, having relinquished the eyeball, was manoeuvring into the first nearside junction to return to the convoy.

"53 now tail end, convoy complete." He pulled in behind him.

"Yes, yes, no deviation, Costcutter and Northcote Avenue nearside, 3 for cover, 25. Be aware, heavy traffic, convoy close-up, shops nearside and offside, Windsor Road nearside." Then, suddenly, "Stop, stop, stop nearside outside PH, name unknown, loss of eyeball. Backup?" The vehicle had stopped without notice in heavy traffic.

"Backup gone by."

Suddenly, they were for the first time without total control of the subject. The car had stopped without warning and the front two cars had driven past without having had the opportunity of stopping.

"51 ahead nearside."

"52 ahead offside."

"54A out."

The DI pulled in behind the vehicle ahead, apparently 54, on their side of a small slope and beyond the rear view of the subject vehicle. A woman exited the passenger seat of 54 ahead of them. Kenny switched on his radio.

He leaned across and said, "Do the log!" and then left the vehicle. He crossed the pavement, removing his earpiece from the box, and stood looking in the windows of one of the cafés on the right-hand side. For the first time he was entirely unsighted and out of radio contact. He saw the car he was in, 55, with the DI, disappear from view down the first turning on the left. He was alone.

*At least it's not fucking raining,* he thought.

He turned on his earpiece and inserted it into his right ear. A cacophony of sound bombarded him – not panic, just urgency; no-one had control, which meant no-one had sight of anything, neither subject nor the vehicle. Two cars had plotted according to the cross system.

A few seconds later, it felt like minutes had passed.

"54A has eyeball," a wonderfully serene, balanced, reassuring female voice came over the airwaves.

"54A, Subject 1 on original, crossing the road opposite the North Star PH, north side of road, Halifax Building Society nearside. Subject vehicle continued on original." This indicated that Shanks had driven-off in the original direction.

"51."

"Yes, yes."

"52."

"Yes, yes."

"To confirm, Subject 2 is driver of subject vehicle."

"No deviation, NatWest bank to offside." Silence and then: "Right, right, right, The Broadway."

"55A your backup".

"53A making."

"Yes, yes."

As he neared the junction he saw the same woman he had seen earlier on the opposite side of the road; she looked to her right, caught Kenny's eye and gently nodded, once. Kenny followed the road around to his right and caught sight of Warden again on the other side of the road about twenty yards ahead of him. 54A had turned right as well, directly behind Warden, and had retained the eyeball.

"54A can confirm, Subject 1 carrying holdall. This is one-way street, subject is walking against the flow."

"51, permission to plot."

"Yes, yes, 51. Confirm stay with Subject 1, let subject vehicle run."

"51 making for ahead nearside."

"52 ahead offside."

"53 rear."

"54 rear."

"55 rear."

"51, units plotted back to you. 54A?"

"54A, yes, yes, no deviation."

"52, permission."

"Yes, yes, 52."

"Subject vehicle continued on original away from plot."

"Yes, yes, 52," then almost immediately, "Stop, stop, stop, subject into TK outside subway." He could see that 54A had stopped and was looking in the front window of an estate agent, about twenty yards short of the telephone box, and that there was movement inside. He moved forward to a bus shelter on his right-hand side, from where he could see the telephone box across the road through the constantly moving traffic. His view was obscured by signage so that he couldn't actually see inside, but he would be able to see if Warden left the kiosk.

He sat down amongst a group of people. *Not ideal,* he thought, *but it may suffice.*

"55A offside can take."

"Yes, yes, 55A, to you."

"55A has the eyeball on the TK but not Subject 1, who is inside. 54A stay rear, 53A ahead to cover junction and Ealing Broadway Tube," he whispered.

"53A, yes, yes."

"54A, permission."

"Yes, yes."

"Subject 1 entered TK, waiting for call, no outgoing. For the log."

"55, yes, yes."

"55A, no change, no change. Be aware that Subject 1 may be being dry cleaned and under obs by a third party at this time."

Kenny had encountered dry cleaning before and had indeed adopted the system himself on occasions. It was a good method of ensuring that the person you were meeting was not being followed or accompanied by anyone else, and this was done by directing the person through a location or series of locations that could be watched and monitored to confirm that he or she were on their own.

"No change, no change. Still in TK. When we have movement there will be no warning."

He knew that the first he would see of Subject 1 would be when he opened the door and walked into view and that he would be able to give very little notice of any movement.

A double-decker bus temporarily obscured his view but he could see through the windows to the other pavement and asked 54A to see if she could tell whether the subject was using the phone. She changed position and was able to confirm that he was on the phone. Warden had been in the TK for about five minutes.

Suddenly, "55A, off, off, off, original direction, Ealing Broadway Tube offside. Come through, 54A. For the log, time now 13:34."

"Yes, yes, 54A has long-distance eyeball, no deviation."

Kenny walked parallel on the other side of the road and slightly behind Warden. This system worked well – two directly behind the subject and one on the other side of the road, nearly in line with the eyeball, provided the following team with flexibility and enabled them to cover junctions and changes in direction.

"53A."

"Yes, yes."

"When we've passed your position, return to TK and log a call to the office."

"Yes, yes."

Standard practice. By calling a known number directly after a suspect call from a TK makes it much easier to subsequently analyse the data from that TK and identify the number called by the suspect. It also allowed for a cursory search of the inside of the TK for any notes or messages that may have been left.

"No deviation, Haven Green nearside, Ealing Broadway Tube offside."

"Park offside, subject crossing road."

"55A has the eyeball, no deviation."

53A informed him that he had re-joined the surveillance.

"No deviation at RA, following the road to the offside, Tesco offside."

"55 permission."

"Yes, yes, 55."

"You are entering Madeley Road."

"To PDX and crossing the road." He looked to his left and could see 54A walking quickly the long way around the RA. Kenny kept on his side of the PDX, hanging back as the road opened up with less street furniture. Warden continued on.

"Right, right, right, Madeley Road." He glanced to his left, 53A was across the crossing as he saw Warden take the second left.

"Left, left, left, road name unknown. Still on nearside." Kenny slowed his pace as he reached the end of the road, which allowed him to have a good lingering look at Warden as he strode away and assess the distance he was from the junction before deciding it safe to call 53A around the corner into the road.

"Hold back, 53A."

Warden wandered on without a concern.

"This is a narrow one-way street, subject is going against the flow."

"55 permission."

"Yes, yes."

"Believed road is Haven Lane."

"Yes, yes, come round 53A."

"Yes, yes 53A has the eyeball." Kenny had walked past the end of Haven Lane and then crossed the road to be on the correct side.

This was a very awkward street – narrow, one way, not a main thoroughfare and no street furniture to speak of. He wondered where Warden was headed. He still had the holdall with him.

"53A no deviation, still nearside, no cover."

Kenny and 54A were standing at the bottom of the road out of sight, hesitant to commit and unsure whether to expose themselves in such a restricted area. He indicated to her to go and she crossed to the offside of Haven Lane.

"54A back up."

"Yes, yes, 54A."

Warden must have been about one hundred yards from the junction when 53A piped up.

"Left, left, left, temporary loss."

"55, maybe a pub – the Haven Arms!"

He was obviously looking at the A–Z and checking maps on his phone.

"53A can confirm, in, in, in to Haven Arms PH, 53A will enter."

He would have removed his earpiece at this point and commentary had to be kept to a minimum.

Kenny crossed the road and spoke to 54A and arranged for her to walk up the street and check for possible exit routes. Kenny followed her but on the right-hand side of the street.

All was quiet; there were no radio transmissions.

Just before the pub on the right-hand side, Kenny saw a lady tending to her garden. She was in her mid-seventies, hair pulled back, wearing a green apron and green gloves. The garden was beautifully tended with wonderful flowers, climbing plants and a small patch of lawn. She was on all fours, seeking out and destroying invading weeds, and had reached the front left-hand corner of the border. Instinct and the necessities of the operation caused him to stand and admire the garden.

She started the conversation. "Good morning."

"Good morning," said Kenny, "I was just admiring your wonderful garden."

She stood up, stretching her back as she did so.

"Thank-you, yes." She pushed her hand into her lower back and her voice showed the strain. "It takes a lot of work but I think it's worth it. Are you a keen gardener?"

"I try. Work gets in the way, I'm afraid."

"Ah yes, I know the feeling."

Kenny leaned over the wall and touched those plants he could reach, allowing his fingers to softly pass over the leaves. As he looked up he noticed that the house next door had a 'For Sale' notice. She saw him looking at the house and the sign.

"It's still for sale, been on the market for about six weeks – probate, I'm afraid. Ken died very suddenly; lovely chap." She clearly liked the look of Kenny because she then said, "Would you like to look inside? I've got some keys."

"Oh, I'd love to, if it's not too much trouble, that would be great, thank you. I'm not sure I could afford it, mind you."

"Well, it's on the market for £750,000; not sure they'll get that, it needs lots of work doing. My name's Joyce, by the way."

She scuttled inside and returned, leaving by the front gate. She joined him in the road and they walked to the adjoining house, a whitewashed three-storey terrace. She entered with a key and he followed, closing the door behind him.

Kenny had a pang of guilt; he needed to come clean and say that he had no interest in the house. There were still no transmissions and everything was quiet.

"Well, Joyce, I really appreciate you taking the trouble to show me the house and I'm really sorry to have interrupted your gardening, but my real reason for speaking to you is that I'm a police officer." He produced his warrant card and showed it to her.

"Oh yes," she said, looking at him quizzically.

"I need to keep an eye on the front door of the pub."

"The Haven?"

"Yes, I shouldn't be long."

At that moment the radio crackled into life, which was clearly heard by Joyce, who looked puzzled.

He lifted his jacket to show her his covert radio and removed the earpiece.

"I'm really sorry to have disturbed you, but it's really quite important."

"Oh, that's alright, how long are you going to be?"

"I don't know actually, could be five minutes or two hours."

"Well, if I give you the key for the place, you can hand it back when you leave, I'm sure it will be fine. Would you like a cup of tea?"

"Thank-you, but no."

"OK, I'll leave you in peace."

Kenny added an important proviso. "I'm not here so please don't tell anyone – that's really important."

"Don't worry, dear." She left.

Kenny locked the door after her and made his way upstairs to find the best vantage point. The house was unfurnished but the carpet remained and it had clearly been recently occupied. Signs of wear and tear were everywhere. He chose the top floor of the building where there was a small dormer overlooking the pub; it was less obtrusive and because the house was set back from the road, it gave a good view of the exit and the road in both directions. People don't generally look up, and height gave more control and distance.

He found an empty tea chest, turned it over and sat

down. This gave him a view of the pub's entrance and radio reception was good. He had been monitoring radio traffic and was aware that 53A had eyeball on the subject, who was alone in the front bar. Vehicles had plotted to cover both ends of the lane.

"55A permission." He heard three clicks from 53A, indicating that it was safe to transmit and nothing else was going on at the time. "55A, I'm in OP opposite PH, I have visual on the front and views to the junctions at both ends." Once again, three clicks.

The pub wasn't particularly busy – a few people came and went, not a roaring trade – but it looked good and very inviting, tucked in amongst the brown-brick terraced houses that lined the streets.

He began an impromptu log to record timings, descriptions, vehicles and anything else that he thought he should record. One man in his fifties came out a couple of times to light up. This was always a little awkward for a number of reasons; smokers outside pubs didn't move a great deal, they weren't engaged in any distracting pastime, like animated conversation, and they had time on their hands to ponder and observe their surroundings. Today, this included looking at the buildings opposite and engaging Joyce in conversation from the other side of the road. He hoped that she had remembered what he had told her. At least, he thought, by chatting to her the smoker was occupying his time and not being too inquisitive about his surroundings.

A couple of men entered the pub at different times and Kenny jotted down their descriptions. Then there was a series of clicks. "55A permission," followed by three clicks.

"Has subject 1 met someone?" Three clicks from 53A showed that he had met someone in the pub.

Kenny looked at his sheet. There were two possibilities.

"Blue jacket?" Two clicks. Clearly the wrong person. That narrowed it down a bit. "Male, forties, dark hair, green jacket, grey trousers, brown shoes?" Three clicks instantly.

"55A to all units, the man meeting Subject 1 is now Subject 3. Does any unit need relay?"

Shanks remained Subject 2 throughout the operation.

No response. So everyone could hear what was going on. Warden had been in the pub now for just over thirty minutes; he had been with Subject 3 for about five minutes. Still the old boy with the cigarette was talking to Joyce, who had stopped what she was doing and was now standing at her front wall.

Several more people went into the pub and the cigarette smoker, who was obviously a local, acknowledged them as they entered.

Kenny tried to remember whether green jacketed man was carrying anything. He thought not but couldn't be sure.

"55A permission." Three clicks.

"Any change?" Two clicks.

He had certainly come from the same direction as Warden, but had been walking, no vehicle.

About twenty minutes had passed when Kenny heard a series of clicks, indicating movement. About thirty seconds later, Warden appeared at the door and stood on the threshold, looking up and down the road.

"55A permission." Three clicks.

"55A has eyeball on Subject 1, standing at pub entrance looking around." He remained there for about a minute. "And right, right, right, direction Ealing Broadway." He was re-tracing his footsteps.

Kenny noticed he did not have the holdall.

"Subject 1 does not have the holdall, repeat, does not have the holdall. No deviation. Be aware that Subject 2 may be in vicinity with car. We will stay with subject 3 at PH. Any change, 53A?"

Two clicks.

*So Subject 3, the green jacketed man, is still in the pub. Good.*

"51 permission." Three clicks.

"Subject 1 has passed us, still towards Broadway."

Kenny phoned Franks at the OP and told him that Warden was on his way back. Apparently, there was no movement at the house. Good evidence.

He and the team stayed in the area of the pub, he hoped that 53A would remain alert and provide him with plenty of warning that Subject 3 was moving to the exit.

Time went on and as it did so, doubt began to creep into Kenny's mind.

Had they both missed him?

Perhaps there was a back entrance?

What would they do if he stayed there for the rest of the afternoon?

All these options seemed unlikely, especially as he had the holdall that Warden had given him.

Forty-five minutes passed; nagging doubts persisted.

What if he was that cute and changed his jacket – would he recognise him?

Then a series of clicks. Movement!

Within ten seconds, Subject 3 was at the door and off very quickly. The immediacy of his actions and the lack of hesitancy took Kenny by surprise.

"Standby, standby. Off, off, off, immediate left, left, left on the nearside away from PH. 55A has eyeball, all units hold. I can control for the next two hundred yards. Can confirm Subject 3 has blue holdall on right shoulder, looking around. Description, IC1, six feet, medium build, forties, dark short hair, moustache, green jacket, grey trousers, brown shoes. No deviation."

He could observe with ease, monitor his movements, without risk of compromise, and was able to take the sting out of what would have been a difficult pick-up from the pub without an OP in place.

Then, without any warning, the subject stopped, turned around and stood looking back the way he had come, and then slowly began to walk back towards the pub.

"Stop, stop, stop. Recip, recip, slowly back towards PH. 53A, remain in PH." Three clicks.

Kenny was suppressing his response to the intensity of the situation, keeping his voice calm, balanced and trying not to show the level of concentration required to maintain contact with the man. He must not lose him. There was no-one else in the street, Subject 3 was alone. He had just completed a perfect anti-surveillance routine, delaying his exit from the pub and allowing anyone following him to lose concentration, become disinterested, and then moving quickly and deliberately at the very outset, unsettling and unbalancing the following team who were trying to react to the situation. This process allowed him to grasp the initiative, take advantage of the unexpected and expose the surveillance when it was at its most vulnerable.

"Fucking bastard – I've got you!" Kenny whispered to himself.

"55A, all units hold. Subject 3 approaching PH to his offside." Kenny could see Joyce in the garden; she had been coming and going, trimming, digging, tidying. The cigarette man was leaning by the door of the pub.

"Subject 3 passed PH to offside, now offside pavement, direction Ealing Broadway, still with holdall. Beware of man smoking cigarette standing at the front of PH." He tried to keep his voice calm and steady but the guy was all about himself and

Kenny could see his head moving slightly to left and right as he cleared the ground ahead of him.

"Units be aware that Subject 3 is surveillance-conscious. We need some piccys of him when opportunity arises. No deviation, no deviation towards Ealing Broadway. Subject is halfway along the road. I will lose control when subject reaches road junction. 53A clear to exit." Three clicks.

"54A permission."

"Yes, yes."

"54A and 51A are covering junction."

"Yes, yes – approx. fifty yards from you on offside, now crossing to nearside."

"51A can take."

"Yes, yes."

"51A has the eyeball, Subject 3 to PDX." With that, Kenny rushed downstairs and out of the front door. Cigarette man had left and Joyce was in her garden. He forced himself to slow down, locked the door and lent over the fence.

"Thanks, Joyce." He held out the key.

"Oh! You've finished, have you?" She took the key.

"Yep, all done. I'll come back and see you when we're done. Don't forget what I said."

"I won't." He wanted to give her a hug.

"Must rush – take care and thanks."

She watched him go and waved.

As he shut the garden gate he turned, saw her looking and waved back. Kenny trotted up to join 53A, who had left the pub. "Everything OK?"

"Yes, great, tell you later." He could hear that Subject 3 was still walking towards Ealing Broadway and the commentary was still coming from the Alphas. *This is a good team,* thought Kenny. *Worth a mention later.*

The cars were adjusting their position according to Subject

3's movements, which were relayed to them by the Alphas. In effect, it was like a constantly moving bubble, with Subject 3 in the middle.

"Left, left, left into Ealing Broadway Tube."

*Jesus Christ, he could go anywhere,* thought Kenny.

"55 permission."

"Yes, yes, make it quick." It was crowded, a throng of people were moving in and around the entrance, great for cover but not if you want to keep contact. Concentration was vital.

"Three options, Central, District or Mainline – give us a heads-up."

"Yes, yes. To the barrier. Oyster, no direction, wait…" and then, "District line, District line."

"55, yes, yes. Who do you have?"

Reception was deteriorating; transmission was broken. They were going below ground; comms would be lost until they re-surfaced.

A quick check. This was the end of the District line and he could only go in one direction – the only mitigating factor, although he could hop onto the Piccadilly Line at any stage.

"54A, 51A and 53A…" Reception faded out.

55 took control. "55. Relay, Subject 3 is on the District line. Who has Alphas?"

"52."

"51 and 53, go to Ealing Common Tube Station."

"51 yes, yes."

"53 yes, yes."

"52 and 54 to Acton Town, second stop."

"52 yes, yes."

"54 yes, yes."

"55 will hold to pick up Alpha." There was nothing on the radio from the Alphas on the tube.

"55A, 55 location."

"Outside the Ealing Broadway Tube."

"Stay there."

Kenny moved to the road so that his position was obvious but he didn't quite know which direction his car was going to come from. He scanned the area and had only been there for about twenty seconds when the boring silver-coloured Japanese car pulled up in front of him. He got in and they moved away, but were then held behind a vehicle at red traffic lights. When the lights changed they turned left down the Uxbridge Road and made up what ground they could against the burgeoning traffic.

The desire to reach the tube station and regain control of the subject was paramount, but it wasn't just the speed, although it was fast, it was the sharp braking, tight acceleration, manoeuvring around slower vehicles and fairly constant blaspheming that reflected that part of the surveillance.

Still there was no contact from the Alphas. The radio was silent.

As they approached Ealing Common Tube Station, the DI slowed down. This was sensible; to come to a halt outside the station in a cloud of smoke with the smell of rubber permeating the foyer of the station would not be conducive to a covert surveillance operation. He turned left just past the station and stopped.

"Out you hop. I'll plot the cars, you give us a heads-up if you see the man or hear from the others."

Kenny got out and the car moved off. He made his way tentatively back to the entrance to the tube, not knowing whether the subject had already exited or not or whether, indeed, he had continued his journey beyond the first two stops, to another station.

As he turned right into the road down which they had just come, the tube station was off to his left. He had to quickly find a position from where he could see the entrance to the tube station without going through the rigmarole of finding another Joyce. He found it without really looking. Directly opposite was a telephone box. Although they didn't know it when they planted these boxes on the sides of roads, in towns and in rural locations, they were a godsend to surveillance officers, allowing them to naturally merge with the environment, shelter from inclement weather, aid communication by using the telephone, and provide, in most cases, all-round vision. He opened the door and entered. He lifted the receiver; everything was working. It was now just a case of waiting. Of course, Subject 3 may well be on his way to another destination, having passed through this stop already, en-route to his suburban hideout.

Kenny confirmed his location with 55 and knew that the Alphas from the other vehicles were on the train; he was alone. He watched the people move around, in and out of the tube, visiting shops, but he needed to concentrate on the entrance. He was half expecting 55 to pop up and say that the subject had arrived at Turnham Green Station, or even Earl's Court.

He could see inside the foyer of the station and noticed a flurry of people moving through towards him from the barriers. A train had just arrived. Twenty, thirty, forty people all coming out at the same time and star-bursting as they reached the street – and there he was, Subject 3 in a green jacket, sliding through the crowd, moving quickly and deliberately towards the street. Kenny would have jumped for joy if he hadn't been in such a restricted space.

"55A contact, contact, contact. Subject 3, Ealing Common Tube, towards the exit." He wasn't sure who else was receiving his transmissions but then heard 55's relay transmission.

"55, contact, contact, contact Ealing Common Tube Station." He knew that other people would be reacting to it but there was no sign of the Alphas who had been on the tube.

Subject 3 hesitated as he reached the outside world, as if he was re-adjusting to daylight and deciding where he was going. At the same time he slipped off his green jacket and hooked it over his arm.

"Stop, stop, stop at the exit. Subject has removed jacket, blue shirt, blue shirt. Wait for direction. Subject 3 still has holdall over shoulder. Left, left, left and crossing the road. No deviation. Park nearside."

Then after a short distance. "Right, right, right, temporary loss, road name unknown."

And after a few seconds, "55, Wolverton Gardens, Wolverton Gardens, residential area." *Slippery bastard!* he thought. *He's removed his top garment at the critical time – at an exit and in a crowd.*

Kenny knew that other units, particularly the Alphas, would be moving to his location. He paused at the junction. It had taken time for them to come up from the tube and there was no cover on the opposite side of the road. He looked around and saw 54A running up on the other side of the road to view the junction and call him around the corner.

Still he waited as 54A moved into position. And then, "Stop, stop, stop. Subject held in Wolverton Gardens, on offside approx. thirty metres from junction." *Bastard!* Kenny thought, but he admired him; he was maintaining the routine of checking whether he was being followed and disrupting any surveillance.

"Moving forward. No deviation. Come round, 55A." Kenny glanced round – still no sign of the others – before moving around the corner. He could see Subject 3 about thirty metres ahead.

"55A has it, no deviation." This was a quiet residential street and he knew the area would be difficult to work.

"51 permission."

"Yes, yes."

"T junction ahead; I have that junction covered."

"Yes, yes, no deviation, on offside, approx. twenty metres from junction." Kenny could see the line of parked cars sideways on and knew that the junction was approaching.

"Approximately ten metres from junction. 51 has the eyeball. Right, right, right, Creffield Road, crossing to nearside, no deviation, approaching bridge. Hold back 55A, open road, no cover." Kenny hung around the corner out of sight and wondered how far ahead the subject would be when he was eventually called round, and how far he was from his destination.

"55A come round." He turned the corner. Subject 3 had crossed the road to the nearside and 54A now took over the eyeball once she had crossed to the same side.

"54A has eyeball, no deviation." Kenny glanced behind him. There was still no-one behind him, but he was confident that the team were maintaining the 'bubble'.

"51 permission to plot."

"Yes, yes."

"51 rear."

"52 with Alpha ahead nearside."

"53 ahead."

"54 ahead offside."

"55 ahead."

"No response 51A and 53A. 51 will contact them on mobile and give location. Back to 54A."

"54A, yes, yes, no deviation."

"55A permission."

"Yes, yes."

"55A, can someone take a photo of Subject 3 when opportunity arises?" He was still unidentified and Kenny needed a photograph.

"55, yes, yes, am ahead, will do."

"54A no deviation, no deviation, Daniel Road to nearside."

"52 permission."

"Yes, yes."

"52, I am ahead first nearside, Western Gardens."

"Yes, yes."

"55 permission."

"Yes,yes."

"I have photos."

"Yes, yes, no deviation."

"Left, left, left, road name unknown. Postbox on offside opposite junction."

"52, that's Western Gardens. I am ahead offside. 52A is out."

Kenny's mobile rumbled; it was Franks. Warden had returned home safely. Franks had nearly missed him; he was on foot, there was no hesitation, door key out and straight into the house. He tried to phone Kenny without response, the conversation was short and sharp.

Kenny increased his pace so that he could see around the corner. 54A was lingering on the junction out of sight. It opened up as he got closer. Western Gardens was straight for about seventy-five yards and at right angles to Creffield Road and then curved to the right. He caught sight of the subject as he followed the road around to the right – and out of sight.

"55A eyeball, no deviation nearside, Western Gardens. Still with holdall. Temporary loss due to bend in road. Come round 54A."

Then, a quiet voice from the ether. "52A has the eyeball, no deviation, still Western Gardens, hold back 54A, 55A." They stopped, they were out of view, tucked around the corner and were unable to see down the remainder of the street.

"Straight road." 52A was talking very quietly as if he was close to the subject.

"Slowing… stop, stop, stop. Looking behind. All units

hold. Looking ahead. Still hold." The transmissions stopped and, in accordance with procedure, no-one spoke. 52A had control; everyone knew that he was in an exposed position.

He was there for what seemed like an age, but it was probably thirty seconds or so, just watching and waiting. All was quiet – no people, no cars, just the distant hum of traffic and the rustle of the leaves in the breeze. Then, very rapidly, "Left, left, left, in, in, in. Subject 3 has entered the last of the line of new houses on nearside, number unknown, blue door."

"55 permission." Three clicks.

"Can you hold your current position?"

"Yes, yes," he whispered, "subject to nosey neighbours."

"55, 55A, do a walk past in about ten minutes to confirm number and any vehicles. I am ahead nearside covering junction. Who has junction at rear covered?"

"54."

"Yes, yes, 54, 54A, return to vehicle, back to eyeball."

"52A, no change, no change."

Kenny returned to Creffield Road, moving out of sight, waiting for sufficient time to elapse. This made sense and he was thankful for the team's diligence and experience. It would have been dangerous if they had been too impetuous and arranged an Alpha to walk past the house to confirm the address as soon as the subject had entered the building, considering his actions that afternoon, it was likely that he would have gone straight up to his bedroom window to look out onto the street to check for any movement – people hanging around, unusual cars in the street. Ten minutes gave the man time to settle down, relax and take his mind off the risks he was taking and the dangers he could possibly encounter, not only from Old Bill but from anyone else who may have been interested in what he had been carrying. Kenny hoped that 52A was tucked out of the way.

He bobbed up. "No change, no change, 55A."

"Yes, yes."

"55A permission."

"55A, yes, yes."

"I'm going to start my walk through."

"Yes, yes." Kenny began walking up the road on the offside. As he turned the bend the line of new houses on the nearside came into view. He paused under a tree, sheltered from sight. The first new house on the nearside was 30 and he could see that the second one was 32; he counted about fifteen houses in the row, he re-checked 30 and 32 and counted the houses off. That made the house they were looking at number 60.

"55A, believe house number is 60, will confirm." He strolled along, counting off the numbers in his head. Some of them displayed figures; others did not. Finally, he was opposite 58, its number on the wall of the building.

"Can confirm, 60. Blue Door. Silver BMW 3 series in drive," he whispered the number to 55, who was maintaining the log in his absence.

He continued walking a short distance ahead and he saw 52A lurking in the bushes, well out of sight of the subject's house but clearly not sustainable for any length of time.

"Did you get that, 55?"

"Yes, yes."

He noticed that a tall hedge separated the drives at the front of 60 and a much older property at 62, and that there was a small medium sized wall separating the drive from the pavement. A short walk and he had re-joined the DI in his car. He settled in – earpiece out, covert radio off.

"So, all good?" enquired the DI.

"I think so." He hadn't eaten all day and leant back to take a sandwich from his box and pour a cup of tea from his flask.

"You OK for thirty minutes? I think 52A will be OK for a little bit longer, but I passed him on the way here; he may need a relief." The DI arranged the changeover.

It was just after four o'clock. He phoned Franks, who told him that Warden had returned to the house at about three thirty p.m. He updated him with his current position and then arranged to meet him that evening.

Apparently, and not unsurprisingly, Warden had been very busy upon his return. Kenny wanted to stay in Western Gardens for a little longer whilst he had the team available and settled on plot. There was always an outside chance that Subject 3 was merely visiting the house and lived elsewhere; the longer they could maintain their position and confirm that there was no further movement, the more likely it was that he lived there. But he just had that feeling that it was his place. Why else would he have taken so many precautions to ensure he wasn't being followed? He had entered without hesitation, probably using a key. Upon that basis it was unlikely to be a friend's house or girlfriend's place or whatever.

"I'd like to pop into the local Collators before leaving, if I may – I just want to check the address, voters' register etc."

The DI agreed to drop him off, and as there was no further movement, thirty minutes later he stood the team down.

The log was passed to one of the DSs to ensure it was signed off whilst Kenny visited the local nick.

He always liked the Met Collators – old boys who knew the ground, knew the faces and could summon up titbits and anecdotes effortlessly.

Whilst he was there he checked the voters' register and address index and then ran the BMW they had seen through the PNC. Before leaving, he checked when the black bin collection was for the street – this Friday. Of course, it would be, wouldn't it. The next day.

Once he completed his checks and finished his enquiries, they drove back to the office and he bade farewell to the DI and the team and thanked them for their help. Before leaving, they were given the memory stick with all the photos taken during the day, including those of Subject 3, and arranged for the log to be dropped off the following day.

He met Franks later, in the office. It was late and they were both tired. Dumping his bag and kit on his desk, he told him what had happened. Franks was immersed in his paperwork, logs, authorities, photos; the list appeared endless – everyone, everywhere, it seemed, wanted their arses covered, whether it was senior officers, prosecutors or courts, by bits of paper.

He told Franks that he thought he had identified Subject 3 but needed clarification. The voters' register showed that a Richard Purves lived at the address in Ealing Common. The vehicle came back to the same person but a different address. The name was on a Collator's card; he appeared to have been convicted of possession of amphetamine with intent to supply a few years ago and was locked up for eighteen months. The Collator had given him a photograph of Purves taken at the time – and it was possibly him, but he wanted to have the photos taken during the surveillance developed to confirm his identity.

He showed Franks the old photo, then told him the bad news:

"Can you come up to London tomorrow morning, first thing?"

"Why?"

"Bin collection in his street – we need to be there early."

"What time early?"

"If we could leave here at, say, five."

"Five?!"

"Well, OK, five thirty. It will give us a chance to clear his bin and perhaps confirm a few things."

Franks agreed reluctantly and was dragged off for a beer before going home.

*A good day,* Kenny thought. *Let's see where it leads us.*

# 7

# DIRTY BINS

Kenny waited outside Franks' house, a Haddock semi-detached in a small cul-de-sac about a mile from the office. He had managed to get-up at half past four without disturbing his girlfriend and showered, and after a quick cup of tea and gathering the kit he required, he had arrived about ten minutes early. He knew Franks would be on time; he was methodical and reliable without being boring and stiflingly oppressive. It had rained overnight and the wind had increased, which, he felt, would be ideal for their task that morning. He had packed kit for both of them, including three bin bags filled with fibreglass and old newspapers that he had hastily bundled together the night before. It was important to miss the morning rush hour, to avoid the waves of faceless commuters intent on arriving at their London offices with the minimum amount of time spent on the road, the train or the tube, and to arrive before the bin-men.

It was dark but he saw the front door of the house open. A small shaft of light silhouetted his friend's large bulk before he saw him click the door closed. The next thing he knew, Franks had opened the passenger door and he felt the waft of cold morning air

"Morning!" he announced as they drove-off.

The journey was uneventful and they arrived at Ealing about forty-five minutes later. The traffic was light and the rain that had started midway through the journey was becoming heavier and more persistent.

Kenny outlined the previous day's activities and took Franks past the underground stations, the Haven Arms and the route that Subject 3 had taken from the tube to the house.

As they approached Western Gardens, Kenny was reassured to see bins outside the houses; some in drives, others by the front door, but most on the pavement. It was black bin day. He preferred black bins to the red recycling bins, and definitely to green garden wheelies, which were utterly worthless to them for the purposes they had in mind. Red bins, although interesting to them, were full of loose material that was difficult to extract and filter, and the process tended to be time-consuming.

It was still raining and was a little blustery as they turned into Western Gardens; the wind buffeted the car as they drove slowly along the street. Here again, black bins lined the street. As they reached number 60, they slowed. The bin was in the drive, halfway between the house and the street and beside the BMW and another car – a red Peugeot. Franks jotted down the number.

When they reached the end of the street, they turned the corner, stopped and swapped over. Kenny got into the passenger side. He was already wearing dirty overalls, and he slipped into a faded high-vis jacket, gloves, a beanie and protective glasses. It was blustery and he tested his covert radio. All good.

They knew what was required of each other and worked as a team to a system that worked and tended to produce good intelligence. They estimated that they were about two hours ahead of the council bin men. It was six thirty a.m.; most people were still in bed or wandering around in a dazed stupor. The weather had worsened and it was squally and wet. This meant fewer people on foot and less dawdling.

Kenny got out of the vehicle and, starting at the furthest end on the opposite side of the street from number 60, began putting the wheelie bins together and dragging them from paths and driveways onto the pavement in front of the houses. This made sense in real life; the bin collection would be quicker and the refuse wagon could take both bins at the same time. He made his way down the street, doing the same thing at each of the houses. When he reached the end, the junction with Creffield Road, he crossed the road and came back up the other side, moving closer to number 60. He had already worked out that if he paired number 28 and number 30 together, he would end up pairing 60 and 62. He moved slowly up the street. The rain had penetrated his high-vis and splattered his glasses. There was still no movement from the suspect house.

He slowed slightly when he reached number 40, wiped his glasses and realigned his gloves. There was no bin outside the house so he continued to 42 and placed the bin on the pavement. As he did so, the door of number 40 opened to the breezy exterior and a singularly attractive lady in a dressing gown beckoned him over. He retraced his steps and walked the short way up the drive.

"You couldn't possibly get my bin, could you? It's in the garage – it should be open." This was unexpected, but he had to assume that the woman may have known Purves. He tugged at the bottom of the garage door and it slid up and over; he wheeled the bin out and closed the door, and looked towards the woman. She was still there but with her arm outstretched. He left the bin and walked over. Her right hand was clutching a crumpled tenner.

"No, it's alright, love."

"I insist."

"No need, all easy."

"You are sweet, thank you. What's your name?"

Kenny thought quickly; he hadn't expected any conversations that morning. "Bert."

"Thank you, Bert – if you ever need a cup of tea, I'm always in."

"Thanks, dear." He returned to the work in hand.

*Lovely lady, wonderful perfume,* he thought.

He quickly reached Purves' house, walked halfway up the drive and tugged at the bin. He knew it wasn't empty. He wheeled it down the slope to the street and moved off to the left in the direction of number 62 and out of sight of the suspect house behind and beyond the adjoining hedge. He then went into the drive of 62, moved the bin onto the pavement and placed it on the other side of the bin from No.60, that was already there.

Before moving on, and ensuring he wasn't being watched, he looked inside the bin belonging to 60. Dirty and smelly, it contained two black bin bags tied at the top, similar to those he had brought with him.

"Two black ones, tied at the top."

"Yes, yes." The remaining houses in the street were older, end-of-the-century semis; most had four-feet-high privet hedges on both sides of the property.

Kenny looked around quickly and, making sure no-one was in view and that he was out of sight of the suspect house, he lifted the lid of the bin, removed the two bags and walked with them a short distance along to the front of 66 and 68. He left them there whilst he continued collecting the bins from the remaining drives. Ahead of him, he saw Franks pull up, open the boot and deposit two more identical black bags a little further ahead on his side of the road, and then drive off towards the road at the far end, Oakley Avenue, and turn left out of sight.

Kenny continued to methodically move the bins and pair them up until he reached the bags that Franks had left. He picked them up – they were light – and returned to the bin belonging to No.60 and placed them inside. He then walked back along the road, picked up the bin bags he had originally removed from 60's wheelie bin and took them further up the road. He was now at 70 and left them there. He continued moving bins onto the pavement and as he did so, after four or six houses, he gradually shifted the bags from number 60 along the road until he reached the junction and then hoisted them over his shoulder and marched away around the corner and was lost from sight. Before leaving he looked back. All the bins were neatly lined up on each side of the street, there were no pedestrians and he hadn't seen a single car, apart from their own, pass along the road. He was still walking when Franks pulled up in the car some distance from the junction; Kenny dumped the bags in the boot, took-off his high-vis and goggles and threw them in beside the bags, and then got in the passenger seat. They drove off.

"You stink!" said Franks.

"Thank you."

They returned to the office and parked the car. Kenny was already in his overalls; he grabbed some latex gloves, put them on and opened the boot. The two bags were equal size and the tops were tied in a knot. He lifted them out and carried them to a well-lit space in the corner of the car park. Franks brought the other empty bin bags. He ripped them open and then sifted through the detritus, depositing the uninteresting packaging – food, tissues and anything else that was not going to tell him anything – into the empty bag. After about twenty minutes, the bags that were empty were now full and he was left with a scattering of items spread over the concrete floor: a large number of receipts, mainly from the local Waitrose for food, ready meals and wine; a number of pieces of paper with phone numbers, calculations and notes; a screwed up half-completed passport application; a bank statement torn into fragments; a number of roach-ends; some small polythene bags; ripped up pieces of a calendar; and some discarded emails.

They tied up the bag with the worthless rubbish and dumped it in one of the big industrial bins that were kept down on that level, put the remaining items that they wanted to examine more closely in an empty bag and retired to their office.

Kenny went for a shower and put his overalls, hat, etc. into a bag to take home, and then returned to the office. Franks was already piecing things together. "What have we got?" he asked.

"OK, considering this is a two-week window of Subject 3's life, quite a lot. Food purchases indicate a single man – lots of pre-cooked food, wine and receipts for take-aways and some restos. A couple of petrol receipts – don't know which car but away from London, looks like Exeter Services, M5, so he's travelling westwards. Bank statement from the local NatWest – he didn't want that seen by anyone so ripped it up into small pieces, but I'm taping it together. Not vast amounts but comfortable; steady credit of around £5000, couple of direct debits, Netflix and BT and mortgage payment, that sort of thing. Payments in from various places, mainly from a company called FI Ltd, regular amounts, nothing huge, statement shows about 5k a month. He smokes a bit of weed, but no cigarettes. Calendar, mainly work appointments for last month, all in London. A few marks and asterisks to remind him to do things without marking exactly what they are – interesting. A few phone numbers we'll have to check, mobile and fixed. Small packages that may have had white powder – we'll have to get that checked – and a couple of emails, torn up but talking about mundane things, maybe connected. We'll have to examine them a bit more."

"Good, is that it?"

"No, keeping the best till last. He was obviously applying for a passport, a replacement or new one, don't know which. He dumped the spoilt application form in the bin half-completed, but you know they're a bit jobsworthy about accuracy. Well, he made an error and couldn't redo it so dumped it, and presumably started again."

"And?"

"So, we have his name, date of birth and address but nothing else. He fucked up the last line of the address."

"And?!"

"Same details that we already have, but confirmation we have the right man. Richard William Purves, 23.03.74, of 60, Western Gardens."

"Great!"

"One last thing." Kenny looked up from his notes.

"Think he's a freemason."

"Why?"

"Discarded ticket to ladies' night at the local lodge. Might not be… possibly."

"That'll upset the guvnor."

"That's what I thought!"

"Wonder what he does with all his dosh, and where does he put it that's safe, secure, retrievable and cannot be found easily? Oh, I've picked up the photos from surveillance." He showed them to Franks.

"That's our man." The photos were taken at a distance of maybe one hundred yards using a telephoto lens, whole length, face on, when he was midway between the tube and his house.

"When you compare them with his mugshot from seven years ago, it's a good comparison. I'd say it's one and the same.

I've asked for his details from NSY. And the DI from the surveillance team called; he's calling in…" He looked at his watch. "In about ten minutes."

About ten minutes later, the DI entered; he brought with him the log, signed and initialled, and the surveillance officer, 53A, who had been with Purves and Warden in the pub. The DI introduced him.

He described the interior of the pub – small yet comfortable, good clientele who all appeared local. Warden bought a drink, a pint of lager, and sat down on a bench seat in the corner by the front window facing the door, giving him a good view of the street, with a large square table in front of him. 53A was on the other side of the bar, nearest the door; he ordered a pint and started talking to the locals who were standing at the bar. His cover story was that he was working for London Underground as an accounts consultant.

"Any boring job for a large organisation that would deter difficult or probing questions," 53A added.

Warden received, or made, a number of calls. He was there for about thirty minutes before Subject 3 arrived, by which time 53A, who had ordered a sandwich, was sitting down directly opposite them. Subject 3 entered the pub and went straight to the bar, ordered a pint and then, before paying, asked whether Warden wanted a drink; he had another pint. Subject 3 paid in cash then joined Warden, taking a seat on his right-hand side on the bench seat. They shook hands.

They had a conversation but 53A was unable to overhear what was being said. The holdall was on the ground between them and beneath the table. Subject 3 received two calls, short and to the point, and did not make any outgoing calls. After five minutes, he stood up, picked up the holdall and walked to the toilet. He was in there for two or three minutes and then returned, taking the same position next to Warden. The holdall was now by his side, not between them. They were talking away and Subject 3 looked around and put his right hand into the left-hand side of his jacket and removed an A4 manila envelope folded lengthways down the middle and placed it between them. Warden picked it up and put it inside his jacket. He then went to the loo and returned a few minutes later. There was further conversation and then Warden stood, shook hands and left. Subject 3 remained on his own but was looking out of the window as Warden left. He sipped his pint, picked up a newspaper and read it. He hung about for quite a while and then left with the holdall. He didn't engage anyone else in conversation apart from the bar staff when ordering his drink. Very calm, very relaxed, he didn't give 53A any attention, perhaps because 53A was having intermittent conversation with blokes at the bar about the London Underground. It was quite an intimate bar and people came and went. 53A estimated that there were eight people in there the whole time, but they were locals and constantly chatting, ignoring everything else around them.

After Warden left, Subject 3 made two calls of short duration. 53A's assessment was that he was 'a cool customer'. Their meeting and the transactions didn't attract any attention, his assessment was they'd probably met there before and the large table they were sitting behind tended to obscure everything below waist level.

"Interpretation of their visits to the toilet?"

"To check that the delivery was good on both sides – the money and the gear. They clearly knew each other; no hesitation in recognition, handshakes and general bonhomie."

"Great," said Kenny. "Anything else?"

"Have you ID'd him?" he asked.

"We think this is he." He showed the DI and 53A the mugshot.

"That's him; that shows him a little younger and his hair is shorter, but that's him," 53A declared.

"Good. But how much gear and how much money?" Kenny said.

"Enough for a week, probably," said Franks.

"OK guys, thanks a lot, good job. We'll keep you posted." They left.

Kenny and Franks sat down together to review the job, to see what they had and to decide the next step.

They had Warden dealing medium to large quantities of crack, and some heroin and smoke, to street dealers from his home address. He was careful and didn't take risks. His main stash was almost certainly in or just beside the canal a short distance from his house, which he appeared to visit once a day or so, presumably to replenish his stock, deposit leftovers and probably place his cash. He met his supplier 'Patch' in London using 'Shanks' as his driver, usually on Thursdays, paid him for the last consignment and then picked up his next delivery, generally using a holdall.

'Patch', aka Purves, lived in Ealing, confirmed by surveillance and intel collection. He was very careful and used anti-surveillance techniques, which tended to reinforce their suspicion that he was criminally involved with Warden.

They agreed to sit on Warden for a little bit longer to finish identifying his punters before taking him out, but they had four questions that the intelligence team might be able to answer:

Where did Warden and his London connection, Purves, first meet?

Does he travel to London more than once a week?

How much money does he take each time?

How much gear does he collect?

They might not get any answers but it may help to clarify

the depth of his involvement and relative position within the organisation.

Several issues regarding Purves were nagging Kenny, and he and Franks had discussed them at length:

Where does Purves keep his gear?

What does he do with the money, which is, of course, always in cash?

And… telephones. How often does he change them over?

Three days later they met again in the office. Kenny had two envelopes on his desk. One contained Purves' full record, convictions, description, MO and the occasions when he was arrested but acquitted. The second envelope was from the intelligence cell. He opened it. They believed that Warden and Purves met when they were on remand and happened to be in same nick at the same time. Warden appeared to travel to London every Thursday and possibly twice a week if the need arose. They were not sure how much he picked up but he had been known to have had in the region of ten thousand pounds.

*This guy is a big player,* thought Kenny.
*Worthy of a bit of attention.*

# 8

# WHAT A COMPLICATED WEB WE WEAVE

The day was bright and inviting, the sun was shining and everything was just as he liked it, organised and under control. Purves lay in the middle of the big white super-king size bed, his head propped up by two very pleasant down and feather pillows; he was warm and comfortable beneath a large white duvet that settled on top of him like a soft light cloud. The room was white, clean and utilitarian. He didn't like unnecessary clutter; everything had its place and he could therefore find anything he wanted, effortlessly.

He'd had a couple of spliffs the night before whilst counting cash and he was more relaxed than he had been for a long time, although, he reminded himself, smoking dope and counting large amounts of cash was not conducive to efficiency, nor accuracy. He would have to check everything again that morning.

Yesterday had been a busy day and he was running late for most of it, something he detested in others and he castigated himself for doing what he disliked in others. But business had been rewarding; he had managed three meets and estimated he'd made a clear profit of ten thousand, six hundred and thirty, or was it ten thousand, five hundred and sixty? He couldn't remember, he needed to check it. Today would be less frantic but he was unsure how much longer he wanted to do what he was doing. Although it was lucrative, it was time consuming and a little dangerous. He was always conscious of the risk. He strove to manage, control and, if possible, reduce it by separating Richard Purves from the immediate and long-term effects of his drug distribution business. He knew that the risks were high – from law enforcement, and equally, his criminal competitors – but by building and maintaining a system of firewalls, he felt reasonably confident that he would remain safe, wealthy and, importantly, out of prison.

Yesterday was an example. He had met Warden and handed over about half a pound of crack cocaine in return for about ten thousand, five hundred pounds, but from that he still needed to pay his supplier. He had taken precautions and they seemed adequate, but what of Warden? He had met him in prison.

Warden had just been sent down and he was on remand. In prison, time is on your side – time to discuss, time to meet other players, time to plan and time to imagine. Warden had been a small up-and-coming dealer with a good client base and plenty of potential, but he had made a stupid mistake – selling to a UC officer – and was caught bang to rights. Greed.

He'd wanted to continue when he got out and presumably saw, through Purves, the possibility of a steady supply link that would be mutually beneficial. Purves spoke a little Spanish and when he was finally convicted he served time with a couple of Brits who had been extradited from Spain for bringing gear into the country, and he realised that there was a niche in the market as a go-be between the Brits organising drug movements from South America to Spain and outlets for the product in the UK.

But that was four years ago. He had kept his nose clean, developed the business and managed to avoid any adverse attention. The other matter, which had been a problem, but one that he felt he had resolved, was what to do with the cash that steadily mounted up from his illicit affairs. Initially this had been, or appeared to have been at the time, an insurmountable issue. He was paid in cash, large amounts of it. If he placed it in his bank account, bought ISAs, gave it to his solicitor or bought a largish car, like a surfacing whale, it would inevitably come to the attention of the law enforcement agencies – and he wanted to avoid this kind of attention and the awkward questions that would emanate from certain quarters.

When he first started, the business had been low-key, less burgeoning, and the amount of time and effort needed to maintain it was, equally, more manageable. He did have an entrepreneurial streak and had developed an interest in property development. It started by buying small plots of land at the right location, obtaining planning approval and then selling the land with the authority in place. After several successful transactions, the plots grew bigger until he was able to follow the projects through from buying a pile of dirt to selling the same plot, some months later, with a four-bedroomed detached house and attached garage plonked on top. Taking out the middle men, wherever possible, provided benefits. Then he was caught selling gear and did time, but he had already salted away some of the profits from his endeavours. When he came out, he continued developing property and bought a small plot of land that had commercial opportunities rather than domestic. He had intended to build a small business complex but that was rejected by the planning authorities and he decided, instead, to level the plot out, tarmac it, fence it off and use it as a car park, enough for about two hundred cars, close to the railway station. It did well, so well that he bought another plot. The same thing happened. Not a massive income but enough to live on. The profits from these allowed him to buy a laundrette in the same area. Again, a good investment, good income, but not enough to retire on.

Distributing a bit of gear had originally been a side-line, an interest, a means of making money. But as the business developed, an acute problem developed: what to do with the money. He knew, from contacts he had made in prison, that this was common to most criminal enterprises where large amounts of cash were flowing through people's hands. His solution was to make the businesses he had purchased, owned and developed, appear more – but not too – successful, by pumping money into them from the cash payments he had received from the drug distribution business, and by doing this, making the money usable once again… in effect, laundering the loot. The car parks and the small launderette were ideally suited to the scam, small enough to be boringly invisible but where the transactions were almost always in that most useful commodity of all, cash. The three businesses he gathered together under a Holding Company, FI Ltd (Freedom Investment Ltd); he was the sole director and managed a profitable portfolio. He'd employed some people to run them and sit on their arses all day, in separate kiosks to collect the money and another to service the machines in the launderette. That was it. Easy really.

His mind was meandering. He needed to separate himself from the illicit side of his business and his personal life from his business life. For all intents and purposes, his money came from good business acumen and sound judgement, he could explain it away, he could cope with the accolades. It was just that it wasn't true. He yawned. It was early. He got up and looked out of the window; all was quiet. It was blustery and raining hard.

No-one about. It was bin collection day; the street was lined with them. He strolled through to the bathroom and had a shower. A great place to think and ponder, same as a bath really, but baths happened at night and took too long. He dressed and wandered downstairs, turned the kettle on and decided to have porridge. His girlfriend, Sam, hadn't stayed the night; she'd left her car at his house and gone to meet a friend. She'd obviously had too much to drink.

He leant against the kitchen worktop, supped his tea and lazily stirred the porridge. He was starting to formulate plans – count the money, stash it, visit the car parks and launderette, collect the money, place it in the bank with a proportion of his ill-gotten gains.

Who would possibly know how much they were really making? All the accounts for the company were submitted on time and in an orderly fashion, everything balanced perfectly. The porridge was done and he sat down, listening to the news on Radio 4. When he had finished he slid the bowl to one side and, checking that the front and rear doors were locked and that the curtains were pulled tight, he lifted the small blue holdall that he had collected from Warden, the previous day, up onto the table. He removed all the cash. He had wrapped all the denominations in bundles of one hundred pounds the night before. He placed the bag back down onto the floor and started counting the money again. A little simpler than the night before but still time consuming. After about half an hour, he had arrived at a figure – ten thousand, five hundred and fifty pounds. He wrote down the amount so as not to forget it, again. He separated the amount into two piles, one of eight thousand pounds, the other of two thousand, five hundred and fifty pounds, and placed them in two separate A3 envelopes which he then sealed.

Time to go. He stashed the eight thousand pounds behind a line of books on the bookshelf and left with the remaining envelope. Once he had driven to the two car parks and the launderette, collected what money was available and counted up, he added the money he had brought with him and then separated the takings into separate amounts to reflect the three businesses and headed for the bank, a NatWest branch in Ealing Broadway. The money then went into the business account, FI Limited. Once completed, he returned home.

He removed the second amount that he had stashed behind the books – he'd need this for future purchases – and put the envelope in the holdall that had been used by Warden. He left the house, this time walking. He made his way to the tube at Ealing Common, went up to Ealing Broadway before hopping on the Central line to North Acton; this was quick and easy with his Oyster Card. He always remembered his anti-surveillance technique and dry-cleaning; don't rush, look around, take your time, do normal things that would help expose their team members, disrupt their system and weaken their ability to maintain contact, and very importantly, don't make whoever was out there think that you knew they were there – stay calm. In short, avoid running off, for, although you would almost certainly lose your tail, you would also expose the fact that you knew, or suspected, they were there. If in doubt, abort. He left the station and via various well-trodden routes walked straight into the small clinically clean warehouse just off Victoria Road, called 'Stash and Leave'. He walked in though the main entrance.

"Good morning," said a cheery receptionist.

"Good morning." Purves tapped in his password and access code and showed the lady his key.

"Thank you, Mr Purves." He took the lift to the second floor and exited into a wide lobby decorated in exactly the same manner as the reception area – a painted grey floor and red and yellow décor. He turned left and left again, as he had done many times before, and entered a long, wide, grey-painted corridor with strip lights on the ceiling. On the right was a line of small red and yellow numbered boxes in three layers that took up the entire wall.

He walked halfway along the passage and then turned to face Box 212, which was at shoulder height in the central line. It was one of a bank of about fifty boxes, which were all painted in the same colours. He knew that the corridor, and therefore his movements within it, were monitored by a camera to his right and at ceiling height on the same side as the wall of boxes. He also knew that the boxes were hinged on the right and that when any door was opened, it obscured the view of the camera, and thence any effective overview that the receptionist, or anyone else for that matter, had of the remaining boxes beyond the door that was fully opened. He had seen the bank of monitors on the receptionist's desk and had quickly identified the potential of obscuring the camera's view of the remaining boxes on that level on the far side of any opened door, particularly those that were immediately adjacent.

This was a box he rented and he knew what it contained: an expensive watch, his mother's wedding ring, one thousand pounds sterling, one thousand euros, his passport, deeds for the house, and his will. Instead he went to the adjoining box, to the left of 212, Box 213. He rented this box under a different name and had a separate key.

There were no other cameras. He stood slightly to his right, further obscuring the view the camera had of the second box he was opening. He removed the second key from his pocket, opened the door and slid out the galvanised container. He opened the lid halfway and placed into it the eight thousand pounds in cash that he had taken with him. He peered in and noticed that the box was almost full. He checked on what he had remaining of his last shipment. He estimated about a kilo, together with some speed and acid. It also contained some false documents, a couple of passports, some cash and a loaded Browning 9mm Automatic. He removed an envelope that contained some crack and then the weapon. He had been meaning to do this for some time, it was just too risky and he had constantly chided himself for delaying the decision to dump it in the Thames. The time was right.

He wiped down the surfaces as best he could, without being seen, pushed the drawer back then locked both boxes. He hesitated.

*A mental note,* he thought to himself. *Getting a little short.*

He would need to contact his supplier, a man he had known for many years. In fact, they had been at university together and had become very close before going their separate ways. The relationship was re-kindled after Purves was visited by him in prison; they had similar political views and both were coming out of periods of difficult personal turmoil and changes in direction, particularly employment. They saw the potential for harnessing and then developing the supply of drugs into a lucrative business, but with safeguards. They were intelligent men with business acumen, and they accepted that any personal contact between them would greatly increase the risk of discovery. Trust was important. They had reached a mutual agreement to remove the middle men, to pare down contact to a minimum and only deal with each other, with no introductions and no third-party involvement, thereby reducing the risk.

He returned to reception and left the building.

When he had come out of clink a few years before, following advice from a fellow inmate, a Jewish man called Joseph, who had been locked up for some kind of long firm fraud, he opened a stand-alone account at a bank and branch that he didn't normally use. Joseph had told him that he always had one account that he had access to that had no direct connection with himself, his businesses, accounts or associates. He used the account to pay for certain things that he wanted to keep at arm's length.

Purves had listened to what he had been told by the older man and thought it was sensible advice. He obtained a false passport, used the utility bills from one of the properties he had developed, and opened an account at Barclays in Acton under the business name Trenchard Properties. The company was nothing, just a shell; the only tangible aspect of the name was the bank account. He picked up the cheque book and bank debit card at the property before it was occupied and then deposited one thousand, five hundred pounds in cash to credit the account.

He used this account and false details to open the Stash and Leave account and to pay for the second box, 213, which was paid by direct debit every month. He topped up the account, usually once a year, with about one thousand pounds in cash. He knew that Box 213 was unused when he went to place the items in his original box, 212, and saw it open and empty. The bank was happy – the account was always in credit, Stash and Leave were completely content with regular payments, and Purves was satisfied because it provided a safe haven for items he wanted to be unconnected with, whilst ensuring they were safe and secure. The only drawback came when he needed to replace his original bank card. This was resolved by deliberately damaging his original card, visiting the branch and arranging to pick up the replacement at the branch several days later, because, as he explained to whomever was trying to help him, he was having quite a lot of building work going on at the house and was concerned it might get lost in the mixture of rubble, sand and cement.

He returned to the tube station with the intention of returning home. As he reached the turnstiles his mobile rang;

short and sharp conversation followed. Purves knew it was business because it was on the phone he reserved solely for his illicit dealings. All he needed to know was who, what, and when, and Purves would determine the price and the place.

The answer was as clear as it always was; his customers knew how the system worked. A few ounces that afternoon. He knew the caller and where he was from and told him to be at the TK beside the florists in Spring Bridge Road, Ealing at three thirty p.m. prompt with the money in a carrier bag. This would enable him to go home, sort himself out and cover the meet.

He had two mobiles. One was used for all his personal calls and FI business calls, paid by direct debit from the FI Ltd account. The second one was pay-as-you-go, a 'burner phone', paid for in cash and used only for his illicit business. He ditched the pay-as-you go phones in the river once a week or so, earlier if he remembered, and replaced them straight away. As soon as a phone was replaced, he phoned his contacts and updated them with the number. They were cheap – off the shelf – and sourced through any retailer. He knew how their system worked and was comfortable with the arrangement, and they with him. Notwithstanding this, he used his false ID. Again, as long as he paid up they were happy, but it separated his bad business from his good business, ensured that his number didn't come up regularly on other people's billing and that he wasn't being listened to, a precaution in case the authorities were giving him some attention; it just disrupted any close scrutiny and made their lives a little more difficult. He had often wondered what he would do if he was ever nicked. The telephone was one of the highest risks; it connected him to some bad people and locations. He had settled on two plans of action. In the first one, if he needed to act promptly, the phone would be placed in the toilet and flushed; even if it didn't flush away, most likely the phone would be completely fucked. The second and more reliable solution was to throw it in the washing machine and turn it on. Once again, water would solve the problem but a prolonged churning in the drum would ensure its destruction, and once the machine was in operation, it would take time to close it down.

He arrived home. Sam was still away; he was alone. He liked the space, the ability to do what he wanted without being influenced by others. He put the envelope with the crack in it in the kitchen sink and checked it. There was no need to weigh it, it was about right; he always went slightly over on the weight anyway; it built up a good relationship with the customer and ensured repeat orders. Short-changing, over-charging or under-weighing, in his view, just drove customers to other sources, reduced loyalty and increased mistrust and animosity. Once this was done he washed the sink thoroughly and stashed the gun behind the books on one of the book shelves, ready to pick up and dump.

He left home at two thirty p.m. with the gear in an orange Sainsbury's bag and, after ensuring he was not being followed, went by tube to Ealing Broadway. On leaving the station he crossed the road and walked along the side of the park opposite, towards Spring Bridge Road. Halfway along was a rubbish bin; he placed his bag inside the bin and continued walking. The telephone box he had directed his customer to was at the end of the path, next to a florist on the corner. He crossed the road and climbed to the top of a small multi-storey car park. He had used this before; it gave a good vantage point for the TK and the rubbish bin. It was ten past three. People hurried around busily filling their days with a series of unrelated movements. He saw nothing of note; no-one hanging around, no sign of any follow.

At about twenty-five past three, he saw his man striding over the bridge from the direction of Morrisons; he was carrying a Marks and Spencer's carrier bag. Within seconds, he had entered the kiosk. Purves waited for a few minutes and checked for any sign of watchers and, when he was sure there were none, he telephoned the number in the box. He saw the man pick up the receiver and they had a short, sharp conversation. As they were talking, Purves moved down the stairs to ground level, where he could see the telephone box. He told him to leave the bag in the box and walk along the path beside the wall adjoining a car park. He then told him that he would see a rubbish bin a short distance away beside the path; if he looked inside he would see an orange Sainsbury's carrier bag. He was told to remove it and continue walking towards Ealing Broadway Tube without looking back, and not to dawdle. Any questions? No. OK.

He saw the man leave the kiosk and walk into the park towards the rubbish bin. Within seconds, Purves was in the kiosk and looking around. Still no sign of any adverse activity. He picked up the receiver, looked behind him and saw the man remove the orange carrier bag from the bin and continue walking towards the tube, at the same time checking that it contained what it should contain. He disappeared from sight. Purves remained in the kiosk for about ten minutes. During that time he did not touch or acknowledge the presence of the bag. It would, he thought, have taken a particularly inquisitive and awkward little shit with time on their hands to realise that the bag initially had nothing to do with him. After a while, he replaced the receiver, picked up the bag, walked into the park and, as a precaution, sat down on a bench to enjoy the sun for a short while. When he was satisfied that he wasn't been watched, he returned past the kiosk, along the same path towards Ealing Broadway.

He was home in fifteen minutes. He checked and counted the contents – another ten thousand, five hundred pounds.

He needed to stash the cash temporarily, so, grabbing a small Pozidriv screwdriver from a drawer in the kitchen, he walked through to the dining room. After moving a standard lamp, he gently lifted the corner of the fitted carpet and underlay, and unscrewed a small section of floorboard that the central heating engineer had taken up when he repaired the system about two or three years before. He placed the bag in the cavity and then removed the weapon that he had hidden on the bookshelf and stuffed that into the available space as well before covering them with bits of rubble, sand and cement and replacing the floorboard and carpet. He made sure it fitted, pressed it down firmly and then put the lamp back in its original position and returned the screwdriver to the drawer. This done, he turned his attention to cooking supper for Sam and himself.

# 9

# THE WAY WE WORK? IT'S LIKE THIS!

Shanks pulled up in the Uxbridge Road near the park; he had spent the last hour hanging around behind Morrisons. He'd had a sandwich, some crisps and a Coke, and was bored. He'd had long drawn-out calls to and from his girlfriend, Roseanne, who was nagging him about where he was, what he was doing and why he wasn't at work. She was on his case all the time, saying that he had a good job, she didn't want him to go back to prison, he needed to look after the baby, and what about finding a place to live? He'd batted her off quite well but then got narky with her, asking her when she was going to start to earn some money and saying that she shouldn't eat or smoke so much. He didn't tell her that he'd pulled a sicky and was just as unlikely to let her know that he was going to be paid two or three days' wages for his troubles.

He'd put the phone down on her – she'd do the same to him – and so it continued all afternoon. His mum didn't help. They were living at her mum and dad's council house on the Duchy Estate, a big sprawling 1950s council estate that was probably a good idea at the time but was now just a soulless dump. Her dad worked for the council, had done for thirty years; Shanks didn't like him and he didn't like Shanks, particularly when they were living under the same roof, but he suffered it for the sake of his seventeen-year-old daughter who had become pregnant by Shanks when she was sixteen. They had taken them in when he was kicked out from home and had nowhere else to go.

He particularly didn't like him using drugs; he couldn't understand it, didn't want to understand it, and knew that it was taking more of his wage than seemed right and proper – so much so that with their smoking, they had little money to spend on food, the baby, or help with running the house.

The phone calls had occupied his time whilst in Ealing and had prevented Warden from getting hold of him.

Finally, after about six attempts, Shanks' phone was answered.

"What the fuck have you been doing? I've been wandering around the streets with a big bag of gear waiting for you, you little wanker. Fucking useless! Where are you?"

"Just down the road."

"I'm in the Uxbridge Road walking towards the North Circular, get your fucking arse down here and pick me up, you fucking shithead." He hung up.

Shanks started the motor and went carefully along the Uxbridge Road, not wanting to miss him and then have the hassle of turning around on a busy road. He saw him on the left near the park and pulled over. He leant across and clipped the door button. Warden opened the door and got in. As he was pulling his seatbelt across, he looked Shanks in the eye and said, "If you ever let me down again, then you can sling your hook, you little tosser!"

"Sorry, it's the missus," Shanks said apologetically. He could see that Warden was seething. He moved off towards the ring road.

"Where to?"

"Just take me home!"

Warden had had a number of calls from customers asking when he would be at home. He'd had to fob them all off because of the delay caused by Shanks. He didn't like to be under pressure and knew he would have a busy evening as a consequence. He removed the envelope from the inside of his shirt and opened it. He looked inside at several polythene bags of small granulated knuckles – rocks.

"Good man," he said.

They carried on along the North Circular and onto the motorway.

"Everything went OK then?" Shanks said cheerily.

"Yes, no thanks to you. You are an idle fucker, you know. If I can't rely on you then I'll find someone else." And then, "Yeah, went fine, smooth as clockwork. But he gives me the shits."

"Why?" asked Shanks, keen to change the subject from his late arrival.

"He was a strange fucker in prison – kept his distance, know what I mean? He wound people up the wrong way. Got bounced in the toilets a couple of times for being a twat – cracked cheekbone, a few bruises, scratches. It's where his nickname came from; he doesn't like people using it because it reminds him of his time inside, I suppose."

"What was his nickname?" Shanks enquired innocently.

"Patch. He wore a patch over his eye, left one I think. It was all blood shot and that. Everyone called him Patch. Didn't like it one bit." They continued their journey.

Warden had clearly been thinking about Patch. "He's a paranoid bastard."

"How come?"

"I met him in prison, right, and I've been working with him for a few years, but he still insists on me going to a phone box and I have to go there and wait for his call like a spare prick at a prostitute's wedding. He calls me and tells me to go somewhere to meet him. I reckon he's watching me when I go to the telephone box to make sure I'm alone and that. To make sure I'm not being followed."

"Fucking hell." Shanks widened his eyes and lifted his head slightly and looked at Warden.

"Mmm... Still don't know where he lives. He changes his number all the time. Cool fucker, that's all I can say... a really cool fucker."

"Mmm," said Shanks in sympathy.

"But I don't think he's going to get done over again."

"Why?"

"He's got a shooter."

"How do you know?"

"He showed me one day. I'd asked him if he was worried about being turned over and he said, 'No, I only deal with people I know and trust.' He looked me straight in the eye and I said, 'But what if you get blagged in the street?' He moved his jacket slightly and I could see the handle of a gun. He was smiling. 'Not again,' he said, shaking his head, 'not again'."

"Maybe it was just an imitation?"

"And the point of that would be? You are a plonker! So he gets turned over and produces a pretend gun, what's he going to do, go 'Bang'?!"

"S'pose not, hadn't thought of that." They continued their journey and as they turned into Barnet Street, Warden turned to Shanks.

"Pull over at the layby. I'll walk the rest of the way." He then placed the envelope back inside his shirt and tucked it inside the top of his trousers. From his jacket pocket he produced a wedge of notes, counted off one hundred and fifty pounds with his right thumb and handed it to Shanks.

"Ta."

"No problem." Shanks was impressed with the flash money; there must have been five to six hundred pounds there. *Business must be on the up,* he thought.

"OK, I'll give you a call; probably in a few days. But next time don't let me down. See ya, bruv." Warden got out of the car and began walking nonchalantly down the street.

Shanks drove off. He was thinking of the hassle he was going to get when he arrived home, but he had one hundred and fifty pounds in his bin. He was pleased.

Warden continued down the hill to his house; everything was normal, no-one hanging around. Halfway down he phoned a boy he knew called 'Danny', a black lad aged about twelve but who looked sixteen, always bunking off school but reliable and keen to earn a buck. He was at home with his mum, kicking cans and looking for a bit of excitement. He answered the phone.

"Dan, it's Warden. Can you do the normal for about half an hour and get back to me? Anything at all, give me a call, OK? I'll drop the money off later." 'Danny' agreed. He jumped on his bike and was off like a ferret up a drainpipe.

He had used Dan for a couple of years as his eyes and ears out on the streets, and phoned him when he was loaded and wanted some kind of reassurance that there were no Old Bill around in cars, vans or on foot, trying to be incognito – or, in fact, anyone that may have an interest in his business. He knew the area well: the back streets, the people, the cars, everything really. Any cars that were out of place, that weren't there normally, anyone standing or walking that he didn't recognise, he could rely on Dan to phone him and let him know. It had happened a couple of times, the odd car, a strange-looking person, and Warden had shut up shop, cleared the decks and cleaned everything down. Both of them had been false alarms, but he didn't mind, he preferred a couple of false alarms to being hit without notice.

He'd had some experience of being under surveillance and had talked to others about it when he was locked up. Lots of shit happened, but it was pretty simple, really. If you were switched on, you could tell Old Bill. They were normally blokes, some women, all aged between, say, twenty-five and forty-five, able-bodied – two arms, two legs, never or rarely together, they would never be doing anything other than walking – no road diggers, no postmen, no road cleaners – and they never wore stand out clothes and usually had their hands in their pockets. So, once you discounted teenagers, old-age pensioners, and mums with children, the field was quite limited. Same as their cars. All grey, blue or silver. All less than three or four years old. Standard make and model. Forget about red BMWs or white Audis.

He dug down into his coat pocket and found the front door key; up the stairs, door open, and in. Just before he turned left to go up the stairs he saw Danny cycle past, cross at the traffic lights and disappear from view behind the old house on the corner.

He double-locked the front door and put on the two opening chains and went into the back room. He laid out a tablecloth and put the bag he had bought onto the table. He went into the kitchen and brought out kitchen scales, and started removing all the polythene bags containing rocks onto the pan of the scales. When he removed the last one, he checked inside the bag that there was nothing left and looked at the weight. About ten grams over the half pound, just about right.

He counted the individual polythene bags – eight in total, eight one-ounce bags. He held the first one up to the light to confirm that it contained separate, tightly wrapped bags of cream-coloured rocks that reminded him of posh sugar that some people have with coffee. He opened the bag and counted the rocks covered in cling film. The first one had twenty-eight. He pulled out the table drawer until it touched his mid-rift, removed a smaller set of scales and weighed each small bag. They were all exactly or just slightly over one gram each. He placed them back in the original bag and did the same thing with the remaining seven bags. He did this every time he returned from London; he was never under-weight. There was one thing he would say: Patch was a reliable man, which was very important. He had put aside about six rocks that were above weight and tried one, heating it and inhaling the fumes. Ten minutes later he was still sitting at the table.

"Dynamite, pure dynamite," he whispered, "as they say in the films." Satisfied, he re-sealed the bags he had opened.

When he had started selling crack he'd had some difficulty finding a place to stash the gear that he felt was secure yet readily accessible. Then an old dope head had shown him where he stashed his skunk that was totally secure, easy to access and out of the way of the dogs that the Old Bill were prone to use. He told him that he had removed one of his old internal doors, carefully drilled out the top across the width to a depth of about three inches, and then chiselled out a slight lip at the top. He had then cut a length of wood to the same size to cover the cavity, browned it so that it blended and then fitted it so that it sat snugly onto the lips and was held in place by small magnetic catches at each end. He said you could use any door but that the old solid Victorian or Edwardian doors were the best – apparently, they were sturdier, more robust and less prone to chip at the edges.

He opened the door that separated the kitchen from the dining room and dragged a chair up against it and then stood on it. He inserted a kitchen knife at one end and gently levered off the lid. One by one he gently packed the individual bags into the cavity, bar one, which he kept on the table. He then replaced the lip of the door and checked it opened and closed without catching, and replaced the chair. The remaining bag he stashed behind one of the kickboards in the kitchen. He then wiped down the table with a damp cloth and cleaned the scales he had used. He was ready for business.

He knew all his customers and kept a rough account book, using initials and numbers to keep track of who had what, how much they'd paid and any money owed, so that when someone phoned, he knew how much they wanted and what price he had been charging them. Not all the prices were the same. He set the price according to the amount that a person bought; the larger the quantity purchased, the cheaper it was, based on price per gram. He didn't, and would never, sell individual rocks; it really wasn't worth the hassle and the crack heads were unreliable payers, had loose mouths and were more likely to rip you off or rob you than buy your gear. He left that to the middle men.

If someone came to the door, and this had happened several times, whom he didn't know or didn't want to know, he effectively told them to fuck off. In fact, it had become so bad at one point that he had a spy hole fitted so that he could vet people knocking at his door. He had considered a camera but this, he thought, was a little too obvious and may attract unwelcome attention.

Everyone eventually knew the system. They phoned him and asked him whether he had gear, and if this was a positive, he would ask how much they wanted. Generally he knew, but he occasionally needed to check the book. He told them the price and they would tell him when they would be around to collect the gear. He didn't like to be rushed – it could lead to mistakes – so anything from fifteen minutes and above was ideal and then he knew who to expect and roughly when they were due to arrive.

Again, occasionally – not so often now – blokes he knew would turn up without phoning. He told them to fuck off as well, and to phone him; if they said they'd lost their phone or something, he told them to use the telephone box around the corner.

Generally, it worked well. No-one, not even well-known players, were allowed into the back room, the dining room or the kitchen; they waited in the corridor out the front or in the front room whilst he collected the pre-prepared quantity that they had ordered by phone.

He always took the money first and counted it before handing over the gear and would never have more than one punter in the house at a time. Two against one could be a problem and it would give them the opportunity to discuss prices, and each would know how much the other was shifting; something he preferred to avoid.

There was little conversation and the transactions were always business-like and rapidly concluded, with just enough time to check quantity and payment.

Late afternoons and evenings were busy, never in the morning – presumably when the dollar dealers had collected enough money to make a wholesale purchase. It was always the same at this level. Consequently, mornings and early afternoons were quiet but visits picked up by about three or four o'clock, and remained busy until eight or nine o'clock on some evenings.

Danny hadn't called, so he called him. He apologised – no credit – but everything was cool. There was no sign of the Old Bill. Warden arranged to drop off forty pounds to his mum in the morning.

Warden's girlfriend, Sharon, knew what was going on; she wasn't really fussed, just treated it as a bit of business. She had a flat of her own anyway so could get away from it if she needed.

Warden's phone rang. It was one of his customers; he wanted four grams. Warden told him the price and told him to come around in twenty minutes. He divvied up the amount and put it to one side. The phone rang again and he did the same; this was a constant theme as he took orders, sorted out prices and arranged visits.

Soon he started receiving callers. A knock on the door and the person would be allowed in, money taken, told to wait and the right amount served to the punter, and then he left, there was very little conversation. Not constant, but a steady flow of customers.

It was important that he kept a record of who had what and how much he received, so that he could balance the books at the end of the evening. By about nine o'clock, things had calmed down. Sharon had called and was going to call back at about ten with a take-away. He sat down and did some calculations.

He'd shifted about one and a half ounces and had, on his calculation, made about eight hundred pounds profit; that didn't include payments to Shanks and Danny. He also estimated that he had about seven and half left, plus any residue that was already in the stash.

And that reminded him – before Sharon came back, he needed to get down there. He gathered his money together and any rocks he had remaining, placed them in a resealable bag, removed the residual air and then sealed the top and placed them on the kitchen table.

Once ready, he poked his head out of the front door to make sure the coast was clear and once satisfied, he returned, collected the packages and stuffed them around his goolies. He left the house.

It was dark, he turned left and walked down the street to a small alleyway, where he paused in the darkness. He lit a cigarette and waited for a few minutes before continuing. He reached the canal bank and turned right onto the path. It wasn't used much these days, apart from by joggers. He walked along a short distance until he reached a green garden gate at the back of one of the houses. He turned and faced the old disused canal and moved forward until he saw the old pole that he had stuck in the mud, about a metre into the water. He paused, looked around to make sure he wasn't being watched and then knelt down under the bank until he felt a nylon rope; he tugged on it and pulled up a glass jar.

He was pleased with himself for choosing this method of hiding his drugs. He used a three-litre Kilner jar that was weighted to allow it to sink to the murky, silty depths of the canal. It was re-sealable, would not rust and would protect the contents. He unclipped the jar lid, and removing the bags from his crotch, he placed them inside to join others that were already there, and then clipped the lid back and lowered it back into the water. The tricky thing was remembering what was there because with the ebb and flow of money and drugs, keeping tabs on amounts was difficult. He kept two figures at the bottom of his book – running totals, one for money and one for the crack – just numbers, no pounds, shillings or pence, or grams or ounces; that would be too obvious.

Once the jar was back he moved back to the alleyway, making sure no-one was about, and returned home.

Sharon wasn't there, but as soon as he returned she phoned and said she'd be back in ten minutes.

Warden ensured there was nothing incriminating left lying around and relaxed. He was done for another day.

# 10

# A STICK IN THE SPOKES

The office was empty and still; the weekend had passed and papers lay where they had been left. It was midway through the day when a key was thrust into the lock, the door was opened with a flourish and the lights turned on, bathing the desks in a fluorescent brilliance. The tranquillity and calmness had been disturbed; the room had reluctantly become one of movement.

They had come into the office to collect batteries and check on their paperwork before diving out into the real world and intended to stay for no more than ten minutes – a quick coffee and a chat. There was a knock on the door.

"Come in!" bellowed Kenny, annoyed that someone was going to disturb them when they were really pushed for time. The door opened and a vision of true loveliness presented itself to the two officers.

"Have you got a minute?" said the woman.

"Yes, please, come in, grab a seat!" said Kenny, rather sheepishly. They knew her well, she had worked on previous cases with them and they had already provided her with the available phone material from their current investigation. She was an analyst within with the intelligence section.

Liz sat down. She was carrying a sheath of papers which she placed on the desk in front of her. She had been an analyst for about eighteen months and her job was to receive data – any data, phone calls, sequence of events, criminal associations, anything really – examine them, analyse their contents and produce charts that could then be easily presented and assimilated to identify key areas that were worthy of further attention.

Sometimes, the volume of data being generated from different sources during an investigation made it difficult to assimilate the contents and link them together. Liz cut through the mist that shrouded the information and presented a clear picture, which is why the analysts used to be called the Anacapa Team, after an island in the Pacific that is often shrouded in mist, particularly in the morning, but becomes wonderfully visible again once the sun has risen high in the sky. Liz brought with her a gentle, quiet, feminine touch, which was completely at odds with the sharp-angled, hard and often awkward environment in which she chose to work.

"Would you like a coffee?" Kenny asked meekly.

"Oh yes, that would be lovely."

Franks clattered around with the mugs and once the formalities of whether she wanted milk, sugar, decaf etc were over, she said, "It's about the phone printouts you gave me last week. One for a bloke called Warden and the other…" She looked at her notes. "Purves."

"Yep, what about them?" Kenny replied.

"Well, with Warden, the same mobiles come up pretty regularly. He's had the same phone that he's got now for just over a month." She passed over sequential and frequency charts.

"The numbers at the top of this list," pointing to the

frequency chart, "are those that are called or received most regularly, and you'll see they occur all the way through the week, consistently, and the duration is usually about fifteen to thirty seconds. However, if you look at the bottom of the frequency chart, and I've only done the last month, there are..." She counted with a pencil, softly, quietly and all the while gently breathing in. "Nine numbers that are phoned only once."

"OK..." Kenny was just about keeping pace.

"Now, if you look at the sequential chart, seven of those numbers are outgoing on Thursday mornings; the other two seem random." They looked at each other and then over her shoulders, consuming her gorgeous perfume whilst at the same time trying to establish what she'd identified.

"OK, you still with me?"

"Yes," they said in chorus, like a couple of mesmerised schoolboys.

"Now, you followed Warden to London last Thursday, with his friend Shanks driving, right?"

"Yes."

"So, on that day he telephoned this number." She pointed to an 07 number. "About three quarters of an hour before he left." This was one of the seven random 07 numbers that she had referred to earlier.

"OK." Kenny had forgotten she had copies of all the logs for superimposing on the call data.

"According to your logs, he left the pub." She looked at the log, "the Haven Arms, at 14:22 hours. At 14:24, he telephoned Shanks' phone multiple times, presumably to get a lift home. He comes here at..." She checked the log. "Three thirty p.m. Although he is making and receiving calls throughout the day, he receives the bulk of his calls after three thirty p.m. when, presumably, his dealers know that he is back."

"OK, so what we are saying is that Warden probably phones

Purves on a different number every week, usually Thursdays, prior to leaving for London?"

"Yes."

"How does he know which number to call?"

"Don't know. Maybe Purves calls him from the number he's about to ditch, perhaps he telephones him from a TK and lets him know. In any event, he knows. Which brings me nicely onto the calls made from the mobile that Warden contacted, the one ostensibly used by Purves last week."

"Yes…" They were still up to speed and enthralled by the charts – and indeed, her perfume.

"I've only got last week's, because the number he was using then didn't exist before last week – or apparently afterwards, in fact; the only usage on that phone was for a seven-day period, which covers the day you followed Warden to London, nothing before and nothing afterwards." She swapped the charts over and showed them two smaller charts, again sequential and frequency.

"OK, so this is Purves' mobile, we think it's probably under a false name. There's far fewer calls. But you'll see that he has an unidentified incoming call at the time that Warden was in London and…" She checked the log. "You saw him in the TK opposite Ealing Broadway between 13:25 hours and 13:34 hours." She pointed to the entry.

"Yep, that's right. Waiting for a call," Kenny recalled.

"At 13:31 hours, that TK number was phoned from Purves' phone whilst Warden was in the TK."

"Fucking great! That means we've got the right man!"

Kenny stood up and then, realising what he said, added, "Sorry, Liz!"

"A little more…"

"More?" they said in unison.

"Yes. If we look at Purves' phone for that week, he contacts seven telephone boxes in the Ealing area, all short duration, all, generally, mid-way through the day."

"Liz, you are a star!" Watching her colour slightly in response to the accolades of her colleagues, Franks smiled.

"I know you're in a rush. Just one last thing. Would you like me to request the billing data for the other six numbers that Warden phoned on Thursdays and see if there is any correlation between them and the calls made last week?"

"If you could, that would be great. How much time do you need?"

"A couple of days."

"Fantastic. Thanks a lot, Liz. I owe you." Kenny looked across to Franks, who had raised his eyebrows and looked to the ceiling as a sign of utter disbelief. She sipped her coffee and was persuaded to take it with her as she left the office with a 'ta ta', and closed the door.

"Lovely, quite lovely." Kenny sighed.

Franks interrupted his mate's thought pattern.

"Back to the subject in hand, that's great. That ties them in nicely and points to a system. Purves appears to be controlling his buyers by passing them through specific TKs. It'll be interesting to see how she gets on with the other numbers."

They were running about fifteen minutes late by the time they arrived at the house on the corner and trudged up the stairs to their room, dark and a little musty, rather like a mushroom farm. Chinks of light spewed through the window blackouts as they prepared themselves for another evening's work, laying out all the equipment – radios, bins, cameras, pee-pots – as normal.

Franks had the first watch and folded up the bottom part of the blackout so that he could see the front door of Warden's house. Kenny had gone across to the far side of the room to look out at the junction and the road beyond, leading into the town centre.

That afternoon, Warden had had a number of visitors, all well known to both detectives but photographs were taken. The purpose of the visit was to try to identify the remaining couple of punters who were not known to them and had resisted all their attempts to put names to faces. Their photos had been circulated and plastered on confidential noticeboards, but no-one knew them. They had had a couple of suggestions but they had been discounted. They were probably outsiders who had come into the area to buy from Warden and then left. If this was right then it showed how widespread his market had become. If they were not identified then they would probably have to leave it and go with what they had, rather than trying to ID people from elsewhere.

The afternoon ground on and, by early evening, Warden had had eighteen visitors, all male and all of whom had stayed for less than five minutes; some stayed for just a couple of minutes and two visitors knocked on the door without it being opened and wandered off.

It was a standard evening really, he'd been busy, very active which supported the investigation and underlined the level of his dealing. It was clear and bright, and traffic was moderate as everyone was striving to get home and avoid the worst excesses of the rush hour.

Warden had had a visitor, Bobby Loader. He was well known to Kenny and Franks from previous encounters, and had been logged as having a strong, long-term relationship with Warden. He was a good street dealer, not particularly violent but quite prickly when cornered, especially when he was carrying. Lots of front, very leery, difficult to deal with, reputedly carried knives. He was one of Warden's closest associates and whom they had currently listed in the second phase of arrests, after potting Warden. His photograph was taken and his description included in the day's log. He had remained at the address for nine minutes, slightly longer than normal. As he was leaving, he met another man wearing a hoodie at the bottom of the steps. The second man had not entered the house and, although they couldn't see his face, the guys didn't recognise his clothes or gait and were reasonably certain they didn't know him and that he hadn't featured previously in the operation.

Loader and the second man talked for a few minutes before walking off together down the street and across the traffic lights in the direction of the town centre.

Kenny opened the slats of the window that overlooked the junction and watched the two of them walking together away from the house. He took a couple of pictures and then noticed a third man walking up the street towards them. He was about one hundred and fifty yards away and, by using binoculars, he knew him as one of the two men they had yet to identify. He took a couple of long shots and saw him close on the two men walking along the street. When the three met, they were on the opposite side of the road from Kenny and about seventy-five yards distant. There was some conversation, use of hands, head movement. The man with Loader was hanging back slightly, as if he didn't want to become involved.

"Looks like a little disagreement down here. The two you've just seen leaving the house have met another; they aren't hitting each other but there's something going on. The bloke whose coming up is one of our unidents," said Kenny.

Traffic was getting heavier now and came in great chunks as the lights let vehicles through and then cut them off like the blade of a guillotine.

"They're head to head." The two men were facing up to each other. They may have been shouting but Kenny couldn't hear anything inside the house and over the steady hum of passing traffic and the static in his earpiece. Occasionally, a heavy bus temporarily obscured his view but he kept his eyes focused on them.

"Better log this with a time."

"OK, 17:05 hours, done," said Franks.

After what was probably no more than forty-five seconds, but felt like five minutes, Kenny saw the newcomer, the unident who had been facing towards him throughout, come very close to Loader. They were about the same height and their noses appeared to be touching, with heavy eye contact. Still the third man hung back; he started looking around, much more aware of what was happening around him than the two opponents. No-one else was about. Traffic passed, unaware of, or ignoring, the altercation. Still Kenny took pictures, he was taking a series when he saw the unident's head rise by about two or three inches, he was on the balls of his feet and his head was thrown back, his mouth thrown open, and then his body settled back momentarily to its normal position. He looked Loader in the eyes until a second violent spasm engulfed him and he again pushed himself onto tiptoe and threw his head back with his mouth open.

"Might need some uniforms down here, Tom."

Kenny was taking pictures with his camera, which was fixed on a tripod, and alternating that with binoculars. Franks scurried over to join him.

Before he reached him, Kenny said, "Fuck, he's shivved him!" He saw the unident settle down on his feet for a second time as Loader took a step backwards. As he did so, he saw Loader's right hand remove a large kitchen knife from the man's abdomen, which appeared to have penetrated upwards, beneath his ribcage. The knife was smeared with blood and the man clutched his stomach, mouth open but unable to speak, still standing. As Loader moved, he said something to the man, who was unable to respond. The third man, on seeing the knife, ran off towards the roundabout in the opposite direction from Warden's house, never looking back, with no hesitation, just keen to get away from the carnage.

Loader moved away and carried on walking in the same direction. Almost as an afterthought, he realised that he was still holding the knife; he looked at it and threw it into one of the gardens facing the road, and then, quickening his pace and, keen to leave the scene, turned left down the alleyway towards the canal.

Franks phoned 999, explained who he was and what they'd seen, and was assured that someone was on their way.

The man who had been stabbed walked forward about six paces, his hands clutching his stomach, and then fell to his knees on the pavement, settling on his haunches. He removed his hands and looked down; his abdomen was bloody. He lifted them to eye level and then looked down again at the mess. Finally his back buckled and he slumped forward and then rolled gently onto his left side.

At the same time, a dark car pulled over, a little way past the prone body. A woman got out of the passenger door and went over, gradually bending down to his level. They could see her touch the man's neck and wrist, presumably to see if there was any sign of life. The hazard lights of the car came on and a man, the driver, joined the woman. He had a mobile clamped to his ear. Within thirty seconds a police car pulled up, closely followed by an ambulance, causing congestion and chaos. Their view was obstructed now by the parked vehicles and they could see nothing more of the curled-up body. They had said nothing to each other. Neither had they considered leaving the building; the risk to Patience if they were seen was too great and if they had acted, by the time they would have reached the victim, they certainly would not have been able to provide any more assistance.

Franks phoned the Control Room Inspector, who confirmed, from information provided by the first responders, that the man was dead, from what appeared to be a single stab wound under the rib cage and into the heart. He added that he had probably died as soon as he had been stabbed, that there was nothing anyone could have done to save his life.

Franks checked with the inspector that their conversation was being recorded and then told him what they had seen and that if they looked in one of the gardens adjacent to where the body was located, they would find the murder weapon; a bloodstained kitchen knife.

"Fuck!" Kenny said with venom as he turned to Franks, his upper incisors clamping themselves onto his lower lip to accentuate the 'f' in fuck and to underline his annoyance and frustration.

"OK, where do we stand now? We are witnesses to a murder; we know who the murderer is, can identify him and have photos of the event. All of this will need to be disclosed – logs, photos, our names, what we're doing... everything," Franks said, pragmatically.

"And Patience?"

"She's protected; we'll never need to disclose where we are sitting, all the correct procedures and authorities are on file."

"Warden?"

"That's a good one. So, the murdered man is one of his punters – he's been to his house before, but we don't know his name. We know who the murderer is, Bobby bloody Loader. When he's arrested and, if he's talkative and tells them where he was prior to the stabbing, that will drag Warden into the maelstrom. If he's very open and tells them about Warden's activities, then that puts our man right in the frame," added Franks.

"OK, but Loader isn't under arrest and may not be for a

day or two, and even then, he may not talk." Kenny was trying to talk it through and look at the various scenarios.

He closed his eyes and then looked at the grimy floor.

"Fuck, fuck, fuck!"

They were still sitting and looking at the murder scene beyond the junction – police cars, ambulances, plain cars. Blue lights pulsing against the buildings.

"No point in leaving at the moment. And Warden? What's he going to do?" Kenny was thinking of ways of salvaging the operation.

"He'll shut up shop. Keep a low profile, keep clean for a week or maybe two. He's not involved in the murder, has no personal responsibility, but there's going to be a lot of Old Bill sniffing around the area for a few days and he won't want to put his head above the parapet," said Franks.

Kenny thought about it. "What do we lose? What does the investigation lose?" He answered himself, "Nothing. Absolutely fuck all… we can evidence the amount of dealing, we can take out his stash at any time of our choosing, and can link him to it and to his man, Purves."

"We lose evidence from the house," said Franks negatively.

"We do, but what is he going to do with any gear or dosh in the house?"

"Put it in the stash?"

"Correct. All in the same place, out of the way, nice and easy. He's not going to get rid of anything unless he really, really needs to – he'll ride it out and carry on when the dust settles."

"And what do we do now?"

"We stay here, see what's going on, and when it gets dark, we leave. When we get back we need to speak to the murder team, whomever that may be."

Franks phoned the nick and was put through to the Duty DS. He explained to him their position and what they intended to do and arranged to meet the DI when they returned. He also told the DS who the murderer was and what clothes he was wearing.

Kenny marked the logs up to date with what they had seen. When he had finished, they resumed their positions. Warden's house was quiet, no visitors. He poked his head out on three or four occasions, as did his girlfriend, to look down at the flashing blue lights and parked vehicles just beyond the traffic lights and Kenny noticed, for the first time, a young black lad on a bike hanging around the area, not getting too close but observing from a distance and then using his mobile phone. He hadn't noticed him before.

"Do you know that black lad on the bike?"

"No, I've seen him about, think he's local. I've taken some pictures before," replied Franks.

It was probably the most mundane period they had had in the OP. There was no action and it was numbingly boring; time seemed to tick along in slow motion. All the time blue lights flashed at the scene; they had erected a tent over the scene and the garden where Kenny had seen Loader throw the knife. Press came and went, traffic flowed.

As darkness fell, one police car remained. The tent had been removed and council workers were hosing down the pavement of any signs of blood and gore.

Within a couple of hours, they appeared to have finished and the police car left, leaving a single yellow sign on the pavement where the stabbing had occurred, asking for witnesses to come forward. As far as Kenny and Franks were aware, there were only three witnesses to the murder – them and the third man who had run away.

They gave it until eight thirty p.m. and started to pack up their kit into their large black bags. Franks kept an eye on the Warden household in case there was any late night movement.

"Hold on a minute."

"What?"

"He's out and walking down the road, towards the scene." The last thing to be removed was the log and he quickly updated it with this most recent movement. They watched him wander across the junction to the yellow sign, hands in pockets, look around for perhaps twenty or thirty seconds and then return home.

"Just poking his nose," said Franks.

They allowed him another ten minutes before clearing the room and leaving. It was eight forty-five p.m.

They arrived back at the nick twenty minutes later, dumped all their bags in the office and went hunting for the duty DI.

They found him in an improvised Major Incident Room along the corridor. He had corralled some of the duty team who were not already committed with prisoners, and they were busily writing statements and completing forms.

"Hello, guys! I've been expecting you, come on in!" They entered the MIR and followed him into an annex, a small room that he had been using as an office away from the hubbub of the main room.

Once the door was closed, he began the conversation. "I just wanted to check my facts. You're running a drugs operation against Tony Warden. This evening a person you know leaves his house, meets another whom you don't know a short distance away down the street and knifes him. The man you don't know was dead at the scene, a single stab wound to the heart. You saw the incident as it unfolded and you maintained a log and took photos. So far?"

They both nodded in unison.

"The murder suspect is Bobby Loader, whom you have identified on your job as a street dealer who gets his supplies from Warden. Am I on the right track?"

More nods.

"OK. Now for the bits you don't know. The victim is a man called Mick Cornwall – I don't think you had managed to ID him to date – minor criminal, comes from Newbury… the ID on him, driving licence. We need to formally ID but it's him. We have the murder weapon, long kitchen knife covered in blood, recovered from garden close by. Not sure but probably a dispute over drugs, money, pitch, something like that, but we'll confirm that later."

"And Loader?" asked Franks.

"We arrested him at his girlfriend's house, hiding in the wardrobe. He'd changed his clothes but we were snapping at his heels and there was a big pile of bloodied clothing in the kitchen. He's locked up. We won't interview him until the morning, but it's not looking good for him at the moment." Silence.

"You have some photos?"

"Yes."

"OK, we'll need them and we'll need witness statements from you."

"Do you know who the other bloke was, the one who ran off?"

"No, not yet, but you have some pictures?"

"Yes, not good, hooded."

"Don't fuck yourself over with this, there is nothing you could have done, either before or afterwards. The woman who stopped was a nurse, we have her statement. She says there was no pulse, no sign of life – he was almost certainly dead within seconds. There won't be a PM until tomorrow, but we're pretty certain that the knife pierced the heart, it's all fairly straightforward. Loader's spoken to his brief who has said that his client is innocent." Kenny and Franks looked at each other.

"Now, your job. We're going to have to speak to Warden, and I would think he'll put the shutters down at the moment, at least until things calm down a little. I can hold off on him for a couple of days, he's not critical, didn't see anything, but we'll need to clear him. This brings pressure on you and your op. Can you sort yourself out by the day after tomorrow?"

"Not much choice, really," said Kenny despondently, accepting the necessity and understanding the priorities.

"Not really. I don't want to fuck your job up, guys, but we do need to speak to him, and if you are able to sort your side out first…"

"Should be doable," said Franks.

"Need to sort out some ninjas in a couple of days."

"OK," said the DI. "By the way, when we searched Loader's bloodied trousers, he had about half an ounce of crack in one of the pockets. I suppose he was panicky and so intent on dumping his clothes that he forgot about it. We can evidence that for your job. The gear's been booked in and is in the safe if you want a gander."

"Thanks Guv, appreciate your help on this. We'll keep you in the loop," said Kenny.

"Likewise, I'll let you know what happens with Loader." They exchanged mobile numbers and left the room.

They wandered through to the MIR, the hub of the murder investigation, to seek out the exhibits officer. When they found him, they asked to look at the drugs that had been found in Loader's trousers. They followed him, a short, squat detective whom they both knew vaguely, to a locked cupboard in a separate room, shelved out with slats that were already beginning to groan under the weight of dozens of polythene bags filled with everything from keys to clothes, soil samples to sweepings.

The man flicked through his register, found the item and offered the book to one of them to sign and date. Once completed, he passed the item to them – a medium-sized plastic bag, sealed at one end. Kenny fingered the item enclosed in the bag with his fingers. The bag contained another smaller plastic bag, which itself contained dozens of small pea-sized cream-coloured balls of rock, each of them tightly wrapped in cling film and tied at the top.

"Where were they – exactly?" asked Franks. The exhibits man referred to the book and ran his fingers across the entry.

"Says here right-hand trouser pocket."

"Anything else on him?"

Once again, the exhibits man returned to the book.

"Set of keys, loose change… oh! And four hundred and twenty pounds in notes – same pocket."

"Mmm… interesting that – just scored off Warden and no time to hide it, or not bothered, and no attempt by Bobby Loader to rob him of it either," said Kenny.

They thanked the exhibits man and left the room. It was late.

"Fancy a pint?" said Franks. "It's been a long day."

"Love one, but we've got to get our books squared away. I'll get a couple of whiskies and meet you in the office."

They met a short while later and spent the next two hours sorting out the paperwork, sipping whiskey and discussing where the job was going. By the time they had finished, they were up to date with the logs, photos and pocket books.

It was about one thirty a.m. when the two men left. It was dark and had been raining. They were tired. There was no further conversation.

# 11

# WHAM BAM, THANK YOU MA'AM

They had agreed to meet again in the office first thing the next morning and duly arrived there at the same time, at about seven o'clock. A big and imposing brick building in the centre of the town, they had driven in through the large metal roller doors which sat, rather imposingly, at the back and below ground level, so that the car park itself was permanently bathed in a bright fluorescent light. Separately, they found parking spaces and, locking their cars, they met in the middle of one of the wide aisles surrounded by concrete pillars, cars and a constant feeling of dampness.

As they approached each other, they knew exactly how the other was feeling. Their eyes had begun to sting, concentration was difficult and their limbs ached. Yesterday had been a long day; they had finished late, a little shocked and a little jaded. They both wanted to go away and get pissed, have an Indian followed by a long sleep, but both men also knew that that was, at the moment, impossible. They were in the middle of an operation, which up to the previous evening was under control, developing well and had some potential. Now, although still controllable, it was driven by events that had been outside their remit, utterly random and completely unexpected.

"Breakfast?" began Kenny.

Franks nodded.

They strolled wearily to the lift and went directly to the canteen on the top floor, safe from the outside world. As they entered, the warmth enveloped them and the smell of eggs and grilled bacon stimulated their senses as they joined the queue. The canteen was buzzing with activity; the early uniformed shift were huddled around two long tables, their belts, coats and radios draped over their chairs, they were supping their tea, devouring fry-ups and reading the old papers that been left lying on the tables for the past few days. Small conversations, shared jokes, laughter, intense listening, empathy and a degree of grizzled exhaustion.

Scattered around the room were others, generally separated into their own small teams; intelligence, interviewers, tac firearms and other officers, nervously checking their paperwork prior to court next door, peppered by occasional spontaneous laughter and gentle ribbing.

They collected their food and took a table in a corner, knowing that the conversation they intended to have was not for general consumption. Bacon, eggs, fried slice, beans, sausage, a cup of tea and generous amounts of ketchup – that would sort out their weariness.

The chatter settled on the events of the day before, where they were and what they intended to do over the coming days to retrieve the situation and preserve something of the investigation in which they had invested so much time and effort. It was agreed that they would need to arrest Warden and Pritchard before the murder investigation developed in their direction, whilst at the same time deflecting any likely impact on Purves, who was, at the moment, probably unaffected by the killing. If they could achieve this over the next forty-eight hours, they could settle down and see if they could rein Purves in and tie him to the other two.

After being reassured by the environment and the ambience, and fortified by the food, they wandered down to their office, unlocked the door and silently entered. Everything was as they had left it. Very quickly they agreed essential jobs that needed completing. It was very unlikely that Warden would continue serving in the midst of so much activity, and the consensus was that he would wait until things had quietened down. He probably anticipated being interviewed or perhaps arrested as part of the murder enquiry and would have cleared his house of any evidence that he may have felt was incriminating. The game plan, therefore, had to be straightforward, and executed fairly promptly to avoid clashing with the murder investigation. They decided that the OP would run as normal on Warden's house that evening and that Kenny would leave to keep tabs on the stash by the canal in the hope that Warden would return to it to replenish his personal stock. Although it was short notice, they would try and organise an arrest team to collar him when he went to the canal. If it went to plan, this would ensure a direct and incontrovertible link between the suspect and his drugs.

Franks prepared the information for two search warrants, one for Warden's house, the other for Pritchard's, and left to arrange a magistrate. Meanwhile, Kenny phoned the ninjas, the local pro-active team, to seek assistance in lifting Warden and, if this was successful, to search the two addresses and a meeting with them was arranged for later that morning.

Franks returned an hour later, warrants in hand. They began to prepare subject files containing photographs, descriptions, distinguishing features; and search files with house layouts, occupants, a plan of the canal site and anything specific that they were looking for at the houses.

At about midday, the local guys came in for a briefing. They agreed to provide eight people to do the hit and then, if everything went to plan, the subsequent house searches. A further briefing was to be held later that afternoon in the office, prior to deployment.

Kenny emphasised that they needed to park away from the plot, wear dark clothing and maintain absolute silence – no mobiles – and if an approach to the stash was made, listen to the lead-in from the OP and, most importantly, detain the subject silently and remove him from the site via the footbridge, not via the alleyway to the main road, and then locate and seize the stash and preserve it for forensic examination.

That afternoon, they finalised their plans, bringing the file up to date and updating the murder team with developments.

At six p.m. they gathered in their small office. Op orders, numbered and completed with plans, diagrams, logistics, comms and command structure were handed out. It was crowded; officers sat on tables and chairs or simply stood. Kenny went through the gameplan once again and answered queries. The normal ones were raised – dogs, knives and firearms – and all were answered with, "The intelligence indicates there are no dogs on the premises to be visited and that none of the subjects carry firearms or knives or have access to them." It was a tense session. Most people in the room knew Warden, and some, Pritchard. They all listened intently and they were all keen to perform, knowing the amount of work that had already been completed and not wishing to cock things up with a wrong move at the wrong time, or by missing some vital evidence or intelligence.

At six o'clock they moved out, Kenny and Franks to their OP and the hit team to a large car park some four hundred metres from Warden's house and on the opposite side of the street from the canal. Franks and Kenny parked their car, walked up to the side door of the OP and entered using the key, and crept up the rickety steps to the room they knew so well. They set up their equipment as normal – cameras, binoculars, logs, radio – before uncovering the window shades.

All was quiet. There were lights on in the house and the curtains were drawn. Traffic was light and it was dry and still. They checked the comms and confirmed that they could communicate with the ninjas (callsign TT20) and vice versa.

After about thirty minutes, Kenny slipped out of the house and, after checking that his covert radio was working and that the plot was clear, he walked down the road and into the alleyway that led to the canal. He had with him a backpack containing his poncho, binoculars and an image intensifier. When he reached the embankment, he raised Franks on the radio. "56A permission."

"Yes, yes, 56A."

"Sitrep."

"All clear, no movement." Kenny made his way to the position he had previously occupied on the opposite side of the canal, slightly offset from the exit to the alley. He found the bricks he had left on the towpath and the upturned petrol can and settled down, once again drawing his old American Army olive-green poncho over himself and tucking his bag in close. He checked his surroundings: undergrowth good, all quiet, no walkers, nothing different from the last occasion. He noted that there were fewer lights on the back of the line of terraced houses he was facing, but all good. He removed the image intensifier from his pack and tested it by pointing it across the canal to the far bank and peering into the eyepiece. What was dark suddenly became green and bright, but it was important there were no artificial lights to spoil the vision. The lights from the houses were sufficiently dull not to affect the image. All good. Next he tested comms.

"56A permission," he whispered.

"Yes, yes."

"In position, all quiet."

"Yes, yes 56A. TT20 did you receive 56A?"

"Yes, yes," came the response.

So, everything was in place. Even the Ninjas could hear him.

"TT20 yes, yes – for the log, time 18:35." Then silence. Kenny felt alone, but he was comfortable although slightly damp. The fresh smell of vegetation and the occasional shuffling of an animal close by disturbed the peace.

He surveyed the scene as his eyes became accustomed to the dark; he could see the alleyway and the slight glow from the street beyond and the occasional car passing the road-bridge to his right. His mind wandered. *I hope this fucker comes down here tonight. Don't let me down, you little bastard,* he thought.

He knew he only had two possible evenings in which Warden could be caught at his stash and this was the first opportunity – they just needed a bit of luck.

Fifteen minutes later, a transmission broke his train of thought.

"OP. No change, no change. 56A?" crackled into his ear.

"56A, yes, yes," he responded.

Silence once again descended onto the canal bank.

After a few minutes, he heard muffled conversation coming from the far side of the canal. The words were indistinct. He strained his eyes and saw some movement between his position and the road bridge.

"56A permission."

"Yes, yes 56A."

"Be aware. Movement, far towpath, voices between road bridge and my location, indistinct."

"56A, yes, yes. TT20?"

"TT20, yes, yes."

Kenny knew that if Warden was already out and about and went straight to his stash, the hit team would be hard pushed to reach it and nab him in time. But that was part of the risk; the longer the operation went on that evening, the less likely it was that he would come out.

Kenny waited. He could still hear the muffled tones, slightly louder now, and he could make out the different pitches – a man and a woman. He saw the dark shapes as they came out of the lee of the road bridge. He brought the scope up to his eye, and could make them out clearly – two people, one larger than the other with dark clothing, the smaller one with lighter clothing, walking slowly side by side, occasionally stopping. They were, at Kenny's estimate, about fifty metres from the stash.

"56A permission."

"56A."

"Couple, fifty metres away and closing slowly."

"56A yes, yes."

"TT20."

Kenny knew where the hit teams were and that it would take them a couple of minutes to reach the stash. They would be out of their vehicles, lined up in a dark corner, checking their kit, with no conversation, no sound, listening intently to developments.

"56A, twenty metres."

The couple dawdled on, busily chatting and unaware that they were the centre of attention and that ten people were concentrating on their every move. The couple passed in front of the entrance to the alleyway. Kenny could make out the bigger bulk of the man and the smaller-framed woman.

"56A approx. ten metres, no deviation, no deviation."

"56A, yes, yes."

"Now directly opposite, no deviation."

"56A yes, yes."

A few seconds passed.

"56A permission."

"56A, yes, yes."

"They've passed the location and my position, continued walking towards footbridge."

"56A, yes, yes."

Panic over, Kenny settled down. He could see the couple meandering towards the bridge; all was quiet again.

"56, no change, no change. TT20?"

"TT20, yes, yes."

The couple drifted on and out of his sight, although he could hear them climbing up to the footbridge to his left and then see them silhouetted against the ambient light from the town as they continued over the bridge to his side and out of sight. A few minutes later they came ambling back along the towpath on his side of the canal and Kenny could now see that they were holding hands and still talking. He knew they would pass within about five metres of his position.

"56A permission."

"56A, yes, yes."

"No transmissions – one minute," Kenny whispered into his mic.

Franks knew that noise was the issue. Perhaps someone was close to him. He pressed his transmitter three times to acknowledge. Kenny could clearly see the couple now, occasionally stopping for a snog and grope as they edged closer to him until they were between him and the stash. *Thank fuck they haven't got a fucking dog,* he thought.

On they walked, oblivious to Kenny, who was stock still, only his head protruding from the poncho, but he felt fairly secure surrounded by brambles. They continued with their stroll and after twenty or thirty metres, Kenny said, "56A, permission."

"56A, yes, yes."

"All clear – couple walking past on my side, now out of sight, back to you."

"Yes, yes. TT20?" Franks said to make sure they weren't feeling left out.

"TT20, yes, yes." Silence.

There were a few desultory transmissions from Franks checking comms and to confirm everything was good. After about half an hour, Kenny began to think that Warden was not going to appear, that he had been scared off.

*Perhaps,* he thought, *he is no longer using this stash. Maybe he has already been to the canal?* There had been no movement nor any indication of habitation at the house. Then he became more pragmatic. More optimistic. He carefully analysed the situation in his head. Warden was a good dealer, he disliked taking risks, he had presumably used this stash for some time and he felt safe, more importantly, he clearly couldn't visit the stash in the daylight – it was too dangerous. He just needed to remain positive, to always believe that the operation, any operation he was engaged in, was going to be successful.

The night dragged on. Kenny knew that the uniform guys would start getting bored and restless, eager to get involved – and the longer the delay, the more chance they had of being blown out. Suddenly over the airwaves came, "Standby, standby! Subject 1 to the front door, looking up and down the street. 56A?"

"Yes, yes." *Praise the Lord. He was always at home, and it looks as if he is going to go out,* Kenny thought.

"Door closed, subject inside, wearing blue jeans, grey hoodie, with hood up. TT20?"

"Yes, yes."

It was quiet on the towpath; nothing stirred. About thirty seconds later came, "Standby, standby. Subject to the front door, same clothes, looking up and down the street, door closed, at the top of the stairs, looking up and down. Towards the gate and off, off, off and right, right, right, away from junction. 56A?"

"Yes, yes."

*Fuck it,* he thought. *He's going the wrong way, away from the alley. Maybe he's having a quick gander around.*

"56A permission," Kenny called.

"Yes, yes."

"He's probably having a mooch around before coming here – make sure 20 are aware and to keep their heads down."

Before Franks could answer, the uniformed guys had acknowledged, "Subject continued on foot, no deviation, and out of sight of the OP. Total loss." The view from the OP looking up the street away from the traffic lights was limited. The adjoining house on that side protruded into the street and blocked the view.

So, once again, silence, and no-one had control of the subject. It was likely he was having a look around but maybe he had relocated his stash, maybe he was going to make another phone call. One of the difficulties was that Franks couldn't watch both the front door of the house and the road past the traffic lights at the same time.

He had opted, quite rightly, to stay with the house on the basis that if he was looking down the street he may miss him re-entering the house. Time dragged, traffic flowed, but still no sightings of the man.

Several 'no changes' were posted by Franks at the OP until, "Standby, standby, possible contact, walking down the street towards his HA and the traffic lights. Wait for confirmation."

And then, ten seconds later, "Can confirm, contact, contact, contact, subject walking towards H/A alone. Same clothes. 56A?"

"Yes, yes."

"Quite briskly, on same side of street as H/A," and then, "Passing H/A to his nearside and towards traffic lights." *So, he's not going home,* thought Kenny.

"Held at ATS, crossing junction, no deviation."

*He's coming back to his stash – game on,* thought Kenny and he tried to imagine Franks scrabbling to get to the other window, the one that gave a view down the street towards the stash.

"Stop, stop, stop and looking back to his H/A, traffic lights, crossing road to the offside." *Fuck it, fuck it.* Kenny thought as he clenched his fist.

"Continued on offside of the road away from H/A. Stop, stop, stop, on offside of road opposite alleyway to canal. 56A?"

"Yes, yes."

"No change, no change, standing back from the road, looking up and down, smoking a cigarette." He stood there for about a minute.

"Off, off, off and loss of eyeball. He's entered the alleyway beside the church on the opposite side of the road from the canal – this leads to some further small alleyways and car parks behind the church. TT20 be aware, he's walking in your general direction."

"TT20, yes, yes."

"56A permission."

"Yes, yes, 56A."

"I think he's having a good look around before coming here; need to ensure 20 is well out of sight."

"20 permission, we are in a car park to the rear of the church, positioned between and behind several HGVs. He would need to jump over several walls to reach our location."

"20, yes, yes. 56A, did you pick that up?"

"56A yes, yes."

Once again, silence, as Warden wandered around in the dark. About five minutes later,

"Contact, contact, contact! Subject recip. Back onto main road. Same location as last sighting. Looking up towards OP and crossing the road, cigarette in hand, into alleyway and total loss."

"56A, yes, yes." Once again, he was out of sight of everyone, but at least they knew where he was and the direction he was moving in.

"56, 20, start moving and hold in churchyard."

"20, yes, yes."

The churchyard was a good holding position – dark, lots of shadows, plenty of obstacles and no chance of discovery. Kenny did not have a view of the subject for several seconds but then he saw him and whispered, "From 56A, contact, contact, contact, subject towards the canal from the alley. 20?"

"20, yes, yes."

Kenny could see him slowly walking down the alleyway.

"No deviation, towards the canal," Kenny whispered. Warden reached the end of the alley where it met the towpath on the canal and paused.

"Stop, stop, stop."

"20 permission."

"Yes, yes, make it quick, 20."

"In churchyard."

"Yes, yes, 20, no change, subject still held at the end of the alley." Kenny could see, as he had done before, Warden's cigarette; each time he brought it to his mouth it glowed more intensely. No-one else was in sight. All was quiet.

He brought the image intensifier to his eye and turned it on; he could clearly see Warden standing at the end of the alley, facing the canal. His cigarette was even brighter now, the intensity of the light magnified many times from normal so that it was like a bright piercing dot that tended to obscure everything around it. Eventually, Warden took one last suck and discarded it onto the ground.

Kenny continued to look at him through the intensifier and could see him looking around him and back up the alley.

"No change, no change," he whispered.

After what felt like fifteen minutes, but was probably closer to thirty seconds, Warden moved to his right, away from the alley.

"Subject, right, right, right, away from alley, moving slowly. 56, is the road clear?"

"56, yes, yes."

"20, move across the road and hold at the end of the alley, but away from and out of sight of the road."

"20, yes, yes."

Kenny could see Warden moving very slowly towards where he had previously hidden his stash.

"20, move into alley and keep to offside; single file, subject is on the towpath approximately twenty metres to the right of the end of the alley. He will not have a view of the alley."

"20, yes, yes."

Warden was standing at the edge of the towpath facing Kenny, at roughly the same place as his stash. Kenny was able to position him more accurately using the night sight: five chimneys in from the alley and directly in line with the church spire that he could see behind the houses where TT20 had been hiding. Still no movement.

"No change, no change. 20, move down the alley and hold on the offside, ten metres from the towpath, you'll find undergrowth to your offside."

He could see dark figures crouched near the end of the alley, solid black masses against the loose undergrowth.

"20, yes, yes."

"56 permission."

"56, yes, yes."

"Road end of alley clear."

"Yes, yes, 56." Franks was telling him that the alley was sealed from the roadside to prevent anyone entering.

Still no movement, until he saw Warden stoop down into a crouched position.

"Subject crouching by the bank edge. Standby, standby."

Once again, the plop of water and the grinding sound. He could see that Warden was prone, stretching forwards with a large item in both hands. Again, the grinding sound and another plop in the water, louder than last time.

As Warden stood up, Kenny transmitted, "Standby, standby, subject standing twenty metres to the right of the alley on the towpath facing away from alley." And then, "Strike, strike, strike!"

Within seconds, Kenny saw a number of large hulks silently move into view from the alley, dark and menacing, and engulf Warden, who was lost from sight.

Muffled screams, slight movement as if a lion was holding onto its prey, and then silence. Then various people standing up, quiet conversation.

"20, subject in custody."

"Yes, yes, 20 – well done. Take subject towards footbridge away from alley. Check for items beside towpath and for object in water, about the size of a small wastepaper bin."

"Yes, yes."

"No nominations until we've done the addresses."

It was important that he was kept incommunicado until the addresses had been entered.

"20, we have the container."

"Thank you. Take it with you, preserve for forensics, do not open, search the immediate area, use illumination if necessary."

"20, yes, yes."

It was time to go.

"56A, 56, I'll meet you at the car."

"Yes, yes."

When Warden and the arrest team had moved away, Kenny quietly picked up his things and placed them in his backpack, and finally wrapped up his poncho and put that on top. A quick scan over the area showed nothing left. He re-joined the towpath and headed for the footbridge. He glanced over to his right and could see the guys scanning the canal bank with a big beam.

"20, nothing further found."

"20, 56, see you at Cloud-Base Alpha."

Kenny crossed the footbridge. His limbs ached, particularly his knees and lower back, and he felt damp and unclean; his hands were wet, clammy and covered in small bits of vegetation. No amount of hand rubbing managed to rid him of the small bits of grass, moss and rotten leaves.

He reached the car before Franks and had a brief wait when he was able to mull over the evening's activities and look at the direction they were going to take that evening and in the next few days. It was like being the recipient of a beautiful Christmas present that you really coveted but were never quite sure you would get. There had always been a degree of uncertainty.

Franks, who was burdened with bags from the OP, joined him. He had vacated the house, cleared the room, handed the key back to Patience and thanked her for her help. He knew it would have been very awkward and probably dangerous to return later. They would arrange for some flowers and chocolates to be delivered at the end of the operation. Once the boot had been loaded in silence, they got in the car, Franks in the driving seat. He started the engine, turned the lights on, cleared the screen and then looked at Kenny.

Kenny turned when he knew Franks was looking at him and they both smiled at each other. "Job done," said Franks.

They both smiled broadly, shook hands and punched the air.

# 12

# THE PROOF OF THE PUDDING

They arrived at the nick a few minutes later and went straight to custody. Bright lights, shiny surfaces, clean floors, video cameras in each corner, smelling of Jeyes Fluid, but comfortably warm, a high stainless-steel coated desk, people milling around, drunks looking ill… and amongst it all, two middle-aged well-dressed men clutching wads of papers in manila folders – clearly lawyers or lawyers' runners.

Warden was just being booked in, having had to wait in a queue; it was a busy night.

The usual questions were asked and responses given. The custody officer – in this case the man responsible for the entire complex, including prisoners, cells, staff and paperwork – had asked the same questions to, very often, the same people many thousands of times; it was pretty much by rote.

When he was satisfied with the grounds for his arrest, he asked if Warden wanted anyone told that he was in custody. Warden asked for his partner of the same address to be informed, but this was withheld temporarily because of the need to search his house, when notification would be made in person, and, finally, he said that he wished to consult with a legal representative. After a thorough strip search, he was taken to the cells.

Kenny and Franks spoke to the arresting team and examined what they had recovered. Warden had four hundred and ten pounds on him and about three rocks of crack. The guys joined the hit team in an adjoining room. There, sitting on the table, in a scattering of water droplets, was a damp medium-sized glass container with a metal clip lid and red rubber seal. Pink binder twine was wrapped around the lip of the glass jar and a long length of cord was lying beside it on the table.

The lead sergeant, dressed in black and known to Kenny, said, "It was tied to a metal rod which had been rammed into the bank. Once you knew where it was, it was easy – just tug on the cord and yank it in. The jar, I think, must be watertight and weighed down by something inside – it looks like a small blue plastic disc with a hole in the middle. No-one has opened it."

They all peered into the container. The glass was relatively clear and they could see various polythene bags containing items wrapped in cling film and wraps of money, again in polythene bags. In fact, it was so tightly packed it was difficult to differentiate the various packages.

"OK, thanks. Place it in a sealed bag and plonk it in the safe; we'll get it to forensics in the morning."

Once this had been done, the two detectives then briefed the teams for simultaneous hits on Warden's house and Pritchard's. Kenny went to Warden's, Franks to Pritchard's.

Entry was made at exactly the same time. Rapid entry, splitting the front doors at both houses and causing uproar with the occupants and neighbours – screaming kids and irate wives. The searches would take a long time, starting with the loft space, insulation, cavity walls, cupboards, carpets, floorboards, bath cavities, kitchen unit spaces, toilet cisterns, drains, gardens, sheds – the list was pretty much endless.

The investigating team relied on the expertise of the search teams, their desire to check every space, every cavity, to ensure that everything that could be used as evidence was found and preserved.

The houses really were quite ordinary, smelling of curry, boiled cabbage and cigarette smoke, both a little weary, lacking care and attention but nevertheless occupied and therefore in need of a detailed and careful search. The team at Steve Pritchard's house finished first, a full five hours after entering, Warden's house took a little longer. They finally returned to the police station in the early hours of the morning, where Kenny and Franks were able to assess the results.

Search teams found no drugs at Warden's house, but about thirteen thousand, five hundred pounds in cash under the floorboards, which had been covered by a carpet in one of the kid's rooms, scales, a number of mobile phones, and various pieces of paper that appeared to contain calculations, drug prices and customer details. The team also seized rolls of cling film, poly bags and a number of phone bills. Interestingly, they also discovered a cavity on top of the kitchen door, empty, but quite clearly used to hide drugs. Very little was found at Pritchard's – a little bit of personal stuff, mobile phone bills, but he was arrested and taken to the nick.

By the time the searches were completed in the early hours of the morning, everyone was exhausted, jaded. Movement was slow and simple tasks appeared to take longer than normal.

Kenny and Franks finally finished at three thirty in the morning. Locking up the office they trudged to their cars, knowing that they needed to be back at ten o' clock to interview the two boys. It was dark when they left the underground car park, their headlights scanned the remaining vehicles and played shadows on the roof. It was the end of another day.

Later that morning, they re-emerged in the office; their eyes were sore from lack of sleep, their bodies ached, and it appeared everyone wanted to speak to them: custody, defence solicitors, family, murder team detectives, their bosses and forensics. They waded on, intent on interviewing both men before lunchtime. The murder team would interview both of them after the current investigation was completed. Custody wanted reassurance that they would be interviewed that morning and that the enquiry was being conducted expeditiously. The families wanted to know what was happening and to visit their loved ones; they were told the bare minimum and access was refused. Defence solicitors wanted to know what evidence the officers had and when they might want to interview them both; again they were told the bare minimum, but reassured they would be contacted before any conversation. Their bosses wanted to know what was happening and how much it had cost, of course.

Finally, forensics – they went down to see them. They had already fingerprinted the outside of the jar and removed the lid and contents. They found about ten ounces of what they thought was crack cocaine separated into ounce bags, each of which contained individual rocks wrapped in cling film; a small bag of what appeared to be LSD, small microdots, perhaps a couple of hundred; a quantity of what they thought was heroin – a bag of white powder that was not separated into smaller bags – but possibly amphetamine; some scales; a small phone book; and four bags of cash, not counted but notes of five pounds, ten pounds, twenty pounds – several thousand pounds. They were just in the process of swabbing the interior for fingerprints.

So, satisfied with the forensic assessment of the evidence that was seized, they arranged a preliminary interview with Tony

Warden, conducted in the presence of his legal representative, John Wyle, a small, thin man with a gaunt expression; he wore a rather scruffy grey suit that appeared two sizes too big. He had represented many local criminals and knew the two officers. He was actually a solicitor's runner, a person who represented a solicitor or solicitor's firm.

In a small, soulless, windowless room in the depths of the police station, where the benches and table were bolted to the floor, the walls had been repainted several times to obscure the years of graffiti, and the smell of cigarette and body odour lingered, Warden made no comment, as expected, other than to confirm his name. This, he said, was on the instructions of his solicitor. The interview lasted about twenty minutes but he did agree to his fingerprints being retaken. Steve Pritchard was interviewed later in the same room but with a different solicitor, a mean-faced man in a three-piece suit who was unknown to the officers. Once again, he said nothing other than to admit that the small amount of drugs found were for his personal use – clearly aimed at deflecting any difficulties for his partner, who lived in the same house.

After the second interview, they went to lunch in the canteen – the warm friendly place that they had come to appreciate, a real formica and lino environment run by a wonderfully jolly black lady who mollycoddled her customers rather like a mother hen – to discuss the situation and decide which direction they should go in. The responses of the two men during the interviews didn't surprise them; there would be further interrogation and more opportunity to firm up what evidence was available.

During lunch they received a call from forensics, who asked them to visit them on the first floor. Eager to find out the result of their examination, they went straight down there and met a man in all-in-one overalls, Andy Partiger.

"Hello, guys, come on in." He beckoned them into the large office.

"OK, what you have in the glass container is…" He picked up a piece of paper with a list which he then read to them.

"One bag containing three hundred grams of what is thought to be crack cocaine, separated into several hundred, maybe a thousand, separate cling film-wrapped rocks. We haven't opened the main bag. About ten and a half ounces all in all, a further bag of crack cocaine, weighing one hundred grams, about four ounces, not separated; a further bag of crack cocaine weighing sixty grams, about two ounces, again not separately packaged; five hundred-odd LSD microdots – the exact number is…" He looked at the list. "Five hundred and thirty-two, the same kind of stuff that came out of Julie, in a polybag; about two ounces of heroin – loose; five hundred and twenty-two Es loose in a bag; and finally, five bags each containing exactly one thousand pounds in fives, tens and twenties. Oh, and some pieces of paper with phone numbers and some calculations, initials, that kind of thing. We've taken photos." He handed them a file of photographs.

"We have Warden's prints on file and have found his marks on the jar, the lid, the inside of the glass, and covering the pieces of paper. Of course, that needs confirming by statement, but I can tell you they belong to him."

"Any unidents?" asked Frank.

"A couple – I'll let you know. Oh, and one other thing, traces of crack on the scales at Warden's house."

"Great. Anything on Pritchard?" Kenny added.

"Not yet. I've submitted samples of what we think is crack cocaine, heroin and LSD to the lab to confirm our thoughts. I've fast-tracked it, so you should have a result by this evening." Buoyed, they returned to the office. Things were looking up – they could link Warden to the drugs, the canal, crack on the scales at his home – lots of drugs, lots of money, lots of evidence.

They arranged for Warden's solicitor to return at three o'clock and Pritchard's at four thirty p.m., which would give them enough time for further interviews that evening and allowed them to wander in to see Liz. Her small office was accessible from within the intelligence cell; she needed peace and quiet and much of her work tended to be confidential.

They knocked on the door, like a couple of wicked schoolchildren going to visit the headmistress. She leant forward to peer through the glass partition and beckoned them in. They both clattered in and sat beside her table, which was covered in charts and diagrams.

"We've nicked Warden and Pritchard and wondered how you are getting on with the telephone billing," said Kenny.

"I saw you'd arrested them. You've got some good evidence as well, I hear."

"Yep, not bad, but it all came on top with the bloody murder, we had to act a bit quicker that we would have liked. Anyway…"

"OK, your numbers. I've looked at a number of areas: firstly, Warden's phone. I've managed to go back a couple of months and the sequence of events on every Thursday, bar one, is the same. Warden phones a random mobile number in the morning, always different, and then in the afternoon and particularly in the evening he receives a series of incoming calls."

"And the one Thursday when there was no contact?" enquired Franks.

"Could be any reason – bloke's on holiday, car broken down, lost mobile – who knows?" broached Kenny.

"OK, I've also checked the six other numbers that Warden contacted on the other Thursdays."

"And?"

"The process is the same on each occasion. About an hour or an hour and a half after each number was contacted by Warden in the morning, a call was made from the same number that Warden contacted earlier, to a TK in the Ealing area. There are other calls to other TKs at different times of the day on different days of the week, but the routine on Thursday appears the same and there were no other calls between the times that these calls were made and received. On the day you followed him it's the same, although on this occasion you know that Warden was in the actual TK when the call came in from the number he had called earlier in the day."

"Interesting," said Franks, trying to keep pace.

"All six of these numbers reveal the same pattern on Thursdays and each of these phone numbers has a lifespan of between five and eight days. No activity whatsoever either side, which indicates that it's turned on, used, and then discarded within a set period, making any investigation and tracking very difficult."

"That's great, Liz, thanks."

"One other thing," she said. "Many of the calls from these six mobiles, the telephones we think are attributable to Purves, are to telephone kiosks. There are some unattributable incoming calls, but few others outgoing. There is an interesting twist that I can't quite work out at the moment. During the six-week period I've looked at, there are three calls made to the same TK in Poundscombe in North Cornwall. I've checked, there are two TKs in the village – this one appears to be up a back lane behind the village, the other one is on the quayside. The calls that are made are all at the same time, midday, give or take a minute or so, and only one of them was answered."

Kenny squinted his eyes and raised his head, as if thinking about the significance of that information.

"And the call that was answered, what duration?"

Liz looked at her chart. "Four minutes, thirty-eight seconds – 11:59 hours on a Monday, three weeks ago. But all those calls were on different days of the week." She again looked at her chart. "A Monday, a Wednesday and a Saturday." Liz sighed. "That's about it really."

"You've been magnificent."

Again, she coloured slightly as they left the room.

Kenny turned back and re-entered the room. "Just a quickie, can you obtain the call data on that Poundscombe TK?"

"Oh, that's easy. Incoming and outgoing?"

"Yep."

"What time span?"

"Make it three months. That OK?"

"Yep."

They made the way back to their office to consider their position. It was now getting on and they had arranged for the solicitors to return later that afternoon; they had until that evening to continue to talk to Warden. They could get an extension but that would only really take them to breakfast time the following morning – not much use really as he'd have to appear at court that morning anyway.

They discussed the current situation. They could tie in Warden to a large quantity of different types of gear, a sizeable amount of money, and, by observation, significant movement to and from his house prior his arrest, and now forensics. He had scales at his home that had traces of crack and another quite sizeable amount of money. They had yet to examine the workings out on the various pieces of paper, but that would keep until later.

Pritchard was different. He had some personal (drugs for his own use) at his home and they could tie him in with Warden on the one run to London, but no large stashes of either drugs or money. He would have to be left until later and would depend on what, if anything, he said during interview. They would concentrate on Warden, but that was always going to have been the case anyway.

And what of Richard Purves? He was an interesting prospect. He appeared to keep a low profile, was connected with Warden by surveillance and telephone logs, had previous convictions for dealing, had been locked up and had probably learnt more during that period than he would have done if he'd remained at large. Purves and Warden met in prison whilst doing time together and he appears to have established a set routine for any contact between them to form a sterile corridor. There was no intelligence flagged to him nationally, but he was quite surveillance-conscious, highlighted during his meeting with Warden and when he was subsequently followed home. But this gave rise to two issues; firstly, his actions simply highlighted the level of his criminal activity and his desire to protect himself and his business, and secondly, this degree of protection was almost an obsession that gave him a feeling of security, impregnability, which in itself may lead to complacency. They agreed that they needed to know a little bit more about him. But Warden came first. They needed to gather all the evidence together and isolate him, and if that was achieved, to deal with Purves before Thursday next week, when Warden would probably have visited to collect his next consignment.

They began preparing for the second interview with Warden that had been arranged earlier and then went down to the cell block where they met his brief. He requested a private interview with his client first, although they had no grounds to refuse anyway. It meant that they were kicking around in the custody suite waiting for him to finish for some time.

After about fifteen minutes, he re-emerged with Warden

and the two officers led them inside the same windowless interview room. The tape recorder was switched on and both began putting questions to Warden about his criminal activities. To each he made the same reply – 'No comment'. But his demeanour had changed since the last interview – he was less confident, less dismissive and the replies, for what they were, were less assured, and they noticed occasional sideways glances to his legal representative, who steadfastly took notes, earning his pay, for the one-sided exchange.

They began opening up the range of evidence against him, like a market stall holder laying out vegetables in the early morning. They referred to the observations at the canal for the first time and where he was eventually captured, the scales with crack cocaine at his home and the money hidden under the floorboards. The contents of the glass jar – drugs calculations, money and the drugs – found on his person. But no reference was made to the surveillance in London, nor the protracted observations at his home address – these, they had decided, would be kept in abeyance.

After about an hour, he stopped 'no commenting'. He was slumped in his chair and clearly felt under some pressure.

There was a knock on the door and one of the custody team poked his head in, announced himself and handed Kenny a piece of paper. He read it and handed it to Franks; they made no comment and, notwithstanding careful scrutiny to look for any indications as to its content from the suspect and his lawyer, there was no reaction from either man. They looked at each other.

"The time is now 4:15, Tony. I have to tell you that your fingerprints have been found on the lid of the jar where you were arrested, the inside of the jar, on each of the various pieces of paper found inside the jar, and on small pieces of paper contained within each of the bags of money." He paused.

Warden was about to reply when Kenny continued, "On the scales at your home address and on the bag that contained the money at the same address. Enquiries are still continuing. Have you any comment to make?"

Warden turned away from his brief, dropped his head slightly, closed his eyes and mouthed the word 'fuck', but inaudible to the tape recorder.

Kenny said, "Can you repeat what you have just said so that it's audible on the tape?" There was no response.

"I think the word you mouthed was 'fuck', can you confirm that?"

Again, there was no response. The solicitor and Warden turned to look at each other and Warden, once again, was about to reply when the lawyer cut him short.

"I think it's time to take instructions from my client," he said, and the two detectives left the room and returned to the main reception area.

"Good news?" proffered the officer who had brought the message into the interview.

"Fucking right!" said Kenny as he looked at Franks.

They both knew that it left Warden two options: the first one, to remain silent and take it on the chin, to accept the evidence and to eventually throw himself at the mercy of the court – but he would be presented as a very active yet un-cooperative main dealer caught with a substantial amount of drugs of different types and a large amount of money, in circumstances that would probably lead any court to deduce, very reasonably, that he had been at it for some time. Alternatively, he could cooperate and tell the guys all about his involvement, thereby reducing his culpability by being able to shift some responsibility onto others – downwards, sideways, and hopefully, upwards – and reduce his sentence with a guilty plea.

The guys made some tea and passed the time of day with the

custody team. Kenny and Franks knew them all and had a huge amount of respect for them and their role. The conversation was abruptly halted when the brief poked his head around the door. "Could we talk?"

"Of course," said Franks.

They walked together to the corridor leading to the interview room. Wyle continued, "My client realises he's in a tight spot and is going to serve a lengthy prison sentence and wants to cooperate with the investigation."

Neither officer made any response.

"The only thing he asks is that his wife and family are kept out of it. If this can be assured then he will, indeed, tell you what he knows."

Franks said, "We have no evidence against his wife and family, although, without a doubt, they knew what he was doing and benefitted from the financial gain. We cannot promise anything but that is the current position; if that situation changes then so will our approach."

"Thank you for being candid; just give me a few more minutes with Mr Warden." He re-entered the room.

The two officers turned to each other, grinning widely, and shook hands. They now knew, for the first time, that they would be able to progress the investigations past Warden and Pritchard towards Purves. Warden did not know that they knew about Purves, or that he had been under surveillance, which had covered the meeting in London. His answers would need to verify what they already knew, and as for his wife – she would be the pressure point needed to elicit the truth.

After several minutes, the interview room opened slightly and the wizened form of Mr Wyle appeared in the gap and beckoned the officers forward into the room with his hand. They entered. Warden was sitting in the same place and everyone took their original positions. His elbows were on his thighs and he was staring at the floor as the tape machine was turned on once again and Kenny did the introduction.

It was agreed that Kenny would lead the interview and Franks would observe, take notes and interject if necessary.

"Tony, I understand that you've had a chat to your solicitor and now want to tell us everything. Is that correct?"

Still looking at the floor, with his head bowed forward, Warden grunted a response.

"Sorry, Tony, we need you to give us clear answers in order that the tape can pick them up – OK?" He repeated the question.

Warden sat up, faced the two detectives and said in a loud, clear voice, "Yes," and then continued, "but I want my missus and family left out of it."

"As I explained to your solicitor, at the present time we have no direct evidence to link your wife and family to your criminal activities – OK?"

Mr Wyle nodded, judiciously. "OK."

"So, are you going to tell us what you've been up to?"

"You know already."

"We need you to make a full explanation on tape, OK?"

"I'm not going to drop anyone in the shit, I'm not a grass. Steve drove me around, he's just a numpty."

"Just the truth, that's all we want."

"Fuck, I wish I hadn't started."

"Started what?"

"Serving gear."

"When did it all start?"

"I'm no Mr Big, I just help out a few friends, you know."

Both officers had heard this approach many times, and had expected it. They called it minimising culpability or, alternatively, playing down one's own involvement.

"We just want you to tell the truth."

"What am I going to get?"

"It's impossible to say, but you're almost certainly going to get locked up. You know this already but it is for the court to decide, we just put the evidence to the court."

Mr Wyle added, "It's right what the officer says, and will depend on a number of factors that the court will need to weigh up to determine your sentence." Warden was trying to lay out the various options in his mind before deciding what route to take.

"OK," he said. He lay his hands face down, flat on the table and leant backwards. "OK, OK." It was as if he was trying to convince himself that he was doing the right thing.

"I need to keep the family out of this. I know I'm in the shit. What do you want to know? I'm not mentioning names!"

"OK, let's start from the beginning, shall we?" He nodded. "We want you to tell the truth, that's all, but it's probably better to tell us everything from the outset rather than dripfeeding us with information that we have to drag from you over a period of time." Warden dropped his head and nodded. There was silence in the room. No-one spoke. He was probably trying to work out what the detectives knew and how not to tell them about things that they didn't know anything about.

After about half a minute, Warden spoke. "OK, let's crack on.

"When did it all start?'"

"About a year ago. It's just got bigger and bigger and spun out of control really. It is difficult to control, once you're known and you're not ripping people off – good gear, good prices, reliable supply, people just get to know you and introduce others, it just spirals."

"What are you serving?"

"Anything and everything, white and brown, some acid,

Billy Whizz, some dope, but there's no money in that. Mainly smack and crack."

"How much?"

"Varies. I don't know exactly, it depends – I keep a certain amount in the pot all the time and keep it topped up. But demand has increased."

"Who to?"

"I told you, no names."

"I don't want names; I'd like to know how you find your punters, what level they are – amounts – that kind of thing."

"I don't serve to anyone I don't know, it's too risky, too many rip-off merchants and geezers like you around, know what I mean?"

He looked at Kenny and smiled; Kenny smiled back. They both knew what each other was thinking. Warden had been trying to protect himself from direct sales to undercover police officers and in so doing, only dealt with known people. Kenny, on the other hand, knew this, and had never considered inserting a UC into the mix but he also knew that, by him tacitly deciding on this course of action, he had moved away from street level dealer to distributor to other dealers, or maybe beyond.

"So, all your punters are known to you?"

"Yes."

"What if someone comes to your door that you don't know?"

"I blank them, tell them I don't know what they're going on about and close the door, don't want to know."

"And if someone you know comes to the door with someone you don't know?"

"Same thing. Blank 'em. Word soon gets around. To be fair I don't get many people knocking on the door that I don't know now."

"What if one of your punters gets nicked?"

"Keep my head down for a bit, be a little sharper, you know, reduce the risks. You never know what they've said – if they grass you up, you wouldn't know until you fuckers start knocking at the door at five o'clock in the fucking morning." He paused, then continued. "It would depend on who was nicked; if it was a geezer who you knew was a bit willocky, you'd be ultra-careful. On the other hand, if it was a solid bloke whom you'd known for a long time, you could afford to be a bit more relaxed."

"How did a normal transaction happen?"

"How do you mean?"

"Well… imagine I'm a punter and I'm known to you, how would that transaction pan out?"

He thought for a while.

"You'd phone me, tell me what you wanted, we'd agree the price and then you'd come around, at a certain time… usually you'd phone about five or ten minutes before knocking on my door. You'd come in, I'd have it ready, you'd give me the dosh and I'd count it and if it was right, I'd give you the gear and you'd leave."

"Where in the house would this usually take place?"

"Depends on who's about, usually the front room or passageway."

"Would anyone want to look at the gear that you gave them?"

"No, not usually, the punters know me and I know them – it's trust really. As soon as I've given them the gear, they just want to fuck off and make some money and to be honest, I want them to fuck off as well. I don't want them hanging around the house."

"And the missus?"

"What about her?"

"Well, presumably she was around whilst this was going on?"

"Yeah, but I made sure I did the business in an empty room, you know what I mean, she didn't need to know anything really. I just gave her some money for food and things. She's never got involved with anything, you have to believe that."

"OK. Fancy a cup of tea or coffee?"

Warden and his solicitor agreed to a coffee break and the tape was turned off.

Coffee was provided to both and Warden was taken for a smoke break and to the toilet. They were allowed a further short period of consultation before the interview continued.

"To recap, Tony, you've been dealing crack, heroin, amphetamines, acid and some dope for about a year from your home to people you know, who are dealers in their own rights, some of them street dealers. Is that about right?"

Warden thought for a while, then said, "Yeah."

"Your wife knew nothing about what was going on?"

"Yes."

"And business has steadily increased over the last few months."

"Yes."

"How much do you think you've made?"

Warden shrugged his shoulders. "I honestly haven't a fucking clue. I made sure I sold for more than I bought, of course, and that varied, but I never kept track, it was pretty random."

"Well, you had just under twenty thousand pounds in your stash at home."

"Yeah, that doesn't look good, does it? I don't know, I really don't know. I paid my supplier, I bunged Shanks a couple of quid for petrol and stuff, but I've got jack shit in the bank. I dip into the cash if I need something or if the missus needs a bung."

"How long have you been using the stash?"

"Christ." He ploughed his hand through his hair, leant back and looked at the ceiling. "Perhaps a year or so. I thought it was safer, keeping the bulk of the gear out of the house when I didn't need it."

"And the money?"

"And the money."

"And the lists?"

"That too. Fucking hell, this looks bad."

"OK, I think we'll take a break for a bit." Warden asked to see his wife, which was refused, and he was allowed time with his solicitor, who agreed to return later that evening. The two officers returned to their office, buoyed by the progress they had made. Much needed to be done but food beckoned and they once again sought refuge in the canteen.

They discussed the next interview as they chomped through their sausages, beans and mash. They agreed they needed to go through exhibits, all the items seized from the house, and the stash, and then delve more deeply into the source of his drugs and what he had spent his money on.

Once they had finished their supper they returned to the office. Once there, they sorted out the tapes for interview, exhibits and the statements from various officers involved in the arrests and searches, and then returned to the custody suite, clutching the various exhibits, and awaited the arrival of Mr Wyle to continue the interview.

They had time to sit and observe the activity. The custody suite was bustling with prisoners, arresting officers, gaolers, solicitors and their runners, all of whom worked under the close and beady eye of the custody officers. It was the constant movement of people in different directions from that one room that always amazed; prisoners to interview rooms, solicitors awaiting audience, officers booking in arrested people, phone calls from all and sundry, and finally, the formal laying of charges against some wretched individual amongst the cacophony of sound and movement.

After about ten minutes, Wyle appeared, a little more dishevelled than he had been earlier... a liquid lunch maybe? He craved an audience with his client, a short preparation before a further interrogation, and this was arranged.

Once again, he poked his head out of the room and waved the officers in to join him. Everyone took their original positions and the tape machine was started.

Franks and Kenny went through each exhibit in turn, describing them and referring to the relevant number, asking the same questions on each occasion: "Does this belong to you?", to which Warden replied on each occasion, "Yes." He was then invited to sign each label, which he did.

The interview was then interrupted whilst Franks removed the bundles and bags and returned them to the forensic team, re-joining the interview a short time later.

"OK, so we don't want you to tell us about the people you are dealing with but we are interested in where the drugs originate," Kenny said.

"Go on."

"Do all the drugs come from the same place?"

"I told you, I'm not mentioning names, I'm not a grass and if I did name names, my family would be at risk and I'd be fucked on remand."

"I'm not asking for names but I am going to ask you questions about the source of the drugs. Do they all come from the same place?"

Warden thought for a while and stared at the officer. "Yes."

"Local or London?"

"London."

"Do you always score from the same person?"

"No comment."

"Is this a regular process? I mean, do you go up regularly?"

"Yes, when I need to top up."

"Any particular day of the week?"

"Usually Thursdays but occasionally other days, if I'm really short, but the bloke doesn't like it. He's a bit cagey, like, always takes precautions and likes to keep everything nice and simple."

"Do you pay up front?"

"Yes, always. I know his prices, and he likes a straightforward business transaction. There was one occasion early on when he laid the gear on me, but he didn't like it and I never did it again. Need to keep him sweet."

"Does he deal with anyone else?"

"Don't know."

"Where did you meet him?"

"No comment."

"Is he sharp, you know, about himself, keyed in?"

"Every time. He's a cute cookie, but I wouldn't cross him."

"Why?"

"I just wouldn't. Nothing particular but he's just got an aura about him, you know, slightly threatening, I'd never get close to him. If he thought you were having him over he would shiv you, and not think anything about it."

"You're scared of him?"

"Not scared, respectful."

"Does he carry?"

"What, guns?"

"Yes, or knives."

"Don't know but I wouldn't be surprised."

"Can you describe him?"

"No comment."

"Well, how old is he?"

"About forty. I'm not telling you anything about him, I

told you. I don't want to be found in a Biffa bin with no head – OK?!"

"Do you score from anyone else, Tony?"

"No, not for years. We trust each other but I can't tell you anything about him, you must understand that. I'll just have to take it on the chin, Mr Big."

"Does Steve know him?"

"No."

"Does he have any contact with him?"

"No, I told you, Shanks is just a numpty, he's off his head most of the time. He gives me a lift and I bung him a fifty. He's never met the bloke, doesn't know him." A natural pause. Franks looked at Kenny. "A couple of minutes, I think."

Kenny turned to Wyle. "We just need a couple of minutes and you probably need a breather as well, and we'll be back. Is that alright?"

Wyle nodded and they turned off the tape machine and left the room. Once outside they walked down the corridor out or earshot of the room. In a hushed conversation they agreed that it was unlikely that they were going to obtain any further information from Warden about Purves on tape, but they would present him with a photograph of Purves taken during the surveillance, note his reaction and then see if they could progress the investigation by interviewing him off tape to gather as much information as possible without it entering the evidential chain.

Franks returned to the office, leaving Kenny to kick his heels outside the interview room. A few minutes later he returned and produced from his pocket a good full-length photograph of Purves taken on the day that he and Warden had met at the Haven Arms.

Franks knocked on the door of the room and both officers re-entered the room, sat down and turned on the tape machine.

Kenny continued, "Sorry we've been some time. We're nearly finished." He paused for several seconds and then pulled from beneath his jumper, like a magician with a struggling rabbit, a colour photograph that he immediately thrust in front of Warden.

"I am showing the suspect, Photograph Exhibit MS 14 (6). Is this the man who has been selling you the gear?"

Warden, who had been slumped in his seat, sat upright and leaned forward to take a closer look, then looked at Kenny and back to the photograph, whilst Mr Wyle bent his head forward and peered at the photograph over his glasses. After some seconds, Warden slouched back, put his head back, closed his eyes and breathed out. Silence. No-one spoke.

"Do you want some time with Mr Wyle?"

Warden nodded.

"I think that would be a good idea," added Mr Wyle. The officers left the room.

Ten minutes later, once again Mr Wyle poked his head through the crack of the door and beckoned them to enter.

Wyle started, "My client would like to know what his options are?"

"Well, two really. We can carry on with this interview on tape and place everything on the table – but I would anticipate that your client wouldn't say anything. Alternatively, we can continue off tape, discussing the various issues, without any of the content of that conversation entering the public domain – and I would think the second option suits your client and it would suit us."

"Have you anything further to put to my client formally in interview?"

The officers looked at each other and Kenny said, "No, I don't think so."

"Well in that case, give me a couple more minutes alone with my client."

The officers once again left the room and then returned a few minutes later. Wyle said, "My client is happy to talk to you – off the record. I won't stay but I have given him strict instructions not to speak on tape and if he wishes to speak to me for advice, he should formally make the request through you or to the custody officer. I would appreciate a phone call later." And he handed both officers his business card.

Kenny took Mr Wyle back to the custody suite and arranged for the prisoner's record to be adjusted to show him out of formal interview and without his solicitor.

Kenny returned to the room where Franks had already made tea for them all.

He looked up at Kenny. "Been watching me, then." Franks nodded. "You knew about Patch then?" he added.

They both nodded.

"Fucking hell, this is getting heavy." He sipped his tea.

Franks said, "Put it this way, Tony, we're going to hit 'Patch' anyway, whether you tell us about him or not. What we'd like is a little clarification on a few points – off the record – which means he won't know, in fact no-one will know, that you have told us things about him. He will know, eventually, that we followed you, which allowed us to identify him. It would help us, and perhaps help you."

"How so?"

"Because we can let the judge know that you cooperated with the investigation." Silence.

"So, how do you feel about it?" said Kenny.

"I'm fucked. Totally fucked. You've done your job well. Where the fuck do I go from here? I have to try to reduce my time!"

Silence.

"You guarantee that this conversation doesn't go to court?"

"Yes," they both said in unison.

"Well, you've got the right man; he really is a sharp cookie, be very careful, he has a shooter."

"Have you seen it?"

"Yep, once, he had it in his jacket. I've heard that he's not afraid to use it – when needed."

"Where did you meet him?"

"In prison. He was doing time for supply and we were banged up together."

"What's he like?"

"Has legit interests, a big player, very, very careful but looks straight if you're with me. Keeps stuff close to his chest. I haven't been to his house but I imagine he doesn't live far from that pub you mentioned."

"Do you know anything about his system?"

"No, he's always got what I want, so I would think he's pretty well sorted. I told you, a cute cookie. In prison he kept himself to himself – didn't mix – it was only cos I was with him day in, day out, that we kind of got on really."

"Do you know anyone else that does business with him?"

"No, he keeps everything really segregated, nicely boxed off. If he got wind of me being lifted, he would close down for a while and be really all about himself."

"Does anyone else know him down here?"

"Don't think so, not that I've heard."

"Married? Single?"

"Don't know."

"Kids?"

"Don't know. I'll tell you something, he's not the cheapest around but he's reliable and there's no snide stuff. It's all good."

"How much did you get off him last time?"

"Half a pound of crack."

"How much was that?"

"Ten and a half grand."

"Fucking hell, Tony."

"I know, I know. In some ways I'm pleased you nicked me; it was getting a bit out of hand."

"Have you met him at any other place, other than the pub?"

"Yes, occasionally, he changes it all the time. We have used that pub before."

"Other locations?"

"Cemeteries, park benches. Once he met me on a bloody double-decker bus, back seat, told me which one to get on and which seat to use and he met me there, did the business, then he got off and told me to wait for two or three stops – bloody inconvenient, I didn't know where the fuck I was."

"If you didn't phone to meet this Thursday, as normal, would he be all willocky, you know, paranoid about you being out of circulation?"

"Yes, he's said before that if he didn't hear from me, he would just assume I've been lifted or taken out."

"Have you ever not met him on a Thursday?"

"Occasionally. But I always phone him to tell him I'll not be up and he's happy with that and vice versa. I think twice or maybe three times he's told me that he won't be around the next week, you know. I suppose holiday or something, I don't know. Can I see my missus?"

"We'll arrange it tomorrow morning. OK, we've got quite a lot to sort out, including Shanks."

"He's nothing to do with it, let him go."

The officers looked at each other, nodded and agreed to call it a day, but reminded him he would be interviewed by the murder team later that evening and that he needed to tell them what he knew.

Warden was returned to the cells and the officers trudged up to their office, exhausted yet jubilant that they had, in the main, achieved their objectives.

Still, phone calls needed to be made to solicitors, the custody suite, and families, and they still had to interview Shanks – Steven Pritchard.

After the calls, Kenny and Franks interviewed Shanks again with his solicitor. He made no comment and it was agreed that he would be charged with simple possession of the drugs he had at his home, and released.

Warden was later charged with possession of cocaine with intent to supply, which needed to be done before the time limit of thirty-six hours expired the following morning. The not-too-difficult decision was taken to refuse bail because of ongoing enquiries.

After a pretty long and arduous day, Franks and Kenny went for a curry and a few beers at a local curry shop before finding their way home. They would return the next morning to prepare the paperwork for Warden's first appearance at court on Monday morning.

## 13

# HOW THE MIGHTY ARE SMITTEN

Sunday came and went without being noticed, hardly acknowledged, a day to recuperate, meditate, gather thoughts and plan for the future. It had been agreed that only Tom Franks would go into work to complete the necessary tasks in order to placate the various interests, individuals, organisations and, of course, legal requirements of having someone incarcerated in police cells.

Forcing himself to rise, he plodded through to the shower and prepared tea and toast in the short space of thirty minutes, before driving himself to the office. He really didn't want to be there but knew that if he didn't present himself and look active he would only receive annoying calls, enquiring texts and concerned contact from people demanding his presence and wanting decisions.

Once in the office he made himself some coffee and sat down at his desk. Much needed to be done if they were to drive the enquiry through the next week. He gathered the case file together and wandered down to the cell block, mug of coffee in hand. The first thing to do was to process Warden – ensure all the documents were completed and placate the custody staff that someone was doing something with the prisoner. Warden was presented to him, dishevelled, hunched and apparently unused to the bright lights in the main suite. He squinted his eyes and then rubbed his face with both hands and groaned. His opening gambit indicated that he'd apparently had a roughish night.

"What do you fucking want?"

Bringing smiles from the various custody staff who witnessed the occasion, Franks arranged a shower and a change of clothes to be brought in by his wife, then it was fingerprints, photographs, swabs and antecedents and noting all his tattoos – he had many.

Warden knew the score; he'd been through it several times before and was relaxed and confident. Conversation was limited and functional.

After a visit from his concerned wife and a change of clothing, he was returned to the cells and Franks returned to his office.

Much writing ensued – fingerprint forms, lab forms, logs, search forms, remand file and previous convictions, of which there were many. He didn't finish until well after lunch and only went home when everything was completed. Nothing was worse that rushing around on the morning of a remand hearing trying to complete the myriad of tasks before court at ten thirty. He left everything neat, tidy and comprehensible. With a last visit to custody, Franks completed his day and wandered home. He slept.

The following morning, the officers met in the office. It was spent clucking around Warden, his family, his solicitor, the court and the CPS. All went rather swimmingly – a mid-morning five-minute appearance without an application for bail and a remand in custody until the following week. That afternoon they sat in their office over tea and wads to gather their thoughts and plan the next week.

It was agreed that whatever they were going to do about Purves, it needed to be done by Wednesday, because if he hadn't received a call from Warden telling him that he would or would not be coming on Thursday, he would presumably assume that something was wrong and close up shop; this was, of course, on the assumption that he hadn't already heard through the grapevine that Warden had been arrested, but he had been pretty certain that he wasn't working with anyone else in the area.

So, time was tight. They regurgitated the information they already had about Purves:

He had pre-cons for possession with intent to supply and had been locked up with Warden. They had covered and could therefore evidence the London meeting between Warden and Purves in which a transaction took place.

Regular phone contact between Warden and Purves over several months.

Informant identified 'Patch' as Warden's supplier Purves.

ID, through bin examination, confirmed his name as Richard Purves, 23.03.74, aka 'Patch', and that he was living at 60, Western Gardens, Ealing, the address he had been followed to, confirmed by voters' register and the local collators. He drove a silver BMW, was the keeper of the vehicle, which was registered to another address in Ealing, and the vehicle was in his driveway.

He changed his mobile phone weekly and he was antisurveillance, may have access to a weapon – handgun, unknown type. In regular contact with Warden's mobile using different phones and then a call into a random telephone box.

Mug shot from several years ago confirmed Subject 3 was

Purves and subsequent surveillance shots of Subject 3 were identical with the mug shot. Later Warden tacitly confirmed his identity when shown surveillance photograph.

And the question was – where to go from here?

They both accepted that Purves needed to be taken out of circulation by Thursday, but the complication was his apparent access to a firearm, which would make any arrest or house entry complicated, and it was a tight schedule. It only gave them two days, Tuesday or Wednesday. The hit would probably be on Wednesday to give them some leeway to complete the task.

Franks telephoned his boss to appraise him of the situation and the likely direction the enquiry would take; he agreed and approved.

Next, he arranged a meeting at Ealing the following morning with the area commander, the local intelligence team and tactical firearms adviser, because they knew any action would need to be led by them, approved by them and – initially anyway – use their resources. Finally, they needed an update from Liz, the analyst, and both sauntered through to her office.

She was on her computer and glanced over as they came in; she raised one delicate finger to show that she needed a couple of minutes. The pair sat down politely.

When she had finished, she rustled some papers and turned towards them.

"I know you've charged Warden now, so congratulations are in order. Nothing much more on Warden's or Purves' phones. I've done some printouts on the six phones that we think Purves has been using and you'll see they appear to run consecutively one after the other and as soon as a new phone is up and running, a call is made to Warden's phone, amongst others – it only lasts for a few seconds, hardly time for a chat, so maybe there wasn't one. That's his current number. There's no particular pattern to the use of the phones; some are kept for two or three days, others for up to ten days. Now, the Poundscombe telephone box. It's located here." She pointed to a satellite image of the village. "Quite remote really, up a lane just outside the village away from the sea, no buildings close by, apart from what appears to be a small building, possibly a barn, on the opposite side of the road. I've dug out all the call records for this particular TK for a three-month period. Very few outgoing calls, in fact, only four for the whole period; the phone box is really not used very much, the numbers appear to be unconnected, completely different – different times and days. But what is interesting is that quite a number of incoming calls were logged. They were all within a minute or two of twelve midday on different days of the week, but I don't have details of the incoming numbers." The two officers looked at each other, a little forlorn.

"However," she said, smiling, "by looking at the call logs of three of the mobiles that we think Purves has been using, we can see that three of those incoming calls logged at the TK were made from Purves' mobile because the times and dates tie in exactly. Always at midday. And only one of these calls was answered."

"Bloody hell," said Franks. "So, to recap, we can say that, on at least three occasions, Purves has called that remote TK in Poundscombe, Cornwall, from one of his mobiles at about midday on odd days of the week, on the off-chance that someone will answer – and on one occasion, during the period we've looked at, it was answered, and…" Franks looked at the call record, "…it led to a four-minute conversation."

"Clearly someone he knew," said Kenny.

"That's about it. I think we can reasonably assume that all the incoming calls made in that three-month period to that one telephone box were made by Purves," Liz added.

"And the last call you have from Purves to that TK?" Franks

asked. Liz looked at the two logs, running her finger down the list of numbers.

"Last week," she replied. "Not answered."

"So, who is that and what connection has she or he with Richard Purves?" said Kenny.

"This isn't urgent, but might help. Could you go back six months on Warden's phone and obtain details of Purves' different phones?" Franks asked.

"I can't because I only have his latest phone and that only enables me to link the six phones we think to have been used by Purves during that period. What I can do is go back twelve months on the Poundscombe TK and see what that brings up?"

"Magnificent!" said Kenny.

"Yep, thanks a lot, tremendous help. If you could put it all in a chart to make it easier to explain to people?" Franks asked.

"I'm doing that as I go along actually, you'll get a copy this afternoon. Telephone boxes are easy so you'll have that at the same time."

"Thanks," they both replied in unison as they moved to the door.

Returning to their office, Kenny started preparing a briefing pack for the meeting the next morning whilst Franks obtained a search warrant for the address in London. These packs contained only information relating to Warden and Purves and the connection between them. No reference was made to ongoing enquiries, particularly in Poundscombe. It was important to look professional and well informed to outside agencies – and he produced sufficient copies for any likely members of the meeting. They were numbered and annotated to ensure that no copies or pages went astray.

"Hold on a minute!" said Franks. They both stopped what they were doing. "We know that Purves, or to be completely accurate, his mobile, called the TK in Poundscombe on a number of occasions, but that only one of those calls was answered and that there was a short conversation. When we searched his bins, if you remember, we found a receipt for a transaction at Exeter Services. Do you think the time and date of the call and the transaction could coincide?"

"Fucking hell mate. Let's check. Can you dig it out?"

Franks went to their store cupboard and delving into the remnants of rubbish bag that they had retrieved from Purves Bin, recovered the receipt. Clutching the piece of paper they returned to Liz and checked it against the phone records she had compiled. The dates were the same and the time on the receipt, later that afternoon, meant that he had made the call, established contact and then left London almost immediately.

"So", said Kenny, "on that day, Purves has called the TK, spoken to someone at the other end, then travelled down to the West Country and, looking at the value of the transaction, paid for fuel at Exeter Services on the M5. We don't know that he visited Poundscombe but it's surely too much of a coincidence?"

They had an early evening, buoyed with the way the investigation was progressing and the real potential for further development.

The following morning they met in the office, collected the briefing files and the extra work that Liz had prepared on the Cornish telephone box, and bimbled up to London through the rush-hour traffic, arriving there with half an hour to spare. They dumped the car in a side street and walked to Ealing nick, presented themselves at the front counter and were then escorted to a big wooden-panelled second floor meeting room, impersonal and a tad chilly, in the centre of which was a large wooden table. The walls were covered in whiteboards. They lay the files they had brought onto the table in front of them and awaited developments. After a few minutes they were joined by a cluster of people including a superintendent, as the area commander. He introduced himself and then introduced the others in the room, the tactical firearms adviser and area intelligence officer. Kenny and Franks introduced themselves and presented them with the briefing packs they had prepared earlier.

They were reminded to return the briefing packs at the end of the operation and Kenny outlined the operational background, the action to date, the intelligence and evidence they had gathered on Purves and their plan to arrest him for being concerned in the supply of controlled drugs. He emphasised the information they had gathered concerning his access to firearms. Finally, he told them of the tight time limitations and the need to detain him before Wednesday evening; any later would probably result in him going to ground and covering his tracks.

The area commander thanked them and asked the intelligence officer if he had any other information that may assist; he said he did not and he then deferred to the TFA, called Mac.

Mac had been flicking through the file whilst Kenny had been speaking. He said they had to assume the information was correct as it had come from two sources, however there was no other information on the subject. No details of what firearms he may have and no previous convictions linked to weapons. He covered the three arrest options: house entry and neutralise inside the building, taking him out in the street at a pre-arranged signal or, finally, detaining him in the driveway of the house, before getting into a vehicle or reaching the road. The third option was preferred. Reasons – open space enclosed by dwarf walls, railings and hedges, with one or perhaps two vehicles in the drive; that restricted movement and there was less risk to the public. The option of entering the house and detaining him there would cause complications of containment and increase the risk to officers. Striking him in the street increased the risk to members of the public and containment would be more difficult. Two OPs were needed, front and back. He would arrange with the area commander to obtain firearms authorisation. After checking his diary and his team's commitments, he said that the next day was preferable. Total resource, eight armed officers, two front and two rear for containment and four in the assault team located in a van in the road but out of sight of the house. He would provide an op order and circulate.

Kenny said that they would provide a search team for the premises post-arrest, that would reduce the burden on local officers and ensure continuity of evidence. The intel officer, a man called Rob, would organise the OPs front and back.

They exchanged cards and phone details and agreed to maintain contact and meet at Ealing nick at five a.m. the following morning.

Kenny and Franks returned to their car less than an hour after the meeting had begun and drove back to their office. It had started to drizzle and the wipers intermittently cleared the screen. Kenny snoozed for most of the journey. They arrived back just after lunch and walked up to their office to organise resources for the following day.

The small proactive team located along the corridor agreed to assist – they would provide five for the search in the morning and would meet Kenny and Franks at their office at four a.m.

In the meantime, they finished preparing for the morning and left for home.

The next day they met in the office. The proactive team clattered through. Chatter was muted. It was four a.m. and they left within five minutes, hopped onto the motorway and made quick time, arriving at Ealing with twenty minutes to spare. They left their vehicles in the same side street and were shown to the same briefing room.

Lots of activity – plain clothes officers, tac firearms officers and uniform. The TFOs carried H&K MP5s and Glock pistols.

They were handed radios and the OP orders, and within ten minutes the room had filled with up to twenty people, including the area commander. He introduced everyone and then went through the op order, detailing the operation, the intelligence and the purpose of the operation and everyone's roles within it. There would be, he said, two OPs, one at the front and one at the back (OP1 and OP2) and control would be from OP1, with the IO Rob, whom they had met the day before. Mac, the TFA, would be in OP1, his team and the search teams would hold off at predesignated location some distance from the premises. At a predetermined time, as directed by OP1, the search team vehicles would be called in to block off the road at both ends. Questions were invited and there were no takers. Finally, he directed all units to be in position at five thirty a.m. with a de-brief at Ealing following the operation, at time to be arranged.

Kenny went to OP1 with Rob and Mac, whilst Franks remained with the search team some distance away. The OP was in the first floor of a house, currently unoccupied and up for sale but in a perfect location overlooking Purves' house. Access was via a rear passage and back door. They settled down in the cold empty room. All of them had earpieces so could hear the transmissions without using a speaker and as they peered out of the only window they could see his house, the low brick wall, railings and the hedge, behind which Kenny had dragged the wheelie bin. The BMW was parked on the left-hand side of the drive, indicating he was in residence, but there was no sign of the red Peugeot. The house was in darkness; there was no outside light. A street lamp glimmered a dull shimmery light.

Over the next five to ten minutes all the units arrived at

their designated positions, including the TF unit whose van was parked about two hundred metres away in a disused industrial unit, out of sight of the road.

Finally, once he was satisfied all units were positioned, Rob said in a quiet voice, "All units in position; subject house in darkness; subject car in driveway." Then silence.

It was still dark and murky and, because the house was unoccupied, the room was cold and damp. No chatter on the radio, no chatter in the room. Silence.

Fifteen minutes passed.

"No change, no change," he whispered.

A couple of cars passed, headlights on, on their way to work and the occasional light was turned on in adjacent houses. One man on a bicycle pedalled through the plot, oblivious to events in Western Gardens. The silence continued.

Kenny's mind wandered. He hoped Purves was at home and that this was not a wild goose chase – if he was at home, he wondered what he was doing, what he was thinking and what the outcome would be when they finally turned for home later that day.

Another fifteen minutes passed.

"No change, no change," Rob whispered.

"OP2?"

"No change, no change, all in darkness," the voice whispered.

Presumably they had managed to find a second location at the rear to cover the rear of Purves' house. Kenny learnt later that an officer had burrowed himself into an overgrown garden that backed onto Purves' garden, and by moving the bottom of a slat in the adjoining fence, he was able to see the rear of the house.

The wait continued. An hour passed with no movement, no sign of life. The room became a little lighter and the curtains were gently pulled closer together. All three of them were sitting back from the window with only Rob having a direct view of the entire house and drive, including the car.

A further half hour passed. The day had begun, the sun was up and people began walking along the pavement in front of the house, clutching handbags or briefcases; some with earphones, others with children.

Kenny hoped that the little shit would appear before children went to school. His thoughts were interrupted.

"Standby, standby, light on White 2/2."

(White was designated as the front of the house, Black the rear, windows and doors on the ground floor, left to right 1/1, 1/2 etc, 1st floor left to right 2/1, 2/2 and so on.)

"OP2 permission."

"Yes, yes."

"Can confirm low light on, interior first floor."

A light had been turned on in the middle of the three first-floor windows.

*Thank fuck for that,* Kenny thought. *But what if it's a girlfriend or a visitor to the house, an innocent party?*

"Movement in that room, no ID."

They could see steam coming from the air vent.

"I think he's having a shower," Kenny said.

Kenny grabbed the binoculars. He could see the steam coming out of the vent on the first floor and slight shadowy movements from within. The windows were marbled; it was the bathroom. He scanned the other windows; all had their blinds down.

"No change, no change."

The light remained on, the vent continued to discharge steam and heat and still people walked past the property, oblivious to the unfolding events.

After about twenty minutes, "OP1. Light at White 2/2 off, light on 2/3."

They could clearly see movement behind the light-coloured blind, back and forth, back and forth, occasionally causing the blind to gently wallow.

"No change, no change. Still only light on at White 2/3. OP2?"

"Yes, yes, no lights, no movement." The person was in the front bedroom, which was out of sight of OP2. The person remained there for several minutes.

The light was turned off and the blinds rolled up and a figure appeared at the window for about twenty seconds, hands on hips, looking down into the driveway, at the car, into the road and at the building opposite, including OP1, before moving away, deeper into the room and out of sight.

Kenny had the binoculars and as soon as the figure appeared at the window, he was able to have a closer look. At one point it seemed to him that the man was looking directly at him. He remained focused on him until he moved away.

"That's Purves! Light blue shirt, dark blue pullover, dark blue jeans."

"From OP1, light on 2/3 extinguished and blinds up. Can confirm we have the subject in the house, no other persons seen. OP2?"

"OP1, yes, yes. No light on Black."

There was a period of silence; no movement was observed and no more lights turned on.

"OP2 permission."

"Yes, yes, OP2."

"Dim light at Black 1/ 2, movement at Black 1/1 and light on Black 1/1. Figure in what appears to be kitchen."

OP1 relayed the message to the other units.

"OP2, you have the eyeball."

"OP2, yes, yes – no change, no change." OP1 knew that OP2 was working from a covert set; transmissions were weak so they were relayed through a third party that was situated closer to him.

"OP2 subject wearing same clothes and moving around in Black 1/1."

*Evidently making a cup of tea,* thought Kenny.

"OP1 permission."

"OP2, yes, yes."

"Light on at White 1/3, blinds down, movement only."

"OP1, yes, yes, you have control."

The movement in the front ground-floor room continued across from one side to the other, causing the blind to move slightly, and then the shadow disappeared.

"OP1 temporary loss. OP2?"

"OP2 no contact."

Once again, everything fell silent. He had been moving around the house now for about half an hour, but the figure had disappeared.

Kenny scanned the front of the building with the binoculars but was unable to see any movement at the windows. Then suddenly, "OP1 lights off in White 1/3," and then, "OP1 blinds pulled up in White 1/3, can confirm subject ground floor." Kenny could clearly see Purves through his binoculars.

"He's wearing a dark blue coat now."

"OP1 can confirm, contact, contact with subject at White 1/3, now wearing a dark blue coat." Kenny could see him looking out of the window, leaning forward to get a better view, left and right and straining his neck to look along the line of the building beyond the shrubs in the border.

"OP 1, be aware, he's all about himself." He then disappeared from view.

"OP2 permission."

"Yes, yes."

"Lights on Black 1/1 extinguished, no light, no movement now on Black."

"Yes, yes." Rob relayed the update to the plotted team. "OP XS11."

"Yes, yes," came the whispered response from the TFT in the van.

"Be aware you may have movement in the near future."

"XS11 yes, yes, moving into position."

Kenny saw the TFT van move up to within twenty metres of Purves' house, on the same side of the road, turn around and then slowly reverse towards the driveway and stop, shielded by the hedge adjoining the two properties, the rear doors were facing the entrance.

Kenny glanced across at the old Renault van being used by the TFT. He noticed that one of the rear doors was slightly ajar. Lights came on in the hallway.

"OP1, lights on White 1/2, hallway."

The OP called for the blocking cars to move into position at each end of the road, to isolate it from vehicles or pedestrians.

Kenny could see movement inside the hallway behind the front door. After about thirty seconds, the front door was opened slightly.

"OP1, front door ajar, standby, standby."

Kenny then noticed a woman walking on the pavement between the TFT van and the subject's house. She was fiddling with her phone and slowed her pace.

"OP1, XS11, you have a female on the pavement between you and the driveway, red coat."

"XS11 yes, yes, seen."

At that moment, the door opened and Purves walked out and stood beneath the small porch, looking out. He was carrying a light-coloured supermarket carrier bag in his left hand.

"Standby, standby, door open, subject in porch and held, same clothing, carrier bag left hand, all units hold."

Mac the TFA, who had been silent up to now, said in a firm voice, "We need him out in the drive with the door closed behind him; he must not be able to return inside."

"OP1, no change, no change, subject still in driveway."

The woman on the pavement had stopped, looking at her phone, apparently texting.

"OP1 woman on pavement now static, between XS11 and drive."

"XS11 yes, yes, we are aware," came the short response.

"OP1, standby, standby."

Kenny saw Purves drop his left hand behind him and close the door, and in the same movement stride out into the drive.

"OP1, door closed, subject towards gateway. Off, off, off, direction of the BMW. STRIKE, STRIKE, STRIKE!" Operational control automatically went to XS11 from OP1; in effect, XS11 called the shots.

At that instant, both rear doors of the old Renault van opened slowly; the first two out held the doors, allowing a further four to jump out and form up against the wall running alongside the pavement, and walk quickly and silently towards the gate. The van's doors were quietly closed and when the entire team reached the entrance to the driveway they split into two groups, one of two and the other of four. The single pair moved straight ahead, towards the woman; briefly showing themselves to her, they propelled her past the driveway to the house and lay her on the ground, between them and against the wall, separating her from Purves in the porch.

Purves was halfway to the gate and about one metre from his BMW when he became aware of figures in front of him and crossing the entrance to the drive. He took a semi-crouching position and naturally moved back and to his left to take cover behind the rear of his car as the dark bulky figures in front of him started shouting, "Armed police! Lay down your weapon! Don't move!" He knelt behind it and at the same time reached inside the left-hand side of his jacket and produced a weapon, which he then fired in the direction of the oncoming team.

They returned fire and there was a series of loud but slightly muffled burps as Purves quickly realised that any attempt to retreat to the safety of his house over the open ground between the car and his locked door was futile and was likely to end in serious injury, or quite possibly, his death.

The woman against the wall began screaming but there was silence in the driveway as the team covered both sides of the car.

The Renault van in the meantime had been reversed in front of the driveway, blocking the only exit.

The OP could hear more shouting out of their view from the driveway on the far side of the car. "Armed police! Drop the weapon! Drop the weapon!" The woman had stopped screaming; the police officers with her were talking to her and had her cradled in their arms.

"OP1 all units, hold your positions, hold your positions," and then, shouted instructions.

"Weapon on the ground, hands out where I can see them. Now lie on the ground, arms outstretched, face down!" an officer shouted.

Kenny could see one set of officers pointing their weapons at something on the ground at the rear of the BMW whilst the second group moved along the right-hand side of the vehicle towards their colleagues.

Two officers bent down out of sight and several seconds later emerged with Purves, his hands handcuffed behind his back and his head and shoulders leaning forwards. He was once again laid on the floor and searched in the light of the streetlamp and a strong arc-lamp that had been produced. All his belongings were placed in a large plastic bag.

"OP1 permission."

"Yes, yes, OP1."

"Any injures?"

"Negative."

"XS11 all units, hold your position, house clearance will commence." The remaining members of the TFT left Purves with their colleagues and entered the house, presumably with a key found in Purves' pocket.

As the house clearance continued, Kenny could see torches, beams of light and shadows at the windows, and lights coming on in rooms as they were cleared, and could hear shouts of "Room clear!" as they progressed from room to room and floor to floor.

After they finished they exited the home and re-joined their colleagues guarding Purves.

"XS11 house clear, subject in custody, no injuries, one weapon seized and made safe. You have control, OP1." Kenny reminded Rob that the arresting officers needed to strip-search Purves for any concealed drugs upon his arrival at the nick and to refuse any phone calls or personal nomination until house search was completed.

"XS11."

"Yes, yes."

"Ensure subject is thoroughly searched on arrival at custody, and no nominations until searches completed."

"XS11, yes, yes."

"OP1, yes, yes. Exhibits officer to XS11 to receive property."

"Yes, yes."

"Remove road blocks, search team to the address."

"Yes, yes."

"XS11."

"Yes, yes."

"How is the female pedestrian?"

"We have her details. No injuries, insisted on continuing to work. OP11 to all units, debrief at Ealing at 11:00 hours. OP1 now closing down." Mac was the first one to speak.

"Sorted then. You happy with that?"

"Yeah, too right," replied Kenny as they packed up the equipment they had brought with them.

They emerged into the daylight and felt a light breeze on their faces; it all felt a little unreal, as if they had been on a small movie set, isolated from the outside world.

Mac joined his team at the van, who were loading equipment into the rear as the traffic began to flow again.

As Kenny wandered over to the driveway of the house, Franks pulled up with the rest of the search team. As he got out of the car, Kenny shook his hand.

"The job's a good 'un; the information was spot on. Glad no-one got hurt." Franks briefed the search team and told them to take their time – they had all day – and they trooped into the house.

Kenny and Franks followed them in. It was clean and sparkly, wooden floors throughout apart from the carpeted dining room, white walls, recessed bookshelves and IKEA furniture. The rear door led into a small garden that backed onto another house and garden, separated by a fence, behind which OP2 had hidden himself during the operation.

After a cursory look around Kenny and Franks left the search team to carry on the good work and telephoned their DI before driving to Ealing.

There they met the area commander and thanked him and his team for their assistance and then had breakfast, before tying up with Mac and Rob in the briefing room prior to the debrief.

At about ten thirty the room began to fill and at eleven, the area commander entered the room.

He thanked everyone for the professional job they had done that morning and confirmed that although rounds had been fired, there were no injuries.

He told them that Purves was in custody and that a loaded Browning 9mm automatic had been recovered from the scene; apparently two rounds had been fired and two empty cartridges recovered close by. The search was continuing at the house. He requested that all statements, briefing packs and any other forms be handed to Franks, who stood up to identify himself, before the end of the tour of duty.

He asked for any questions; there were none.

The whole de-brief lasted for about ten minutes and at its conclusion everyone dispersed, leaving Kenny, Franks, Mac and Rob to collect the paperwork and tidy the room for the next briefing.

# 14

# THE NET WIDENS

Their plan was to complete the searches during the day and then examine the results before returning with Purves and all the exhibits to the local nick that evening.

Not interviewing the suspect would give them extra time to consolidate, review and extend the period in which they could keep him in custody. They went down to a small room that presumably had been, or was still being, used as an interview room; a small black tape recorder sat forlornly in the corner and the two benches and table were firmly bolted to the lino floor. The room had been commandeered by the exhibits officer for the duration. She was surrounded by four or five sealed clear plastic bags containing miscellaneous items.

She went through them individually without breaking the seals.

"This is what he was carrying."

They could see an empty Morrison's carrier bag.

"And this is what was inside." She showed them a large amount of cash in fifties, twenties and tens.

"It's been counted." She looked down at her log. "Eight thousand pounds. The weapon." She showed them the weapon, a Browning 9mm Automatic. The magazine had been removed from the body and the workings had been locked open; loose rounds were contained in a smaller bag within the larger bag.

"Two keys."

She produced two separate bags containing a key each, both seemingly identical and both attached to a red circular Bakelite fob, one marked 212, the other 213, but with no other identification marks.

"One in his jacket pocket." She checked her log. "212, and one in his right sock, 213. Two phones." She showed them the phones. "One inside jacket pocket, second outside jacket pocket. Oyster card, wallet with various cards, bank cards, pieces of paper, some cash. Two spent cartridges. These were on the ground by the car, expended when he fired at the TFT. The magazine of the weapon appears to have been full before he fired the two rounds."

"Is that it?" asked Franks.

"Yep, I'm just waiting for the expended cartridges from the TFT guys. They fired four rounds so there should be four, also the various bits of paper – briefing document, OP orders, authorisations and OP log, and that should be about it. When I have everything I'll give you a call and I can sign everything over to you."

"Great, thanks for your help."

"Pleasure, best of luck with the enquiry."

It was mid-afternoon by the time they had returned to Western Gardens. There were several cars still in the driveway. They entered and met the Sergeant in charge of the small team.

"Anything yet?" Franks enquired.

"No, nothing. We've done the loft, two of the bedrooms

and the bathroom. We'll be down on the ground floor in a few minutes."

"Before you do the ground floor, can you clear the garden, drive and car before the light fails?"

"Yeah, OK."

"And any bank and business documents, seize please. Let us know if you find anything and I'd like it photographed in situ," said Franks.

"OK."

They left the team to continue the search and returned to Ealing nick to begin to collect the paperwork and tie things together for the return trip.

During the afternoon, Franks' phone rang; it was the search team. They had searched the loft space, garden, front drive, vehicle and first floor – completely negative, nothing of note other than some bank documents. They were going to start on the ground floor, which was probably going to take, in their estimation, four or five hours to complete.

Kenny made a quick phone call to Liz to update her with developments and ask her about the result of her enquiries with the TK in Poundscombe. She hadn't completed the analysis but she had identified a further three incoming calls to that TK; they were un-attributable but had called the number at twelve midday or thereabouts, the same time as the others. She added that she had been unable to link them with any of Purves' phones because she hadn't yet received his phone details for that period. He thanked her and asked her to phone him with any further developments and added that they intended to return that evening.

Next, he phoned the forensic team dealing with the Warden seizures; he updated them and asked them to compare any outstanding prints with Purves.

As soon as the conversation finished, his phone rang

again. It was a member of the search team; they had found two thousand pounds in cash behind some books on the bookshelf. He thanked them and then went with Franks to the house. The lights were on and as they approached the front door they could see movement behind the blinds on the ground floor.

A knock on the door was answered and they entered. It was clear that the search had been thorough; each individual book had been removed and stacked neatly on the shelves, the kickboards in the kitchen were off and the appliances pulled out to check behind them.

The only room on the ground floor with a carpet was the dining room. On top of it was a sideboard, table, standard lamp, four chairs and a rug.

"Have you done the dining room?" Franks cried to the search team.

"Yes, negative, nothing seen," came the shouted back reply.

He entered the room and bent down on all fours and, as he often did during searches, tried to look at it from the perspective of the person who wanted to hide something close-by, that would be difficult to find by a third party, yet relatively easy to retrieve.

Most of the ground floor had beautiful solid wooden floors and were therefore difficult to lift and replace. The house was generally very clean, utilitarian, quite sparsely furnished, and the floor was pristine. He ran his hands over the carpet.

He thought, *If I was Purves and stashed something beneath the floor in this room, I wouldn't be wanting to remove the tables or chairs and sideboard on every occasion, or pulling up the entire carpet.* He drifted over to the corner. Moving a small standard lamp, he felt around the edge of the carpet in the only visible corner and jammed his fingers between it and the skirting board, which allowed him to lift the corner forty-five degrees from the edges, whilst avoiding the razor-sharp gripper rods. He tugged it so that the edge of the carpet sprung from the inverted tacks and then pulled it further back into the middle of the floor, revealing the loose underlay beneath. He pulled this back as well and then looked carefully at the dusty floorboards beneath. He ran his hands over the boards and noticed that a small section had been cut after the floorboards had originally been laid, probably to access a central heating pipe or wiring beneath. It had then been screwed back down again onto the joists. All the other floorboards in that section were virginal and complete.

He shouted through to the team, "Have you got a screwdriver?"

The Sergeant brought through a small toolkit, which he opened, removed the Pozidriv and handed it to Franks, who began removing the screws from the small section of board. The Sergeant, who was leaning over, had been joined by the other members of the search team, who all peered over Franks' hunched body beyond the triangular section of carpet and underlay onto the floorboards below.

Franks had noted that the screws were shiny as if they had been recently used and removed, and asked someone to take a photograph before he removed all of them. He finished with the remaining screws and lifted the board, a light, cold, dusty breeze drew up into the room as he peered into the void but couldn't see anything particularly interesting, other than two copper pipes running along the length of one of the joists. The cavity was quite shallow and was covered with dust, wood shavings, bits of plaster and pipe offcuts and he ran his fingers along the gap between the joists, but by lying fully prone he was able to extend his arms fully into the hole and let his fingers run over the detritus that was out of his sight, beneath the floorboards. Almost immediately he felt something smooth with straight edges. He asked for and was given a torch, which he shone down into the gap, and he was able to see the corner of a polythene bag. He stretched down and, brushing some of the rubble to one side, saw that it contained cash.

*Mmm, what have we got here?* he thought and took a photograph of the item in situ, and then drew himself back on his haunches and placed his hands on his knees.

"Money," he said.

"How much?" asked Kenny.

"Don't know. Difficult to tell. Can you get the local forensic team down to take some photographs and remove it? There may be some more stuff down there, although I couldn't see anything obvious."

He then said to the Sergeant, "And if you're going to do a bloody search, do it properly or not at all. Clear?"

It had annoyed him that after all the hard work that had gone into the investigation, a bit of sloppy searching had missed some vital evidence.

About half an hour later they were joined by two of the forensic team, who took a series of photographs of the cavity and its contents, dusted the cavity floorboard for fingerprints and then removed the bag and placed it in a second clear plastic bag and held it up. It contained several wedges of cash, separated into folded sections.

"Several thousand, I would think," said Kenny. "Anything else down there?" They peered over the hole and removed a further, smaller polythene bag containing creamy coloured crystallised powder. Once again, they placed that in a separate bag and handed both to the exhibits officer.

Instructions were given for the team to lift the entire carpet and check for other sections of chopped floorboards. Kenny and Franks remained in the house until the task was completed and when nothing further was found and the search had been completed, they left the house, closed and locked the door and returned to Ealing nick, where they collected all the exhibits, including the weapon, expended cartridges and the prisoner, and went home in convoy. Purves was escorted in the back of one of the proactive vehicles, with the officers being given strict instructions not to engage in any conversation with the suspect.

They arrived at about midnight and whilst Purves was being incarcerated, the exhibits were safely secured for the night under lock and key.

Both officers meandered home and returned to the office early the following morning. Much needed to be done. The first visit was to the forensics team, once again, to deliver all the exhibits seized from Purves at his home; these included the weapon, expended cartridges, the money, suspect drugs, phones and the various bags and fingerprint lifts. They promised to update the officers with the results as they came in.

They then went through his personal items and the general paperwork found on him and in his home.

Later that morning they received a call from a Mr Goldstein, from a London firm of solicitors, who said he was representing Purves and demanded to see him and to be present during any interviews or examination. He also demanded to see all the evidence and to have a private audience with his client. They found this a little surprising since he could have unfettered access to Purves whenever he wished. He was evidently a London brief and would presumably take some time to travel out of town, but he was told to phone Kenny's mobile when he arrived. They knew this would give them some time to sift through the paperwork found in the house.

What intrigued both officers were the keys that he'd had with him when he was arrested. Two identical circular red fobs with the numbers '212' and '213' etched onto the side of each one.

Were they room keys for a hotel?

Safe deposit boxes?

Left luggage lockers?

They presumably didn't have an historical context otherwise he wouldn't have had them with him when he was arrested.

They also needed to be patient with the results from the forensic team, so they busied themselves with the various papers recovered from the house. They trudged through them methodically, putting to one side those documents or items that were not of interest and retaining bank documents and papers that contained calculations.

"He appears to have two accounts, personal and business. The business is called *Freedom Investments Ltd* – quite a number of transactions, particularly cash deposits every few days, and then credit transfers into the personal account – probably drawings. His personal account – a few outgoings, nothing too ambitious, fed by the business account. Rental agreement on a property that appears to be a launderette, payments out to cover the rent from the business account and some regular payments to individuals and companies – out of the business," said Franks. "Anything from what you have?"

"No," said Kenny disappointedly.

Just before lunch, the solicitor contacted Kenny and they both met him in a small annex of the custody suite. He was small and wore a smart brown three-piece suit, a fob chain, cufflinks and fake brown crocodile shoes. They explained the circumstances of the arrest. He made no comment other than a request to see his client. The officers waited outside in the main concourse and watched the world go round. Some thirty minutes later, Goldstein walked through with Purves, who hadn't seen the two officers before and stared intently.

"Would you like to see my client?" asked Goldstein.

They entered the nearest interview room and asked Purves

a number of questions concerning his arrest, the firearm and the money. They did not reveal that they had found some more money and almost certainly drugs beneath the floorboards in the dining room. To all the questions from both officers over a period of forty-five minutes, his only reply was, "No comment." When the interview was concluded and Purves was returned to his cell, Goldstein turned to the two detectives. "He thought he was being mugged, you know." They didn't respond but arranged for the solicitor to return to the police station later that evening to be present during a further interview.

Meanwhile, they went up to their office, where they spoke to the forensics team and enquired on progress. The drug found beneath the floorboards was crack cocaine, the firearm was a Section 1 Firearm and therefore prohibited, and they were waiting for printouts on the call data from both phones.

They re-examined the documents they had recovered and particularly the bank statements. Franks made copies and then ran his finger down the transactions and underlined those of interest. He noticed that a regular payment was made to 'Stash and Leave' every month. He leant across to Kenny. "What's 'Stash and Leave'?"

"Don't know... hang on." Kenny tapped the name into a terminal. "It's a self-storage company. All over the place. There's one here."

"Where's the head office?"

"Wait one..." He looked again. "Chiswick, why?"

"He's making regular payments to Stash and Leave, fifty pounds a month, goes back as far as he has statements. Have you got a phone number?"

"Yep." He gave Franks the number; he dialled it and looked at Kenny. He brought his finger up to his mouth to indicate that he should be quiet.

Kenny listened to the call. Franks suggested that he had

found two keys on a fob, described them and wondered whether they belonged to a customer of the company. Their view was that both keys belonged to a customer and that they matched the shape and colour of a standard company product – but that they wouldn't be able to establish the name of the owner from the keys alone; every branch was laid out in the same way with the same numbering system. He did discover, however, that they had a central customer database that contained details of all of their customers and past customers across the country.

Once the call was finished: "So, he's got a couple of storage boxes somewhere in the UK and they're probably close to each other. He's not going to rent a couple of boxes in Cardiff or Scunthorpe though, he needs somewhere close to home, But where?"

"OK. The next interview, we ask him about them and give him the opportunity of telling us where they are located." They were just planning the next interview when one of the forensics team knocked and entered.

"OK, guys. We're about finished for the day." It was edging towards five o'clock.

"An update. This is a printout from both his phones." He handed them two sheets of paper.

"There is." He looked at his sheet. "Ten thousand five hundred pounds in cash in the bag that we recovered from beneath the floor, and the crack cocaine weighed in at approximately two hundred grams."

"Great," remarked Franks.

"One more thing – we have one print belonging to your man on the underside of the floorboard that was covering the stash."

"Fantastic!" They both punched the air.

"Have a good evening, see you tomorrow."

"Thanks, guys, best of luck!"

"Looking good," said Franks. "We have possession of a

firearm, possession with intent to endanger life, and possession of cocaine with intent to supply. Can't be bad. But I think there's more to come. I'm interested in these boxes – if we could find them…"

The phone rang; the solicitor was waiting for them. They closed up shop and walked down to the interview room. Once again, they went through the evidence and the exhibits they had available (some were still under examination) and invited him to sign the labels confirming that he seen them. He declined.

Finally, at the end of the forty-minute interview, Franks produced the two keys and asked him what they were used for. To all questions Purves made no reply.

Following the interview, the solicitor was requested to return first thing in the morning. He grudgingly agreed, although he had some doubts over the necessity following the second interview.

Leaving Purves to the care of the custody staff, Kenny and Franks went to the canteen for a cup of tea and a bun whilst they contemplated their next move.

They had little further room for manoeuvre with Purves; if he continued to make no reply during the interview they would charge him with the offences they had at that time and put him before the court. He was incommunicado, unless the solicitor contacted anyone on his behalf, which they thought unlikely. They had not heard anything from the girlfriend, but she wasn't implicated and they'd probably waste time and energy tracing her and interviewing her about their relationship without any particular gain.

The keys were a good line of enquiry. They were, as they had already established, probably storage units in a 'Stash and Leave' warehouse somewhere in the country, and they pondered the questions:

Why did he have two keys?

Were they adjacent to each other?

Were they, in fact, at the same warehouse?

These questions needed to be bottomed out and would require a visit to the head office of Stash and Leave. They also needed to make further enquiries into the telephone box in North Cornwall.

Why there?

Presumably linked to the drug trafficking. But how?

Who answers the phone?

Would the local Old Bill know anyone in or around Poundscombe that may fit the bill?

The questions all needed answering, but the initial problem was Purves. He was arrogant, self-centred, confident, but very exposed to a series of serious offences, including firearms charges, for which he would, if convicted, face a long gaol term, but was apparently oblivious to the consequences.

Why didn't he cooperate?

What was his raison d'etre?

Who was he trying to protect?

And his businesses?

Car parks and a launderette? All cash heavy. Was this a way of laundering his loot? They needed to get financial investigations involved, give them a heads-up and provide the documents so that they could rummage around in his bank accounts and businesses.

They decided to leave the Cornish connection and the storage company until they had finished with Purves. They just didn't have the resources and time to cover everything and needed to prioritise. Purves first, rest later.

They tidied their desks, cleared the paperwork and prepared the remand file that would inevitably be required the following day. After a brief visit to the lovely Liz, who couldn't provide them with any further information, they went for a pint.

The next morning, Kenny had already received a call from the suave and sophisticated Mr Goldstein and they agreed to meet in the custody suite. The time was eight thirty a.m. They arrived before the solicitor and sat on the long bench facing the custody staff. Purves was brought out in anticipation of interview and sat beside them. There was no acknowledgment on his part, not even a turn of the head; he looked straight ahead with his arms resting on top of his thighs. When the custody officer told him that they were just waiting for his solicitor, he did not acknowledge the comment.

Although they didn't speak, both officers had the same thought, which was that the third interview, unless there was an unexpected change of heart, would be a repeat of the first and second – silence or 'no comment'.

Goldstein arrived a few minutes later, apologised for being late, shook himself down – it had apparently been raining outside – and, after a short private audience, the formal interview progressed.

As expected, all the questions posed by the two officers had the same response – "No comment." Forty-five minutes later the chat finished and they left him with his solicitor. This gave them a chance to speak to the custody officer, whom they both knew, discuss the evidence and proffer charges that reflected his culpability at that time. He suggested charging him immediately, which would enable a remand court appearance that morning. When he emerged with Goldstein, he was charged with the relevant firearm and drug offences and told that he would be going to court within half an hour, he made no comment.

This apparently flustered Goldstein, who protested that he hadn't enough time to prepare and asked what the application would be. He was told it was for a remand in custody. He told the officers he would be making an application for bail on behalf of his client. At the subsequent hearing that both officers attended, Purves was remanded in custody – hardly surprising for the offences for which he had been charged, a view not shared by Mr Goldstein.

# 15

# UNDER LOCK AND KEY

The arrests of Purves and Warden and their subsequent remand in custody released some of the pressure and the two officers were able to continue their enquiries.

Their priority was to identify the two mysterious keys that were on Purves when he was arrested. Franks had contacted 'Stash and Leave' during the day and arranged to meet their managing director, a Mr Simmonds, at their head office in London the following Monday.

The weekend passed lazily, the pace of life slowed, the sun came out and the two detectives were able to stabilise, recuperate and recharge their batteries.

Monday morning saw them battling through traffic on the motorway to keep their appointment.

The office was in a rather non-descript building hidden behind the North Circular in a light industrial unit. It was small yet efficient, with a number of people sitting behind computer screens and in front of rows of filing cabinets. On arrival, they were ushered into an office in the corner of the building with

Venetian blinds, stocked with posters, brochures and odd files, and were joined by Simmonds – a tall, featureless man – and a woman, whom he introduced as his wife.

The officers explained the nature of the enquiry and wished to establish if Richard Purves or his company, Freedom Investments Limited, had any security boxes rented from their company.

They showed them the keys and copies of the FI Ltd bank statements they had recovered showing the regular monthly payments.

Simmonds said that although this was a new area of investigation for Kenny and Franks, they had in fact encountered issues like this before. He explained that when people rented a box or room to store items, they were required to sign a declaration to the effect that there was nothing illegal being stored – this included drugs, weapons, proceeds of crime etc. In the contract as well, often missed by renters, was the fact that if it was 'suspected' that a box or room was being rented for this purpose, the company would cooperate with law enforcement agencies, and if it was established that a storage facility was being used for illegal purposes, the contract would be terminated. He handed a blank copy of a contract and underlined the relevant section.

"So," he said, "Mr Purves has been charged with drug trafficking and you think he may have something in one or both boxes?"

"Yes, that's right," Franks said.

"OK, I can check the database and see whether he or his company are renting any space from us. If you can give me a couple of minutes…" He left the room.

The officers were offered and accepted cups of tea and a short time later, Simmonds reappeared.

"Can you just come through?" They followed him to a desk in the main office, where he sat down in front of a screen.

It was open on the page of Freedom Investments Ltd and the name of the only signee, Richard Purves.

"Mr Purves rents Box 212 in our North Acton Branch, under the company Freedom Investments Ltd, and has done for two and a half years. It is regularly used and was last visited a few days ago." He explained that any person renting a box has to enter their individual password and access code before entering the building.

"Box 213, at the same branch, is rented by a separate company and has been rented for about the same length of time. There is no apparent connection between Purves, Freedom Investments Ltd and Box 213, although they would be side by side. I can tell you, however, that Box 213 has never been visited since it was originally rented." They thanked him for his help.

"If you want to open either box and examine the contents, you will need a search warrant, one for each container." They nodded; they had anticipated this response.

"If you have one or indeed two warrants, please let me know and I'll meet you at the branch, and I'll be happy to help in any way I can." They thanked him once again and moved to the exit.

As they reached the door, Kenny asked a final question: "The key for box 213. Would it open any other Box 213 in any of your other storage facilities?"

"We have fourteen storage facilities, and all the boxes or storage units at these units have individual keys. The keys you have would be unique to, in this case, Boxes 212 and 213 at that specific branch, and would not open any other boxes marked 212 or 213."

They reminded him that their conversation and any reference to Purves had to remain confidential and returned to their car. They drove to Ealing nick where they had had the original brief and debrief for the Purves operation and met Rob, the intelligence officer who had helped them with the original enquiry. They updated him with the progress so far in relation to Purves and he arranged for them to obtain two search warrants for Boxes 212 and 213 at the Stash and Leave site in North Acton. A couple of hours later, with the warrants in hand and having already contacted Mr Simmonds, the three of them drove to the storage facility.

It was mid-afternoon when they arrived and Simmonds was waiting. He was shown both search warrants and given copies. He waved them through and accompanied them in the lift to the second floor, where they turned left and left again and walked down a passageway past a bank of numbered boxes on their right-hand side, all of them the same size and colour. Although Simmonds had a Master Key for the boxes at that facility, it was important for evidential continuity to open both boxes with the keys that Purves actually had in his possession at the time of his arrest, to negate any later suggestion that they may have related to any other unconnected locks. Kenny slipped on some disposable gloves and tried the first key, marked 212, in the lock of Box 212; it opened and he slid the tray out slightly. It was full. Box 213 was to the left and directly next to 212 on the same level and he then tried the key marked 213 in that lock. It opened and he slid the tray out about two inches. It also contained several items.

They left the boxes half open without examining the contents and Kenny asked Rob to request a forensics team from Ealing to ensure all possible evidence was captured prior to items being removed. They arrived a short time later.

Franks told them what he wanted – photographs of each stage of the search, and fingerprint examination of the box, door and contents of each, starting with 212. Kenny then asked Mr Simmonds if the cameras that had a view down that particular corridor, the lift and reception were working. He told him that they were; he also confirmed that the recordings were kept for seven days and he invited them to accompany him to reception, leaving the forensic team to continue their examination of the boxes. He spoke to the receptionist and then went into an office at the rear where a bank of eight cameras covered most of the site. At a terminal, he entered Purves' personal record.

"He came on site on Tuesday this week at 10:05 hours and used his code and password for Box 212 to enter the building."

He then turned to another terminal at the same desk and typed in 10:00hrs on that day to start the viewing. The screen began showing activity at the counter and entrance door. Several minutes passed. A couple of people entered and left. As the on-screen clock turned to 10:05 hours they were glued to the screen.

Suddenly, "There he is!" Kenny pointed to the screen.

They could see Purves having a short conversation with the receptionist and then enter his details. The door opened. He was carrying a carrier bag. They then switched to the camera in the lift and they could clearly see Purves entering the lift and exiting on the second floor.

A further adjustment and they saw him walking away from the camera, down the corridor towards the boxes. When he'd reached the boxes that were at chest height, he turned to face them and produced a key from his pocket, and then turned his back to the camera and by so doing obscured the actual box. They saw him sliding the tray out, removing something from his carrier bag and placing it in the box, and then removing something from the box and placing it in the same bag. He then closed the lid and slid the box back into the cavity before locking it and retracing his steps, enabling the team to get a good front view of his face, clothes and bag, which contained something weighty – the hand holds on the bag were strained and the bag ends had been sucked in. He returned to the lift and through reception and disappeared from sight once again.

"Good. So, we've got him coming in on Tuesday, we can link him to 212, but not 213. We can't see which box he opens and we can't see what he's depositing or removing," said Franks.

"But we've found Box 213 and the key was with him when he was nicked, as was the key for Box 212," added Kenny. "Let's hope we find something interesting."

They returned upstairs to where the team was examining the boxes. They had removed the drawer for 212 completely and had removed the contents and bagged and sealed them individually. It contained a passport, some cash, jewellery, paperwork and a watch.

"The passport is in the name Richard Purves," said one of them.

They were busily dusting the box lid, the interior of the storage unit and door for fingerprints.

"We've found quite a number, mainly thumb and forefinger and some palms. Just about finished." They waited whilst they placed the tray in a large plastic bag.

They then turned to the second box, 213. They opened it and removed the tray, placed it on the ground and lifted the lid. They removed each item using pincers and placed them in individual bags whilst Kenny, Franks, Rob and Mr Simmonds looked on.

The first item that was removed, mainly because of its bulk, was a large polythene bag containing a slightly off-white crystallised powder. It was placed in an exhibits bag and labelled. Then a smaller bag of white powder and then a similar sized bag of small dark dots, both of which were placed in separate bags and labelled.

Two UK passports, both with Purves' photograph but

under different names, and then a large envelope of cash, mainly sterling, were once again placed in separate bags. And finally, some bank documents that were also sealed. The guys then took very small swabs of the interior and then dusted for fingerprints inside the container around the lid and exterior, and then the inside and outside of the door.

"Pleased?" asked Rob.

"Bloody right," said Franks. "Jackpot!"

After taking a statement from Simmonds, they recovered, and signed for, the various exhibits taken from the two boxes and handed the local team Purves' details for comparison against any lifts they had taken from in or around either of the boxes. Now that they had satisfied Mr Simmonds that both boxes had been rented by the same man, he gave them details of the person who had signed the rental agreement for Box 213, a Paul Winchcombe, who gave an address in Hammersmith and signed on behalf of Trenchard Properties. The rental was paid by standing order from an account with Barclays Bank in Acton. He gave them the account details.

They returned through the London traffic onto the motorway and to the office, arriving late, at around nine o'clock.

By the time they had booked in the exhibits and left all their paperwork, it was ten o' clock in the evening.

When they returned to the office the following morning, much needed to be done. The first thing was to update the hierarchy, the powers that be, of developments, what was planned for the coming week and how they thought the enquiry would pan out. Franks had inserted into the conversation the possibility of progressing the investigation further in Cornwall. To his immense relief, the DI was supportive, but placed a time limit on the two men. If they were going to pursue the chain of evidence and intelligence, then he insisted that it was completed by Friday that week; other jobs needed their attention and money was tight. Franks agreed.

Warden and Purves were locked up and unlikely to get bail; other evidence would undoubtedly unfold from the forensic teams and there would be no point in re-interviewing Purves until they had secured further evidence and presented it to him in one package to allow him the opportunity to either deny all knowledge, make no comment, as he had done so far, or accept responsibility – an unlikely scenario. All the exhibits had been submitted and were in the process of being examined at various establishments.

The one area that justified further examination was the Cornwall connection. All they had gleaned to date was that Purves had phoned a telephone box just outside a north Cornish village three times at twelve noon over the past three months. Only one call had been answered, and the conversation had lasted for about four minutes. There had been a total of eight incoming calls to that same telephone box over that period; the other five calls were unattributable. They had no idea who was fielding the calls. It was likely to be someone local, but there was always an outside possibility that it was someone coming in from another area. This was considered unlikely because of the tightness and relative remoteness of the community.

Anyway, they thought, it was worthy of investigation, especially since it was in a beautiful part of the country and perhaps, just perhaps, it may lead to something more interesting. They knew that any overt enquiries in a small Cornish village would provoke a ripple of interest amongst the local community, so they had to tread carefully, disguise the real purpose of their visit, particularly in mid-winter, and have a settled and plausible explanation for being there. They also knew that the best plan was often the simplest. They arranged to take walking boots, waterproofs and maps of the area, which would support the story that they were mates who were walking parts of the coastal path in sections. They would use their own Christian names but adopt different surnames. Everything had to be paid for in cash; any paper trail would tend to undermine the legitimacy of their story.

Their backgrounds needed to be bland and uninteresting – they would be insurance managers for the biggest insurance company they could think of, with huge offices and a myriad of staff. Large, anonymous, impersonal and untraceable. Finally, any means of identification needed to be safely stashed away from prying eyes.

Franks had made the call and booked rooms at the only place in Poundscombe that had accommodation available for that time of year, The Anchor pub. It was small, with only four rooms available, but central to whatever was going on in the village.

As a matter of courtesy, he also telephoned the intelligence section in Devon and Cornwall to say that they had found a possible connection between their drug investigation and the area around Poundscombe and to enquire whether they had any likely suspects. The initial response was negative but he was assured that systems would be checked and he would receive a call within twenty-four hours.

They drew sufficient cash and made a quick dash home to collect enough clothes and left for Cornwall that afternoon, exchanging the more cosmopolitan lifestyle for the rural West Country. The journey was boringly unspectacular and after stopping for tea and a sandwich they left the motorway around Exeter to cut up around Dartmoor and on to the north Cornish coast. Hugging the coastal road, they found the signpost for Poundscombe, and, following a winding narrow lane that was bordered by steep walls and high hedgerows for several miles, they entered the rear end of the village and followed the tight lanes and streets to the harbour.

It was a bright afternoon in mid-winter and the wind was rolling the clouds in from the sea. The hamlet was grouped around the harbour, mainly low two-storey solid granite houses with their front doors facing the quayside, intermingled with others painted pink, yellow and blue. In the middle of the cluster was The Anchor, granite faced with black window frames, slightly larger and broader than the adjoining buildings, with its sign, exposed to gusts of wind, squeaking gently on its hooks. They parked up on the quayside.

They estimated the village had about fifty houses, some of which would be holiday lets or second homes for wealthy commuters, but it was nonetheless a small community where many of the residents had lived in the village for several generations. As soon as they arrived they saw the second phone box next to the harbour edge.

They left the car and walked over to the front door of the pub and entered the large flag-stoned front bar, with its smouldering fire, settees and polished counter. It was empty; no customers, no staff. The walls were hung with hunting scenes and photographs of the village in bygone days. It had heavy drape curtains and panelled walls.

Their movement and the thud of the door closing behind them prompted a response and a woman came to the counter.

"Good afternoon, how can I help you?"

"We've booked a couple of rooms for a couple of nights – the name is Kilroy," said Kenny.

"Ah yes, I've been expecting you. Two double rooms, with breakfast. Will you be eating with us tonight?"

Kenny looked at Franks. "Yes, I think so. What time?"

"Seven until nine, and what time would you like breakfast?"

"Eight would be fine," replied Kenny, looking at Franks, who nodded.

"OK, you're in number one and number two." She handed

them their keys. "Straight through that door." She pointed at a non-descript dark-coloured door, "up the stairs and turn right. You'll have views of the harbour. I hope you enjoy your stay."

They both thanked her and she added, "Do you want a hand with your bags?"

"No, we'll be fine, thanks. Is the car OK at the front?" said Franks.

"Oh, you'll need a card! Hang on!" She scuttled away and returned with a sign that said 'Guests, Anchor Inn'. "Put that in your windscreen and you'll be fine." They returned to the car, lifted the bags out, put the sign on the dashboard and returned inside, and, after agreeing a time to meet, went to their rooms.

They were comfortable, warm and cosy with a view of the entire harbour. They met at reception ten minutes later and wandered through the village to get an idea of the layout and have a look at the suspect phone box before darkness folded over. It was breezy and the wind was whipping up a light mist of spray that was curling around the harbour wall and drifting across the moored vessels towards the pub. They knew the general direction they wanted to go in and sauntered along the quayside past some small shops, a café and the post office, all facing the harbour. In the summer they would probably be thronged with people but now, apart from the post office and general store, they were closed, with sad little notices on their doors indicating when they would be re-opening.

Once away from the wider expanse of the harbourside, the roads, lanes and alleys became tighter, more intimate, and less inviting to an outsider because, of course, they didn't go anywhere. They moved on past the small church to a narrow lane that led up to the high ground beyond. Both sides were steep-banked with vegetation, lush and sheltered from the prevailing wind. As they turned a wide corner, the pavement petered out, and on the left stood a magnificent phone box, recently painted a brilliant red with all the glass panels intact.

Franks pulled open the door, went inside and lifted the receiver; he replaced it and then allowed himself to back out of the booth, his ass pushing the door behind him, and then turned to Kenny.

"It works, but it's out of the way, isn't it?" Kenny looked at the box. It was strange to imagine that the phone had been used for multiple illegal transactions with a major drug distributor in London. He looked around, there was nothing beyond it.

"It bloody is!" Kenny replied, wondering how they were going to manage to keep an eye on it during their stay.

They decided to explore a little further and walked up the tarmacked road around a right-hand bend. The pavement had frittered out and the road then returned to a gravelled muddy cart track that kept turning right and up an incline towards a small chapel, which sat above and sideways on to the lane and was partially hidden by a thick bramble hedge. They followed the path up to the gates of the building. Hugely overgrown, it sat above the village but completely out of sight in a strangely serene sense of isolation.

The solid granite building and the road leading up to it probably dated from the mid-nineteenth century, having been built to satisfy the pastoral needs of the community and allow worshippers up from the village and down from the surrounding farms. The telephone box had probably been added later to allow the same people to use the phone after a service, before the advent of home fixed lines or mobile phones.

Kenny opened the small, rusted, wrought-iron gate and walked into the grounds, bordered by a semi-derelict metal fence that had been overwhelmed by brambles and small sycamore trees. The building was in the middle of a square plot. They trod carefully around the structure, avoiding the invasive plants. The large oak front door under a small porch was locked and solid. They walked away from the roadside and to the rear, where there was a second, smaller door, less imposing and not as well protected from the elements as the main door. The frame was rotten and the bottom of the door had succumbed to many years of sun, frost and rain. Looking through, Kenny could see the interior.

The cross panel at the bottom of the door had given way completely, allowing him to slide on his back under the door and into the inside of the building, followed by Franks. The floor was tiled and the roof stretched to the ridge above. Each side of the building was lined with three leaded windows that let some light into the interior. The square-sided pews were still in place and faced a small simple pulpit on a wide plinth at the far end. In the centre, a passageway led to the large oak door that had confronted them when they had first arrived. It was clearly unused – dirty, unkempt and full of echoes. They moved across the building to the far side, which would have a view of the telephone box. Dusk was beginning to reduce the light and they needed to check what they could see before darkness fell. Franks jumped onto one of the pews and looked out of the middle window, but the view was obscured by a hedge and brambles.

There was a segment of glass missing in the next window, nearest the pulpit, and by moving another pew slightly closer and standing on the seat, Kenny could see the top of the box. Franks joined him. If they could push down a few of the brambles overhanging the perimeter fence they would probably be able to see the entire structure. Franks went outside and began pulling down the highest brambles to improve the view. He returned to the window where Kenny was standing.

"OK?"

"Yeah. Fine. Really good. Can you go down to the TK so I can see what I can see and then walk down the road slightly?"

Franks did as he was asked and then looked up at the chapel and the window being used by Kenny. He couldn't see Kenny and the missing windowpane was unobtrusive; the OP was safe. He waited for Kenny to join him.

"OK?"

"Yep, really good, I can see the entire box and the lane leading up to it, but I can't see the area immediately left or right." Then he added, "But I think it'll be fine." They walked back towards the harbour, passing the village church on the right. The early evening mist was settling on the village and after wandering around the quayside they fell into the shop that doubled as a post office. The doorbell announced their arrival and they quietly found what they were looking for – toothpaste, some chocolate and a large-scale OS map.

An elderly lady was in the post office cubicle and came out to serve them.

"That's all, is it?"

"Yes, thanks," replied Franks.

She tallied up the money. "That'll be eleven pounds eighty-five pence, thank you." He handed her nearly the exact money.

"You're from outside, aren't you? I'm sorry the weather's not better!" She opened the till and scooped out the change.

Kenny and Franks expected inquisitive questions. "Thank you, we'll be fine."

"Are you walking?"

"Yes, just doing a bit of the coastal path, we'll be here for a couple of days."

"OK, well, have a good time." She carried on with her calculations and paperwork in the little cubicle that was the post office.

They left the shop and the door dinged once again. They wandered back to the pub and entered the cosy, friendly atmosphere. The fire had been stoked up and was now flickering pleasantly, bringing warmth and ambience to the room. It was becoming cold outside and they appreciated the feeling of homeliness. They slipped up to their rooms.

Franks was the first to the bar. He ordered a pint of bitter and, grabbing a newspaper from the rack, sat down on a comfortable settee facing the fire. He was joined later by Kenny, who had ordered the same drink. They agreed to take a walk early the next morning after breakfast to support their legend of being casual ramblers, but needed to return to the village by eleven thirty in order to cover the twelve noon deadline at the telephone box. If someone kept that appointment, they would attempt to maintain contact to house the individual.

A short while later, the landlady, whom they later discovered was called Peggy, brought some menus for them to peruse. They had a pleasant evening, kept their own company and avoided the rear bar, which was far busier and clearly filled with locals. They were keen to avoid answering any awkward questions as they still didn't know anything about the mysterious phone box visitor, who could well have been amongst the local group. They changed their breakfast time to seven a.m. and had an early night.

The following morning, after a solid cooked breakfast, they made their way out to the harbourside. They had already decided to take the path towards Moorworthy and trooped off towards 'Bullhead Point', the headland to the west of the village. The weather was fine, the wind had dropped and the sun was shining. They reached the cobbled path at the far end of the harbour and climbed steadily to the top, above the cliffs, and took a breather halfway up to look back at the village tucked into the cove. They could see the church and The Anchor pub from their vantage point, and when they reached the top they followed the path around the headland and steadily down to the next cove. The sea was calm and the tide was in when they passed through the inlet and then carried on upwards to the next headland, marked Devil's Head. When they had reached the rocky promontory they turned and headed back to the village, retracing their steps down into the little cove and back up towards 'Bullhead Point', reaching Poundscombe about twenty minutes before the deadline. By using the back alleys and run-throughs, they avoided the harbour, reached the parish church and carried on to the telephone box.

Kenny went straight to the chapel, slid under the rear door and hopped up onto the pew to peer out of the window with the broken pane. The gap in the undergrowth still provided a good view of the box. The time was eleven forty-five a.m.

Franks returned to the hotel and, complaining of an upset stomach, went to his room, which gave him a good view of the harbour. The weather had remained fine, with hardly any clouds in the sky as they settled down to watch. They would communicate by phone if the need arose.

Kenny had to concentrate on the telephone box, which was visible between two thick entanglements of brambles, but he knew that he only had to maintain that level for about twenty-five minutes – as long as they covered the critical time period. Time dragged. There was no-one in sight, no movement, no vehicles, no noise, no distractions whatsoever.

Franks settled into a chair at the window of his room. There were a few comings and goings – a Post Office van, some small boats entering the harbour using the high tide and the odd person walking around the outside wall.

Neither man had a description, not even a height or age; it would all depend on who, if anyone, went to the telephone box at about twelve noon.

Kenny looked at his watch. Eleven fifty-five and still no sign.

*Have I missed the person?* he thought.

*Has he changed his system? Has he been scared off by some other event? Has he picked up on the arrest of Patch?* These issues passed through his mind as he patiently waited, leaning on the wall, peering out of his three-inch squared hole.

He thought he had picked up some movement in the lane leading down to the village but he couldn't be sure because it was in his peripheral vision; he had no idea what movement, just movement.

The lane was so still and lacking any form of animation that he thought it could have been a bird. Then he saw further movement and a different colour present itself near the phone box – grey. That hadn't been there before, otherwise he would have noticed it. The colour moved – it was a person, just grey, no other features but he could only see their top half. The figure moved towards the box and pulled the door open and entered. Kenny checked the time – eleven fifty-eight. He could see it was a person with a grey top with the hood over his head, and no distinguishable features. He was wearing brown gloves and lifted the handset and then replaced it.

He tried to contact Franks. No reply. He tried again. No reply. The person remained in the box looking around and up to the chapel. He was of quite big build, but the hood was pulled well forward of his facial features so he was unable to see the person's nose, chin, eyes, hair or cheeks. He was still looking around, perhaps sensing danger.

Kenny tried Franks again – nothing. The time was twelve noon.

The clock ticked by. He considered altering his position to get a better view, but he risked alerting the stranger to his presence and losing him completely, because he would have to slide under the church door and come around to the front end of the chapel again, in which time he may have left and their quest would have failed. He tried Franks once more – nothing. It was two minutes past twelve. The door to the kiosk opened and the stranger removed his gloves, showing that he was white, and then ducked out of sight for a few seconds, put a small blue backpack over his shoulders and returned towards the village.

Kenny was out of the building and by so doing, lost sight of the person for a brief period. He passed through the chapel gate, around the bend where the box was positioned and down the lane towards the village. He tried Franks once again; this time he answered.

Kenny blurted out, "White male, big build, grey hoodie, small blue backpack, to you." The connection terminated.

Franks became more alert; although he could cover the whole harbour front, he had seen no-one fitting that description earlier and no-one had come into his view since the phone call.

Another phone call from Kenny. "Do you have him?"

"No."

"Well, he walked in your direction. I'm walking down the lane towards you." Call terminated.

At that moment, he saw the man again, still with his hood up, coming out of the lychgate of the parish church, carrying the blue backpack and with a dog, a coffee-coloured spaniel, alongside him. He closed the gate and continued into the village. He was about fifty metres ahead of Kenny, who phoned Franks.

"Been to the church, should be with you shortly," he whispered.

Still Franks could see no-one fitting that description. He didn't want to phone Kenny in case he was compromised. Within seconds he saw Kenny beneath him, having come from the direction of the church, but still no subject.

Kenny continued walking, glancing up at Franks in the room. Their eyes met but there was no other acknowledgment. He continued to the far side of the harbour and stood in front of a house that was for sale. At that instant, from his right and below him, Franks saw the person described by Kenny. He phoned Kenny, saw him bring his phone to his ear. "Contact, contact, directly below me." Call terminated.

He saw Kenny turn slightly and then his phone rang.

"That's him." The subject now had two full plastic carrier bags and was walking straight towards the harbour wall. He left one bag at the top of some railings, walked down some tight sea steps and then whistled for the dog to get into a boat that was moored at the base of the last step. He put the first bag in and then returned for the second, loosened the ropes, started the outboard engine and then whirred away into the harbour and towards the exit.

Franks phoned Kenny. "Do you see him?"

"Yes, grey RHIB."

Before the conversation had finished, the RHIB was out of the harbour entrance and between the headlands that squashed the village and harbour between them. The vessel had a low profile and was quickly lost from Kenny's sight, but Franks, who was in his room and therefore in a more elevated position, saw the RHIB go out to the open sea and then lean left and disappear behind 'Bullhead Point' and out of sight.

The two officers met at the harbour's edge. Aware that they may be being watched by inquisitive eyes, their body language was toned down and there was less animation in their voices.

They faced out to sea as they spoke. Kenny spoke first.

"That's a fucker then!"

"Mmm… but we now know he exists and that he's probably not local to the village. He can't have gone far, maybe a few miles. He went in a westerly direction," Franks said.

"OK, what have we got? He exists, came at the right time, white male, quite large build with a grey hoodie and blue backpack, and has a cocker spaniel. Uses a RHIB and probably lives close by."

"Been here for some time, knows the coast, owns a boat, knows the village and has a dog, all of which indicates some degree of stability and permanence. Where did he go between me losing him and you picking him up? He seemed to disappear, which was really odd," Franks added.

They strolled back to the pub and the post office and retraced the route he had taken from being last seen at the parish church, before being picked up at the harbour by Franks.

"He went somewhere, but where?"

"And why did he go to the parish church?" said Kenny.

"Did he have carrier bags with him when you saw him?" asked Franks.

"No," replied Kenny.

"So, between those two points he visited somewhere and picked up the bags. But where?"

"There are a number of options. He may have visited someone local, between the telephone box and the harbour, or may live close-by – there's a number of houses in the frame. Or he could possibly have left the bags at a place he knew and retrieved them before going back to the boat."

"And the churchyard?" Kenny said.

They wandered up to the church and entered through the lychgate. It was a small but well-tended with a higgledy-piggledy assortment of gravestones reflecting the occupants of the village over the last three hundred years. The church was locked and was surrounded by yews, hollies and ivy, but nothing that struck them as suspicious, or at the very least, out of place.

They left and returned to the harbourside. Franks loitered outside the post office and then joined Kenny.

"If he had gone into the post office, I wouldn't have seen him, it's set back from the road a little – and if he had entered straight away, I definitely wouldn't have seen him."

Kenny viewed the relative positions and agreed that that was a possibility. Normally they would have decided to speak to the shop owner/postmistress and risked exposure, but in this tight community it wouldn't be possible – it was far too risky.

The weather was turning. The wind buffeted the windows facing the harbour, the small fishing vessels began to agitate on their moorings and a light drizzle began to hit the faces of the detectives as they entered the front door of The Anchor.

"Good afternoon, gentlemen, I trust you've had a good morning. It's getting a little blustery out there. It'll be like that now for a day or two," Peggy declared.

They shook themselves down and welcomed the warmth of the fire and the comfort of the surroundings.

"Can I get you something?" she went on.

"A couple of pints of bitter, please." Kenny looked at Franks, who nodded. "Thanks."

The drinks were served and they took to reading the local papers. It was a lazy afternoon; the weather had shifted and they had sandwiches for lunch and then moped around until supper time. A few locals came and went and Franks, on a fruitless quest, went to see if the RHIB had returned to the harbour. After dinner, they went to bed early, a little downhearted by the lack of progress during the day.

The following morning they were up early, and after breakfast, set out to walk in the other direction, eastwards towards Black Rock. They climbed out of the village and up a steep path, past a couple of bench seats to the craggy end of the rock outcrop. They stopped and looked back. The weather had cleared a little allowing blue skies and a gentle coastal breeze. Poundscombe was far below them and in the distance they could see beyond the headlands, Moorworthy, about six miles away. They continued their stroll but again, eager to return for their noon deadline, they turned around and scrambled down to the harbour once more. It was eleven thirty.

Kenny wandered off to the chapel whilst Franks continued walking around the village and up to a small bench seat that overlooked the harbour and was just two hundred metres from 'Bullhead Point'. He took with him binoculars and from that point he could see any movement in the harbour and the quayside. He could also see the roof of the chapel and the churchyard, but not the telephone box. He continued his stroll to the rock outcrop of Bullhead promontory. If the suspect used a RHIB again, he could monitor its movement from the harbour in either direction, but particularly westwards, all the way to Moorworthy. He soaked in the view. He looked at his watch – it was eleven fifty.

His phone rang. It was Kenny.

"Good, I've got you. I'm in position. Nothing going on here. You?"

"No, all calm, no movement."

"OK, I'll give you a call if I have anything." The call was terminated.

Time passed. Eleven fifty-five came and went with nothing to report and silence from Kenny. Eleven fifty-eight, still nothing, no sign of any RHIB or indeed any person wearing a hoodie or holding a dog.

Twelve midday passed without event and at five past twelve the phone rang again.

"Yep?" he answered.

"Nothing here, all quiet, no-one at all. You?"

"No, nothing. Nothing in the harbour, nothing on the quayside."

"OK, I'll meet you at the post office at twenty-past."

"OK." The line went dead.

Franks walked down the slope towards the village. He looked ahead of him towards the quay as he walked.

*This bastard is going to be difficult,* he thought, *and we haven't got much time.*

In the meantime, Kenny jumped off the pew, slid under the rear door and walked down the lane towards the harbour.

They met in front of the post office, both a little disconsolate and feeling that having reached this far and been within touching distance of their goal, it would be tragic if the operation finished at this point, without a satisfactory conclusion. They were both feeling the pressure of time and cost. One of them needed to phone the boss to update him and see if they could extend their stay for at least another day. If he refused they would need to return home.

Kenny wandered back to the hotel whilst Franks made the phone call from a bench at the harbour's edge, ensuring he wasn't being overheard. After about ten minutes he re-joined Kenny in the bar and relayed the decision. "He agreed to an extension until Friday, but no more. If they hadn't detained the mystery man by then they would hand whatever intel they had over to Devon and Cornwall. It was on their patch and they'd look at him as a stand-alone target."

They agreed that he had been supportive and flexible throughout and understood the decision.

To cheer themselves up they ordered a cream tea for two and were merrily munching their way through the scones when Franks' phone rang. He answered it and told the caller to hold for a few seconds and walked outside. He returned to the pub for few minutes later and re-joined Kenny.

"That was forensics – an update. They've counted the cash in Purves' box, the dodgy one, 213 – sixty-seven thousand pounds and some euros, plus one kilo of crack cocaine in one bag that was separated into several hundred smaller ones." He looked down onto a scrap of paper where he had recorded the main points of the conversation.

"Two thousand-odd acid microdots, a quarter kilo of Billy Whizz. The two false passports both had Purves' photograph and showed some foreign travel. The bank documents related to Trenchard Properties, which was, if you remember, the company renting Box 213 – that appears to be a shell company. And I thought I'd keep the best part 'til last…"

"Go on," said Kenny.

"Purves' prints have been found inside the casing of Boxes 212 and 213, on the inside and outside of the doors and around both trays and flaps. In addition," he referred to his notes, "they were on the bag containing the cash, the bag containing the crack, on both monkey passports and on the Browning automatic, including the inner workings and the magazine. In effect, as the forensics guys said, everything was pretty much smothered in his dabs."

"Bloody hell! That's good. Nothing on Warden?"

"Oh yes, sorry, I forgot." He looked at his list again. "His prints were also on the bag of cash in Box 213 – just a couple, I think, but a nice touch nevertheless."

They continued scoffing their scones and supping the tea and the conversation turned back to the mysterious man. They agreed to follow the same routine, the next day, with Kenny in the OP and Franks up on the hillside to the west of the village. They finished their tea, remained in the lounge and tried to avoid too many prying questions from Peggy or her husband, Reg. Night fell and they adjourned for the evening.

In the morning, they prepared themselves for what was to be their last attempt to ensnare their man. It was squally, wet and miserable and they didn't venture any further than the post office midway through the morning to buy some newspapers before returning to the pub.

Later, they checked their phones and left the building. The weather hadn't changed as Kenny made his way to the chapel whilst Franks clambered up, against the driving rain, towards 'Bullhead Point'. His head was down and his hood was billowing with every gust. The track was difficult; steps had been added, but the surface was still muddy and slippery. He paused halfway up and turned around to look at the village; it was shrouded in driving rain and he could barely make out the church or The Anchor inn. He turned to continue his climb when he saw some movement ahead of him. He stopped. It was a cocker spaniel, an orange roan, wagging its tail and eager for attention. Franks bent down to stroke it but after a few seconds it trotted on down the hill towards the village. He stood upright again and glimpsed a person following the dog. As the track was narrow, he stood to one side to let the person past, a large man in a red waterproof with the hood up. On his back he was carrying a blue rucksack.

*Is that our man?* Franks pondered.

It was difficult to identify him as he passed Franks on the harbour side with his head down and continued walking down the slope with the dog lolloping about twenty metres ahead of him. Franks watched him go; he didn't turn around nor did he slacken his pace.

A little bit further on, he saw a bench off to one side. He sat down and looked back. He could see that the man had nearly reached the harbour's edge.

He called Kenny, sheltering the phone inside his hood. "You in situ?"

"Yep."

"I think I've just seen our man, on foot, walking down towards the harbour from my side, 'Bullhead Point', with the dog and blue backpack, wearing a red waterproof, hood up." Silence.

"Hang on, I'll call you back." Franks retrieved his binoculars and focused on the man in the red anorak. The dog was now on the lead as he moved across the harbour in front of The Anchor, and after tying the dog to the outside railings, he went into the post office.

He phoned Kenny again.

"He's in the post office, I'll let you know when he exits." There was no response.

"Are you there?"

"Yep, got that," Kenny whispered. "This place is really echoey, I'm trying to keep the noise down."

"OK." Franks finished the call.

He remained on the bench watching the front door of the post office. Rain came in lumps and the wind gusted, making it difficult to remain still and focus the binoculars; the distance was perhaps a thousand metres and he was trying to keep the lenses clear of water.

After about ten to fifteen minutes, the man emerged, untethered his dog and turned immediately right and out of sight. Franks phoned Kenny once more. "To you, red waterproof, hood up, blue backpack." Silence and call ended.

Kenny was waiting in the chapel. The rain had been hitting the large thin windows and the wind was billowing around the old building, making it difficult to hear the phone ring and any conversation. The mystery man was on his way.

After a short while he saw him, the man in the red top, walking up the lane. He paused by the telephone box, looked around and then put on his brown gloves. He entered the box, lifted the receiver and then replaced it. He checked the time; it was twelve midday.

The man loitered in the box for a few minutes, probably pleased to be out of the rain, and then opened the door and left.

He phoned Franks. "Been in TK. Now out and recip, back to you."

No response necessary. Franks brought the binoculars up. He couldn't see the person but had a view into the churchyard. He then saw the person in the anorak enter through the gate and move to the right, through the graves to the right-hand wall; he hovered there for a few seconds before returning to the road and walking back towards the harbour. He was then lost from sight before reappearing at the bottom of the lane and turning immediately left, and after tethering the dog once more, he re-entered the post office.

Franks phoned Kenny, who had already slid beneath the chapel doors and was in the grounds. Against the squall and the buffeting wind he managed to shout, "He's in the post office, stay where you are, I've got it covered, I'll call when he moves." No response, call ended.

Franks by this stage was thoroughly soaked through from his head to his boots and he wasn't looking forward to moving, but move he must once the person re-appeared.

Whilst he was waiting, he formulated a plan. He didn't want to risk encountering the person again so he needed to keep ahead of him and his dog, observe him from a distance and try to establish where he went after turning 'Bullhead Point'. He would wait ahead of him, above the path at 'Devil's Head', the next headland. From there he would be able to see him come around the far side of Bullhead from Poundscombe and down into the next valley, and then around his position and on towards Moorworthy, where, hopefully, he could then follow him at a discreet distance.

He waited. The man came out of the post office, collected the dog and turned left, retracing his steps towards Franks' position. He phoned Kenny.

"OK, he's out of PO and turned left towards me. Do not phone me."

"OK, be careful." Franks moved immediately. He put the

bins back in his inside pocket, stood up and felt the water running down his legs and back, his boots squelched. He headed around Bullhead and down the other side, over a small stream, past a small cottage and up the far side towards 'Devil's Head'. He had about five or ten minutes to find a good location where he could see the person and the path, whilst keeping out of sight and avoiding any attention from the dog. He left the path and climbed upwards through the bracken, gorse and ferns.

He found an ideal spot about thirty metres above the coastal path, near the top of 'Devil's Head', but below the skyline so that he wouldn't be profiled, and where he could see the path leading down his side of Bullhead into the cove and then up the other side towards him. He rearranged some ferns so that only his head would be showing. When the man passed in front of his position he would be able to keep him in view from the same spot as he rounded the headland and then, when it was safe to do so, he could clamber down on to the other side of 'Devil's Head', out of his view, and follow him at a distance of a couple of hundred metres or so as he moved towards Moorworthy, and then call Kenny through to assist.

Water was running down his face and he was constantly wiping his eyes to clear his vision, and his hands were cold and wet, but he found that by remaining still, keeping out of the wind, minimising movement and using body heat, he was able to maintain some warmth around his body by heating the water that had settled between his skin and his clothes. A few minutes later, he saw a stooping red figure come slowly round the point on the other side of the small cove and down the path on the far side. Franks very slowly cleared the water from his eyes. The man was still carrying the blue backpack and two carrier bags.

He stopped halfway down, as if he had heard something, the dog behind him. The man looked around, his body still but his head moving gently from side to side. He didn't move, looking back up to the headland he'd just passed. The clock ticked slowly and Franks held his breath, trying to remain still against the wind but determined to keep him in view. After about thirty seconds, seemingly satisfied, the man continued his walk and reached the cove, where he crossed a stream vigorously spewing out water onto the rocky shoreline. Once again, he stopped, looking around and out to sea. The dog had gone ahead of him and bounded up a small footpath to the cottage; the man followed and, unlocking the door, allowed the dog in and then entered. A light flickered from within. Franks stayed where he was and could see movement and shadows inside the building.

He phoned Kenny and whispered, "Don't move, don't phone, I'm OK, give me half an hour." Franks thought he must have remained there for about thirty minutes before moving. The wind and lashing rain were unrelenting as he focused on the tiny cottage and its small cove. The man was clearly careful; he'd twice checked that he wasn't being followed, or maybe he had heard something out of the ordinary, but having got this far, Franks wanted him to settle in, relax, dry out. He was determined not to be hasty and spook him. The wind gusted and the rain walloped across the small cove towards the cottage.

He phoned Kenny. Keeping the phone tight to his ear and hoping it still worked, he said, "Everything good. Stay where you are, I'll be back in about twenty. No calls. Got that?"

"Yep." The call ended.

It was mid-afternoon. There were no other walkers, no boats out at sea, and he decided to move. He slid down to the path below him on the opposite side of 'Devil's Head' from the cottage, and having re-joined it, he back-tracked and headed in the direction of Poundscombe.

He knew he had to pass the cottage again, but this time from the opposite direction that the man had taken. He was going to take it very carefully, but if challenged he would say that he was walking from Moorworthy to Poundscombe. He slowed down as he approached. The light was on but there was no sound. Smoke darted from the chimney. He looked to his left into the rocky cove and there was the grey RHIB, pulled up, slightly hidden by the rock overhang at the top of the scree slope. The engine had been removed.

He glided past, his boots splodging as he climbed the far slope. Avoiding the temptation to look around, he turned the headland and carried on down the path into Poundscombe, where he met Kenny sitting on the harbour wall. They walked back to The Anchor, entered and went straight up to their rooms.

Kenny allowed Franks some time to shower and change – he looked cold and soaked through. About twenty minutes later he knocked on his door and entered. He looked cleaner and warmer and was now in dry clothes.

"So?" said Kenny.

"Straightforward really. Didn't get a look at his face but his house is the cottage in the cove on the other side of 'Bullhead Point'. The grey RHIB was in the cove. After the second visit to the post office he walked straight there. I gave him about thirty minutes in case he was just visiting, but the dog knew where he was going and the RHIB clinched it."

"So, who is he?" asked Kenny.

"Absolutely no idea, but..." he unfolded his 1:25 OS map, "...he's living there." He pointed to the cove and read it out. "Southcott Mouth." He looked closely.

"Looks as if there are some outbuildings and a small track leading up to a minor road that runs parallel to the shoreline and about half a click inland. No other buildings, let alone houses anywhere near – very remote – difficult to work on."

Kenny fired up his iPad and via Google Earth focused down on the small cove.

"That's about it. Nothing much more than you've described. A couple of sheds. You can clearly see the coastal path going past the front door. But who the fuck is he?" Silence.

Franks continued, "We can hardly go to the locals and say, 'Oh! we need your help to raid this cottage, this is the address and we don't know his name, we don't know who's living there, no telephone number, no mobile and actually we know fuck all about him. We don't even know what he looks like.' Has he got pre-cons? Is he violent? The only connection we have with our operation is a contact number at a remote telephone box – no other information, intelligence, or indeed, evidence."

"We need to get things moving," said Kenny.

It was three o'clock. He phoned the intelligence team at Cloud Base Alpha and requested any information on anything or anyone with a connection with Southcott Mouth, north Cornwall – telephones, electricity supply, tax returns, anything before close of play. He then phoned the DI, updated him with the situation and asked that he check national records for any intelligence regarding drug supply of any importance in and around Poundscombe, Southcott Mouth or Moorworthy in the past three years. Any drug seizures, with or without arrests, suspicious activity – anything at all really.

There was nothing else for them to do really – just wait and see.

Within the hour, they had received a call from their intelligence cell. It was not good. There was no trace of anything at Southcott Mouth, it may as well have not existed – electricity, gas, water, council tax, internet – nothing apart from some historical wreck references. They decided to get pissed, there was nothing else to do, so they went to the bar and ordered two pints of the local brew to start the evening.

The following morning they woke a little jaded and stuffed down breakfast. Kenny had been thinking about the way forward, particularly the problem of identification. He proposed a course of action to Franks.

"The post office might hold the key."

"How so?"

"Well, he won't have mail delivered will he? I mean, what postie is going to trudge all the way out to his place to deliver a postcard? He must pick up his mail from the corner shop here and we know he's visited when he's come into Poundscombe. So, the postmistress would know everything about him – how long he's been there, how often she sees him, how much mail he has, etc. She appeared really chatty and she would probably be more than happy to engage in conversation. It was quiet, few customers, and it would be interesting to have a chat away from counting stamps."

"So how are you going to engineer that?" Franks said, sceptically.

"It's something we don't do enough of, local knowledge and simply talking to people."

"Yeah, but how?"

"Dogs. He had a dog." Franks looked doubtful. "What do we have to lose?"

"Nothing, I suppose. Game plan?"

"Let me go first, give me five minutes and then come in. I'll take the lead, you just follow the cue."

"OK." But Franks still remained doubtful.

After breakfast, Kenny went around to the store and entered to the dingly bell. The postmistress looked up. "Hello, dear."

"Good morning." Kenny had it in mind to browse in the shop and pick some items randomly – a chocolate bar, a postcard, and a small chewy dog bone. He placed the items on the counter.

"Will that be all, dear?" She looked at him, her left hand on the till and right hand poised to hammer the buttons.

"Yes, thanks."

"A bit chilly out there this time of year," she added.

"Yes, but it's lovely today." As she reached for the bone, he asked whether she had any other dog edibles.

"I'm afraid not, we don't get many dog owners coming in here, they would normally go to the supermarket."

"We're returning today but it's a treat for my dog at home, he's always looking for something when I walk in the door."

"I know, our dog died a few years back, thirteen years old, a Labrador. We didn't replace him; he was irreplaceable really."

"Ours is a cocker spaniel."

"Oh right." She had finished totalling the bill. "Anything else?"

"I don't think so, not at the moment, thank you." That would give him the option of adding an item later if the conversation progressed and he needed more time, or alternatively, if it started to grind to a halt and he needed more time to develop the relationship.

"That'll be three pounds sixty-three, please."

He fumbled around in his pocket. As he was doing so, he said, "In fact, I saw an almost identical cocker spaniel at the door here yesterday. I said hello but I didn't know its name."

"That'll probably be George. Lovely dog, very friendly. You were lucky to see him, he only comes here occasionally."

"A tourist like us?" he laughed. He found the money and handed it over.

"Oh no, he's been brought up here, he knows the area well. He lives over at Southcott Mouth." She pointed up towards the west.

"Ah yes, I walked past there yesterday or the day before, the other side of Bullhead Point."

"That's it, a little cottage. His owner, Mr Tompkins, has owned that for a little while now, keeps himself to himself, but the dog is lovely and he brings him when he picks up his mail and groceries."

The shop remained empty. She was perfectly happy to gossip with Kenny. He sensed he needed a little more time.

"I tell you what. I'll have a bar of your Kendal Mint Cake, that'll help us on our way."

She stretched across, and lifted the bar. "Four pounds fifty, please."

Again, he scrabbled around and presented a fiver. "Funny that. I knew a bloke called Tompkins, he moved down here… gosh, fifteen years ago. It won't be the same bloke, but it's a small world."

She nodded. The door opened and Franks entered to a loud ringing of the bell. "Hello, mate, sorry I've been a bit longer than I thought," said Kenny.

"What's the name of that bloke who moved down here? You know, big chap, worked in the office?"

Franks looked blank. "Surname Tompkins," Kenny prompted.

"Don't know, can't remember," replied Franks.

"God, that is so annoying, it's on the tip of my tongue."

"Well, he has an unusual Christian name, you wouldn't forget it," she replied.

Kenny looked at her.

"Brumber," she replied.

"Brumber Tompkins… no, that wasn't him."

"He used to be a banker and moved here when he split with his wife," she added.

"No," said Kenny, "definitely not him, my Tompkins was in insurance. Anyway, lovely chatting to you. Have a lovely day." As a gesture, he put a one-pound coin in the RNLI box.

"Thanks," she said. "Have a nice day. See you around." She returned to her duties.

Kenny and Franks left the shop and walked around the harbour.

"In case you didn't catch everything, his name is Brumber Tompkins, he bought the cottage at Southcott Mouth about ten years ago, ex-banker, divorced or separated from his wife. Dog is called George. A bit of a loner, collects his mail and groceries from the shop, doesn't appear to have a set routine."

"OK," said Franks. "I want to go and have a look at the graves in that churchyard. He's been in there twice now."

As they were walking through the village, Kenny was speaking to the intelligence cell and asking them to do checks on Brumber Tompkins. He didn't have a date of birth but his strange Christian name would undoubtedly narrow the field. They promised to call back.

When they reached the churchyard, Franks went over to the right-hand side where he had seen the man walk. A number of gravestones followed the lines of the ancient wall. Several were leaning, others were upright by the wall.

"He came up onto the right-hand side here. But I can't see anything." There was nothing out of the ordinary and no signs of digging.

"May have been a dead letter box – a way of dropping off or picking up that protects both parties and is reasonably secure," suggested Kenny.

His phone rang. It was the intel cell.

"Your Brumber Tompkins. One conviction for breach of the peace twenty-three years ago – brawl outside a pub in Chiswick. Fined twenty pounds. Six feet two and a half, large build, no tattoos, date of birth 06.02.63, had his occupation then as a student. Looks like he got into an argument with someone over a girl and lumped him." Kenny was writing as he was being told.

"That's great, thanks a lot." Kenny immediately phoned the forensics team and asked them to compare Tompkin's prints against any outstanding marks.

They returned to the hotel to plan their next move; they had only received authority to work on the operation until the end of the week but things had moved forward and they needed to approach the DI.

Franks phoned him. He was in a relaxed mood. He updated him of the developments and requested permission to extend the operation for a couple more days, explaining that their game plan was to arrest Tompkins and search his cottage with help from a local team. The DI hesitated but then told him that he had received information on some non-attributable drug seizures in the vicinity of Poundscombe and Moorworthy that might be connected. Three years ago, a bale of drugs was washed ashore in the cove between 'Devil's Head' and Moorworthy. It had been stormy and it was generally thought that gale force winds had washed the consignment overboard from a passing vessel. It was reported by a person walking the coastal path the day after the storm. It was ten kilos of cocaine in a watertight vacuum-wrapped container. It appeared that it had been attached to something because a frayed blue nylon rope was found dangling at one end. It was weighted, ensuring that it didn't float. Customs made the seizure, photos were taken, but the package had since been destroyed.

The second event happened about a year ago. Fishermen dragged up a second package about a kilometre offshore, attached by a rope to a buoy. They brought it in and informed the police. This one was about five kilos. No-one was arrested and as it wasn't evidence, it too was destroyed.

The DI continued. "So, I'll give you sufficient time to arrest your man, search his house and interview him. But that will be the end of this operation – no more arrests or searches.

You've done well. Call it a day with Tompkins. And keep me updated – I'm being asked questions, as well you know."

Franks thanked him and assured him he would call him.

As a passing shot, the DI said, "Give Pete Lee a call; he's the DI in charge of the drugs team down there. I know him well, we've done a couple of courses together and a joint op last year. He'll be able to help you. I think he's in Launceston."

Franks thanked him, updated Kenny and then phoned DI Lee and arranged to meet him in Launceston at lunchtime. It was now eleven thirty.

They'd agreed that Franks would cover the meeting with the local team, whilst Kenny continued the vigil on the telephone box from the derelict chapel.

They reserved their rooms for a further two days.

Franks met Pete Lee in his office. He related the facts of the case to him and their connection with Brumber Tompkins and Poundscombe.

He was diligently taking notes throughout and then called through one of his DSs to find out if they had any intelligence on Tompkins. He asked what he wanted and suggested to him that a small team of three would suffice – it was only a small cottage – and a search warrant for the premises and grounds. He then asked what his plan was, something that Kenny and Franks hadn't actually discussed in detail.

Franks explained that there were four options, all of which were made particularly difficult because of the remoteness of the cottage and the closeness of the community. The first option was to simply raid the cottage. It would be extremely difficult to get the raiding party sufficiently close to ensure surprise and the dog may alert Tompkins of any movement or sound. The second, arrest him when leaving the cottage. The same difficulties arose, and keeping any raiding team in place and hidden for a prolonged period of time would be almost prohibitive. Three, arrest at the post office. However, it would be difficult to maintain observations and retain a covert team close enough to effect an arrest, and if an arrest was made the locals would know instantly but timings would be more manageable. Four, arrest at the phone box, evidentially the preferred alternative, being able to keep a strike team in the chapel for the short critical period necessary but also to keep them out of mainstream village life, and it would be easier to control the subject once he was in the TK.

Lee and Franks both preferred the fourth option, evidentially and tactically. Lee arranged for a team of three to meet the two detectives in the chapel at eleven thirty a.m. the next day, with a search warrant, which would include the cottage and surrounding buildings on the same land.

In order to maintain the integrity of the operation, Franks suggested that they park away from the village and walk to the chapel separately. He gave him directions and instructions on how to enter the building.

They were given the names of the officers and exchanged mobile numbers.

Before they left, the DS tasked with finding out whether there was any local intelligence on Tompkins returned. There was nothing recorded under the name or address.

The meeting finished. The DI wished him well and Franks returned to Poundscombe, where he met Kenny. His observation of the telephone box was fruitless; no-one came near it during the period he was there. It was early evening and the rear bar of the pub was more animated than usual, but they stayed at the front, had something to eat and went to bed.

# 16

# THE RED BOX

The following morning was squally, the wind drove in from the sea and great wafts of spray shivered against the windows of the small pub.

The two detectives breakfasted together. They quietly discussed the forthcoming operation but both sensed an increased tension in each other and were approaching the morning with some apprehension.

They ventured outside and agreed that it would be unlikely that Tompkins would use his RHIB. The sea was choppy and unkind, and it was probably too dangerous to navigate around the headland. He would walk, if he was coming. They strolled along the harbour wall, watching the waves battering the boats moored in the lee of the wall. There was no sign of life but, reassuringly, the little shop was open, there didn't appear to be any customers inside but they could see Nancy moving around. Only the orange lights from the pub glistened on the cobblestones leading up to the harbour edge.

Today was the only day they had to catch Tompkins if they wished to bring this inquiry to a close and perhaps use it as a launching pad for further investigation. If he didn't appear, they had already decided that they would execute a search warrant on the cottage anyway and hope to find further evidence to link him to the drug distribution network.

After a short stroll they returned to the pub to dry off and soak in the warmth and comfort of the roaring fire. They read the morning papers over a pot of steaming coffee that Peggy had brought through to them.

At about eleven, they returned to their rooms and then made the final preparations for the operation that morning – phones charged, binoculars in pockets. Within fifteen minutes they were out and into the midst of the blustery weather. Franks cut right around the harbour's edge and then started climbing up a narrow passage towards 'Black Rock' on the opposite side of the harbour from 'Bullhead Point' and Tompkins' cottage. Kenny turned right and away from the harbour, inland and in the direction of the church and the chapel.

As Franks reached the top of the headland, he suddenly faced the full force of the incoming wind, it was stronger, fiercer and, with no natural barriers, was whipping up the spray peppering the rocks below. He looked down. He had come too far around the headland; he couldn't quite see the harbour, but could make out the small path as it tiptoed its way down the gentle slope of 'Bullhead Point' towards the village on the far side of the bay. At the head of the point, where the cliffs met the sea head on, huge waves were hurling themselves against the weary rocks before being thrown back whence they came.

He moved away from the headland and back down the path towards the village; it was less exposed, quieter and it gave him a view of the entire harbour and village. He sat down in a small natural hollow at the side of the path that reminded him of an armchair in the way it moulded around his entire body and gave him added protection from the wind and noise. He scanned the area before him: harbour, post office, pub and the path up to Bullhead. If Tompkins walked from his cottage to the village this morning, he would see him descend from the far headland beyond the harbour and into the village, and this would allow him ample time to warn Kenny of his arrival.

Kenny wandered up towards the chapel without seeing anyone on the way. He passed the church and followed the trail past the telephone box and up to the OP. Once again he slid under the door and took up his position on a pew against the far wall. He peered out and was reassured that he could still see the telephone box and part of the road as it left the back end of the village. He looked at his watch. It was eleven twenty in the morning.

He phoned his mate. He answered. Kenny could hear the wind thumping in the background. Comms were good.

Within five minutes, he saw a tall languid figure walking up towards the chapel and then he heard the crack of broken sticks and the sound of waterproofs against undergrowth as someone waded through the vegetation at the rear of the building and then pulled themselves head-first under the door and into the relative shelter of the chapel. It was the first of the local team. He introduced himself and told Kenny that his two colleagues would be arriving shortly. Kenny showed him the view from the window and the relative position of the TK to them.

The others arrived shortly afterwards and Kenny once again showed them his view from the window and the relativity of the two positions. He stressed that if an arrest was made, only the minimum force was to be used to suppress the prisoner; there was to be no shouting or talking apart from the arrest procedure. It was to be conducted in a quiet, efficient manner. He didn't want to attract local interest. Everything was set. Kenny phoned Franks and told him that the team was complete. It just needed the actor to step onto the stage.

Franks strained to see the far headland through the mist caused by the spray, his view sometimes temporarily blocked by an incoming wedge of grey. Time was creeping forward. He looked down at the harbour, the vessels moored in the lee of the two granite outcrops and the dark angular shape of the village and harbour. Nothing stirred. He couldn't see any human activity and no-one passed him on the path about a metre or so in front of his armchair. Occasionally, he pulled his hand down over his wet face to clear the build-up of moisture on his eyes and eyebrows.

There was still no movement, but then he noted a small figure on the path on the other side of the harbour. He brought his binoculars up to his eyes and focused. Too blurred. He cleaned the lenses with his handkerchief and then wiped his eyes and brought the binoculars up once more. He could see nothing, but by removing them once more and using direct sight he once again saw the figure. Immediately he refocused with the binoculars where he had seen the figure. It was a dog! Same shape, same colouring as Tompkins' dog. But where was the man? He scanned the path. Nothing. The dog lolloped down the path, half trotting, half walking, occasionally stopping to smell something, but not looking behind him. And then, there, about fifty yards behind came another large, slightly stooping figure. Franks once again focused on the larger figure. *That looks good,* he thought, *red waterproof, blue backpack, hood up.* He phoned Kenny.

"Possible contact, walking down from Bullhead with the dog. Red waterproof, blue backpack, hooded. Will confirm." Kenny didn't reply but passed the update to the guys in the chapel, and the call ended.

The figure continued down the path until he reached the edge of the harbour, where he joined the dog, who had already stopped and put the lead on. He continued walking across the front of the harbour, stopping occasionally to look at the boats and out to sea, but always closing the gap with Franks.

When he reached the shop he stopped, patted the dog and tied him to the railings at the entrance, and entered.

Franks once again phoned Kenny.

"Almost certain it's our man, in shop, dog outside. Wait for update."

Again, no response and the call ended. It began to rain heavily. The mist had closed in, he was still able to see the entrance to the shop but the opposing headland was now shrouded in grey and this would make observation of the far headland very difficult, if not impossible. He was still quite sheltered and protected in his armchair. No-one had passed and he was intent on concentrating on the doorway that was some distance below him. Someone else, an elderly man, entered and was lost from view. Rain began lashing against his waterproof and particularly the hood, pushing it occasionally over his right eye. Time passed. Franks waited; the dog waited.

It was eleven fifty-five. Franks saw the door of the shop open and Tompkins emerged, and for the first time he saw his head briefly before the hood was drawn over again. He patted the dog, but leaving him there, he strolled around the corner towards the church and chapel. Franks phoned Kenny. "To you. No dog." The call finished.

Franks rose, shook himself down and walked down the path towards the village.

"He's on his way," Kenny turned around and loudly whispered to the three detectives who were sitting on the pew behind him.

They began zipping themselves up and jamming beanies onto their heads in preparation for braving the elements once again.

Kenny waited. Nothing. He could feel the tenseness in the chapel as the local team stood waiting for the order to move. He waited. Still nothing.

Then his phone rang. It was Franks. "He's returned to the shop," he shouted. Kenny could hear the rain lashing against his friend's hood.

"He's unhooking the dog, not entering the shop, heading back to you, with the dog." The call ended.

Kenny relayed this to the waiting team. "He's gone back to get his mutt!" he said, in a rather exasperated voice.

Silence descended once again and the tenseness returned, then Kenny saw movement to his left side.

Without turning and intent on keeping his eye on the telephone box, he whispered, "Standby, standby, approaching TK. Red waterproof. Hood up." The three gathered by the exit door, ready to slide underneath once the command was given.

"At the TK, looking around, hold, hold." The three men were waiting for the command to strike.

"Hold. Still looking round."

"Into TK. Go, go, go!"

The three men slid under the door one after the other. The door shuddered and shook on its hinges, making what Kenny thought was a hugely uncharacteristic noise. Then he heard the thrashing as they ran through the waist-high undergrowth at the rear of the building to the gate, and then silence.

He maintained his view of the TK and hoped that Tompkins hadn't heard the noise. He saw him lift the receiver and then replace it, still looking around from the shelter of the box.

He looked at his watch; twelve noon exactly. He should be there for at least a couple of minutes, which would give the hit team plenty of time to move from the chapel to the box. The seconds passed. It seemed to take an inordinate amount of time.

He couldn't see the strike team running down the lane

in front of him towards the box – his view was blocked by undergrowth – but he did see the TK door open and the man being pulled backwards away from the receiver, his hood fell backwards and he was able to see the look of horror on his face as he looked to his right, automatically flinging his hands out to counter the backward movement. The dog barked intermittently as he reacted to the sudden movement, but satisfyingly there was no shouting and the minimum of fuss.

Kenny immediately phoned Franks.

"Potted. By the TK." He jumped down from the pew, eager to see what his quarry looked like, what he sounded like, what his reaction was and what he was carrying. He slid under the door and trotted towards the telephone box. He could see the three men standing over a figure dressed in a red anorak, face down and prone on the ground with his head to one side, his left cheek lying on the pavement. One of the team held the dog and was gently stroking him. Beside him lay the blue backpack. His hands were handcuffed behind him. Franks joined the little huddle from the other direction. The man had his head down, but Kenny could see that he was mid-forties, about six feet tall and quite stocky, with medium-length brown hair and a light stubble.

One of the three, the detective sergeant, said, "We've arrested him for conspiracy to supply controlled drugs, he's been cautioned and said nothing, cursory search – nothing on him apart from loose change, a couple of keys and some clothes in the kitbag. He hasn't said anything."

"What's your name?"

Tompkins looked up at him and said nothing. Kenny turned away and, as he did so, heard, "My name is Tompkins, Brumber Tompkins. Who are you?"

"Detective Constable Kenny. Drug Squad." He showed him his identification and Tompkins raised his head to get a better view and then looked up at the officer.

"Will you help me up?"

There had apparently been no resistance and this was a conciliatory tone from Tompkins. Kenny helped him up onto his feet. They lingered in the rain, no conversation, no movement, which fermented a slightly nervous and uncomfortable atmosphere in the little group following the last frantic minutes before the arrest and compounded by the fact that, of course, apart from the local lads, none of the party knew one another until Franks joined them.

Out of sight of Tompkins, Kenny winked at Franks. He had a feeling of elation but it was important to avoid any form of celebration in front of the prisoner; they still needed to interview him at some stage, and any friction from them that may cause anger, animosity or resentment on his part would probably reduce his level of co-operation in the future. They were also keen to avoid contact with the locals before they had searched the cottage; they were still unsure whether there had been any other collusion within the community and, anyway, wanted to carry on the enquiry without interruption. One of the local cars was brought to the top of the cul-de-sac and Tompkins' hands were repositioned to his front to make it easier to transport him. Tompkins, Franks, two local men and the dog drove out of the village and up to the road that ran parallel with the coast.

At Tompkins' direction, they took the high road, skirting above Poundscombe, and parked at a small layby shaded by some trees on the road above Southcott Mouth and then crossed the road to a small and well-hidden path that weaved its way down, around rock outcrops, small streams and ferns to Tompkins' cottage at the foot of the valley, where it opened onto the cove bordered by the coastal path that Franks and Kenny had walked along over the last couple of days. Franks opened the front door with the key that Tompkins had with him and entered the cottage.

Meanwhile, Kenny and the third detective went to the post office. They collected the shopping and the mail that Brumber had already put to one side, explaining that they were collecting it on his behalf. They began walking around the harbour's edge when Kenny realised he hadn't checked the churchyard. Tompkins always went to the churchyard after his visit to the telephone box, and Kenny wanted to check it before continuing to Southcott Mouth. He explained the situation to his colleague, and they returned together to the church, re-entering through the lychgate. Kenny made his way across to the right-hand wall. He walked along the graves backing onto it, checking each one in turn, front and back. As he reached the second gravestone from the end, the grave of Lillian Pitcairn, he noticed a small polythene bag wedged inside the recess between the back of the stone and the wall. He reached down and retrieved it. It was a small sealable bag that had been folded in half to further protect its contents. He was certain it hadn't been there when he and Franks had visited the church a few days earlier.

He held it up. It contained a small white piece of paper, on which there was some writing: *17th/1430 RED 4.* There was nothing else on the paper, but he was reluctant to open the bag to look at the inside section.

He read it out aloud two or three times, trying to make sense of it and interpret the meaning.

"What date is it today?" His colleague looked at his watch. "Seventeenth."

"Time?"

"Twelve forty."

"So that could mean today at two thirty, but what the bloody hell is 'Red' and 'Four'?"

He put it in his pocket as they continued to sweep through the churchyard and around the church. When they had finished, they continued to the cottage, walking along the coastal path round 'Bullhead Point'. The weather had calmed. A light breeze came into shore and the sea was quieter as they turned down towards the cottage.

# 17

# WHAT NEXT IN UTOPIA?

He rose early that morning and put the kettle on the stove before opening the front door. George ventured out to firtle in the undergrowth and, as he did so, Tompkins joined him, taking a couple of steps beyond the threshold to observe his domain. It was blustery out, the sea was angry and the wind encircled his face. He stretched out his arms, arched his back and sucked the salt-laden air into his lungs, surveyed the horizon and the rocky outcrops that wrapped around the cottage, glanced at George and then turned to look at the cottage. It was in his soul, his very being. He was comfortable in this environment and wanted for nothing more.

After lingering for a few minutes he turned around and re-entered the house, leaving the door open to allow the dog to enjoy his liberty a little longer. He prepared George's breakfast, refreshed his water and then poured himself a cup of tea before turning on the radio and putting a saucepan of milk on the stove, adding some porridge and then gently stirring in some sultanas and local honey.

When it was done, he went to the table and sat down, gently stirring the bowl's contents and blowing the surface. The dog wandered back in, gently sniffed his dog bowl, seemingly appreciative of the food but ignoring it, slurped some water and then curled up beneath Tompkins and brought his head to rest on one of his feet whilst gazing longingly at the open door and the distant horizon.

He knew that he needed to visit Poundscombe that morning. He hadn't been for a couple of days and he wanted to replenish his supplies and pick-up any mail that was waiting for him at the post office, give the dog a walk and then check the telephone box and the graveyard. He wanted for very little, his needs were minimal, but he enjoyed the walk and the occasional contact with the locals.

His mind meandered, recalling his past and smiling at events or situations that had influenced his life and thrown him in unexpected directions, those that had moulded his future and, inevitably, his current lifestyle. His halcyon days at university, parties, relationships, drugs, banking, money, marriage, property ownership, cars, divorce. Some rather worrying, others cringingly embarrassing, but in the main rewarding and challenging. He settled on his current situation, the world of drugs and his relationship with Purves, whom he had known since university. They had both studied Politics and Economics and were, literally, thrown together at a party one evening, when both vied for the attentions of a pretty girl. Each had objected to the other's presence and they eventually tumbled outside to settle the dispute with an alcohol-infused fight. It was a pathetic display of rutting, no real harm was done as neither wanted to get hurt and both desperately wanted to return to the fun. Somehow Tompkins managed to land a blow on Purves' left eye and he fell to the ground, a little dazed. He was about to get to his feet, albeit a little reluctantly, when a policeman arrived on the scene, and, sizing it up, arrested him for assault and carted him off to the local nick. There, in the urine-permeated cell, with the room spinning, he contemplated, in an alcoholic haze, his demise and realised how stupid he had been. He was charged the following morning with causing a breach of the peace, appeared before the Beak, and was fined. He accepted the punishment in good grace.

Once released and still feeling very hungover, hungry and a little dishevelled, he sought out Purves and found him, later that morning, still at the scene of the party, lying in a comatose state and surrounded by a sea of bottles, cans, glasses and discarded items of clothing. The girl had gone – fled the scene no doubt, not wanting to be the trophy of either drunken buffoon. He dragged him to his feet and supported him whilst they embraced, chuckled at his black eye and talked about the events of the previous night, and then went on a pub crawl.

They became close friends but eventually went their own ways, following separate career paths but maintaining contact with the occasional tenuous link, and hearing of the other's life changes through mutual friends. After some years, he heard that Purves had been arrested for drug dealing and was serving time, and as he was in London, he decided to visit him in prison. He found him in a depressed state and urged him to contact him when he was released. The prison visit had been a salutary experience for Tompkins and not one he wanted to repeat, it had stayed with him for some time and had reminded him of the overnight stay in the cell a few years before. He shuddered at the thought of the black metal grills, the pallid occupants, bare magnolia walls, locked doors, and the constant smell of boiled cabbage that permeated everything, even his clothes. When he left Purves and returned home, he showered and washed everything he had been wearing that day to rid himself of the clinging odour.

Several months later there was a knock on the door. He answered it and standing on the raised step was Richard Purves, looking a little pale and carrying a holdall. He ushered him inside.

He had just been released and had nowhere to go. They talked for most of the rest of that day over coffee and then in the evening, with a glass or two of wine and an ordered-in takeaway. He made up a bed and Purves stayed the night.

By that stage, Tompkins was finalising his divorce and needed to sell the house and move elsewhere. He felt that the Cornish coast looked appealing. Money, although not tight, was not as plentiful as it had been, and he was contemplating extracting himself from the banking world and living another life away from the financial core of London and the home counties.

It was clear to him that Purves wanted to continue trading in drugs; he explained that he had maintained some contacts and developed further links whilst in prison, which he was keen to explore and exploit, but insisted he would be more guarded, much more careful and a lot less gung-ho. He trusted Tompkins and told him that he intended to build a sterile corridor around himself, protecting himself and his business, but most importantly, to make enough serious money to maintain an un-precocious yet comfortable lifestyle.

The concept intrigued Tompkins. It came at a critical time in his life. He desperately needed a challenge and was attracted by the idea that Purves presented, which he considered low risk and high yield.

But would Purves offer him some small niche within the web he was developing in which to flourish?

The following morning, over breakfast, further discussion developed the subject and Purves outlined his idea of developing an overarching organisation that arranged the importation, distribution and supply of cocaine and/or heroin to the UK, through a tight, well organised team that involved very little physical or personal contact between the constituent parts. He explained that this would reduce the risks, as the product passed from one person to another, and that his plan would protect the people and organisation and reduce the chance of any outside interference. He also explained that minimising the number of people in the chain would protect the key movers from any likely interdiction from law enforcement and increase the potential yield.

Purves left later that day to re-establish his life and Tompkins continued with his plans.

A few months later, the house sold, he bought a small cottage and adjoining land on the north Cornish coast and with his dog, George, he moved down and started his life again. Before he left, he fielded a call from Purves and they met at a local pub. Purves had not been idle in the intervening period and put to him a simple proposition.

He had re-established contact with some good level suppliers in the United Kingdom and mainline distributors and importers on the continent, particularly Spain, and wanted to restrict the number of links or interlocutors between the point of entry and the distribution point in the United Kingdom to just two people, who would be firewalled against each other and outside parties by the use of breaks in the line of communication, using, in particular, dead letter boxes, telephone boxes and 'burner phones' that would be used to isolate the main players. Tompkins listened carefully. Purves had clearly been doing his homework and there was logic in his practical suggestions, but he wondered what role he envisaged him playing in this plan.

After a while, and sensing he had a receptive audience, Purves outlined what he thought his role would be. To simply monitor the delivery of the gear when it was dropped by boat off the coast, recover it, and warehouse it until a request was received to pass some or all of it up the distribution chain. Contact would be made by an agreed DLB with both sides of the chain and communication would be via public telephone at an agreed time on a daily basis. Calls would be made at the same time each day until answered by the recipient. If no calls were answered or made over, say, a seven-day period, then the link would be severed on the assumption that someone had been taken out of the chain. He listened carefully. He liked the idea, but particularly the safeguards, and told Purves that he would think about it and let him know his decision.

A couple of weeks later he phoned Purves and agreed with the proposed plan on the proviso that he could withdraw at any time, particularly when he had gathered sufficient funds for the purchase of more land surrounding his property from local famers, thereby protecting his smallholding against incursion.

They met and finalised plans and about a month later the first delivery was made by boat. It was relatively small quantities at first, but over time this steadily increased, using a DLB in the local churchyard and the isolated TK above the village. He never met the boat crew and, as far as he was aware, never saw the vessel, but he knew that it dropped the merchandise overboard just off the coast after leaving a message at the DLB that a delivery was to be made, detailing the time, date, place and quantity using one of the marked buoys out to sea, usually that day, or the following day.

When Purves required another consignment from the 'warehouse', he would telephone the TK at twelve midday each day until it was answered by Tompkins. He would tell him what he wanted and gave him an indication of when he would collect the package, and Tompkins would then leave it behind a gravestone DLB in the churchyard, in its place Purves left the payment. He presumed that Purves travelled by car or, occasionally, used public transport to break up the routine. The next day he would return to the church and collect the cash, and so it went on. He never knew how Purves made payment to the continental connection; he didn't ask, didn't want to know and, in reality, didn't need to know, but presumed once again that it was through a similar system using a DLB.

Once the system was in place, he had never met Purves again, and he had never received any calls from him, apart from the calls to the telephone box, when, during short conversations they were able to discuss any issues that had arisen, particularly prices and availability. They had maintained the 'sterile corridor' to ensure clear separation, protection for each other and the maintenance of security.

When he had finished his meal, he went out to the small cove with George, as he generally did after a stormy night, to collect flotsam and jetsam, wood for the stove and anything that had been thrown or lost overboard from passing vessels that he might find useful, like nets, buoys and rope.

He looked at his watch, it was nearing eleven o' clock and when he had gathered enough wood for his needs, he stashed what he had collected and returned indoors to collect his waterproof and backpack. He had decided that it was too choppy to take the RHIB, small rain drops had begun to patter against the window panes and, anyway, the dog needed the exercise. He decided to walk to the village. George, used to the routine by now, took a last noisy drink of water and they both ventured outside, and, after locking the door he made his way on foot to Poundscombe, with George bounding ahead up the gentle slope out of the cove. As he reached the headland he stopped, looked back and reminded himself of the beauty of the location, and then continued around 'Bullhead Point' and down the far slope towards the village. The dog had trotted ahead, more interested in the scents and smells of the path.

Once they had reached the edge of the village, he put his lead on and slowly made his way around the harbour's edge to the store and post office, and, leaving the dog tied to the railings outside, went inside. He had a quick chat with Nancy, bought a few provisions, collected his mail, and, after arranging to return a short while later, he left. George sat up at his reappearance at the front of the shop, but instead of grabbing his lead he walked past him and on, up towards the telephone box, but then had second thoughts and returned to collect him. He didn't want him to feel ignored and his keenly wagging tail told him he had made the right decision.

As he approached the telephone box, all was quiet; there was no-one about. The path and verges were damp from the sea mist and George dawdled as he picked up scents from the wet grass. When he reached the kiosk he put on his gloves and opened the door, and George sidled in and sat in a corner. The door pushed in behind him as he lifted the receiver and brought it to his ear; the gentle buzz confirmed it was still working and he replaced it on the hook. He looked at his watch. It was just eleven fifty-nine a.m. He waited as he had done so many times before and scanned the space in front of him – instructions, emergency numbers and a little graffiti. The capsule protected him from any noise, including the blustery wind. Silence.

The first thing he became aware of was the door opening behind him. He was immediately unbalanced and his body moved backwards through the gap. But then another force intervened and he felt arms around his torso and pressure pulling him back onto the pavement, an irresistible movement that he was unable to prevent. His vision blurred as he was turned slightly and forced, face first, onto the ground with his arms trapped behind his back, and he was aware of someone telling him he was police, showing him a card and telling him he was under arrest for drug trafficking. His hands were cuffed behind him as he felt someone searching his waterproof and trousers. He could hear George barking and saw him, from his prone position, leave the booth with his lead loose, come over, and sniff his right ear. He felt hands moving around his body and fingers exploring his pockets. He asked them who they were because he wanted confirmation that they were Old Bill. The ground was damp and he was uncomfortable and he asked to be lifted up so he could the see a group of men surrounding him. There was some conversation between them and he could feel a presence behind him, someone was holding the handcuffs behind his back; presently one of the cuffs was unlocked and his arms were moved to his front and his hands re-cuffed in a more comfortable position.

Within a few minutes he was ushered into the back of a car behind the front-seat passenger and was joined by another on the back seat. George was wedged into the front passenger footwell and they moved down into the village and then up behind the buildings onto the top road that ran parallel with the coast. They told him they were going to his cottage and he showed them the best place to park, in a small layby that lay directly above the valley that ran down to his house.

Everything was happening fairly rapidly; he had been with them for less than a quarter of an hour and the car journey had taken less than five minutes. The small group were immediately buffeted by the onshore wind as they crossed the road and he led the way down the overgrown entrance towards the cottage. They were now on his land and he had allowed the undergrowth to smother the track to deter walkers and trespassers. The wet ferns swept his legs as they carefully navigated down the steep slippery path and he took the opportunity to occasionally glance out towards the sea and the thin lines of surf. Ten minutes later they were at the front of his house and were more exposed to yet more gusts of wind that were funnelled into the cove. One of the men opened the door with the key and entered, and then pointed to the chair in which they wanted him to settle.

George joined him and lay at his feet, and after a short while they were joined by other men who had walked from the village, carrying his shopping and the mail that they had collected from the post office.

He was shown the search warrant for his premises that included all his land, the boats and the buildings, and was asked, only once, whether he had anything on his property that would be deemed illegal, including drugs and firearms. He made no reply.

From the moment he had been dragged backwards out of the telephone box, his mind had been working at a frantic pace, trying to logically answer the questions that he had spinning around in his head.

How much evidence did they have?

Why had some of the officers apparently come from so far away?

How did they even know of his existence?

What had happened to Purves? Had he been arrested as well?

How did they know about the telephone box and its significance? How long had they known about him?

Did they know about the Dead Letter Box? How thorough would the search be?

What were the likely consequences for him?

What about the house itself, George the dog and the property as a whole?

What about damage reduction?

He wondered how he could reduce the impact of these events on himself and his lifestyle. He had considered his position and quite quickly established that he had only three options. He could try and escape. Not feasible – he was handcuffed, there were five of them and where would he go?

Front it. Say nothing at all. Let them prove their case in a court of law. But presumably they had established a firm link with Purves, the telephone box and drug trafficking already, and if he failed to cooperate he could be digging a larger hole for himself.

Cooperate. If he decided to take this route, it would need to be total – there couldn't be any hidden corners and he would need to act promptly to take full advantage of this position in the future.

As he pondered these questions he looked around him. The group were searching methodically, systematically; they had started with the outside, skimming the ground for recently turned earth and had called for a dog to speed up the process. They were checking everything – tapping walls and floors for hidden cavities, checking the roof space, removing cupboards and electrical sockets. This was going to be a thorough search.

# 18

# THE NAUTICAL CONNECTION

When Kenny and the rest of the team arrived at the cottage, Tompkins was sitting, still handcuffed, in a chair in the lounge. As they entered the dog bounded towards him, tail wagging and seeking attention. He leant forward and stroked him on the nape of the neck before Tompkins tapped the side of the chair and the dog returned and curled into a ball next to him.

The inside of the cottage was small. It had thick granite walls, small windows, flagstone floors, a few rugs, and low ceilings. A small narrow staircase led to two bedrooms on the first floor. A wood-burning stove was gently glowing at the back of the living room. The sitting room was utilitarian but cosy. There were a few items on a bookcase with some paperbacks, a sofa, and a couple of loungers.

Kenny beckoned Franks to join him outside.

Franks confirmed that they had found nothing and Kenny showed him the note that he had found in the graveyard and he read it over, as Kenny had done, several times.

"What's it mean?" said Franks.

"Dunno." Then he added in a hushed voice, "But I think we need to be heads-up at 14.30hrs."

"But it could mean anything, anywhere."

"Yes, but think it through – we found it at what we believe to be a DLB, we think he checks the drop regularly, he's pretty static, not going to go very far, no mobile phone that we know of, and everything revolves around this place, so…" He paused. "The seventeenth is today, right, and fourteen thirty…" he looked at his watch, "…is in an hour and ten minutes. He hasn't seen the note, but we must assume that it's drugs-related. Something is going to happen somewhere close at two thirty. That will be either a drug drop, a money drop-off or a meet. The grave is probably being used as a DLB for messages only."

"But what is Red Four?" enquired Franks.

Kenny shrugged his shoulders, "Red could mean a specified meet point – you know, using a code, blue, green, yellow, etc – that each side have identified and can recognise."

"Four?" asked Franks.

"No idea. But let's suspend what we're doing at 14.00 and see what happens. It could be out at sea, or inland, so if we go to each headland, we can keep an eye open for any suspect movement or activity. But remember, he hasn't been to the DLB, we arrested him beforehand. If he had seen it he would have removed it and probably destroyed it, so he doesn't know about it."

They returned to the house. Tompkins was still sitting in the chair with his dog next to him. Kenny called the three local men out and explained to them the 14.00hrs game plan.

The search continued. Franks was impressed by the thoroughness of the local team. Nothing, it seemed, was left unchecked. A dog had arrived to check the adjoining land and any possible cavities, beneath and behind kitchen units, the bath, wardrobes. All the flagstones had been checked for resonance and the mortar for recent repair.

But throughout, Tompkins had remained calm, answering a few questions when necessary whilst stroking his dog. He was, Franks thought, confident that they wouldn't find anything incriminating.

The guys had gathered a few pieces of paper, mainly bank statements and stockbroker's notes, but no utility bills. Amongst the papers in one of the kitchen drawers, they found a second note: *27th/1100 BLUE 2*.

It confirmed to the detectives that the system had been used before, the coding was consistent and that it was probably something to do with drug supply.

At two o'clock, both detectives and one of the local team left the cottage. Tompkins watched the change in emphasis with interest and had allowed them to use his binoculars. Franks still had the pair that he had used earlier with him. The weather was pleasant with a light breeze and blue sky, completely different from earlier that day. Franks climbed to the top of 'Devil's Head'; visibility was good and he could see from Moorworthy to 'Bullhead Point'. Kenny, meanwhile, clambered up to Bullhead and had a view from 'Devil's Head' right around to Poundscombe Bay, Black Rock and beyond. The local chap went up the path behind the cottage to where the car had been left and could see the valley behind Southcott Mouth and the two headlands where Franks and Kenny were. When they were in position, they settled down to wait.

Out to sea were a few small fishing vessels and, on the horizon, two larger ships steaming towards the Bristol Channel. Kenny trained his bins on the smaller vessels. Most of them had fishermen with rod and line, but these were closer to the coast. The others, slightly bigger, were in effect small trawlers and he could see the nets draped over the sides of the hulls.

Franks looked at his watch. Two fifteen p.m. Still no unusual movement, no walkers on the coastal path and no-one in the bays. He could see one of the small trawlers edging closer to the coast, perhaps half or one mile out – light blue hull, white superstructure, red lid on the cabin. It had no nets out and no rods in view. He brought his bins up. No-one on deck. The vessel was heading for shore rather than plying parallel to it.

He phoned Kenny. "Do you see that blue and white trawler?"

"Yep."

"Heading for the coast. Keep your eye on it – no nets, no rods, no-one on deck."

"Might have finished for the day."

"But why then is it headed for the coast rather than a home port?"

The vessel came closer and started to pitch and yaw as it reduced speed. It then veered right and slowed. Both men were focused on it.

The vessel was wallowing as it turned at right angles to the shore and slowed. It was about half a mile off the coast when it appeared to stop and had positioned itself so that it was directly beside a buoy and between it and the shoreline, making it difficult to see any activity from the land. Two men emerged from the cabin and started pulling on a rope that was attached to it and when they reached the end, they pulled it onboard. They attached something to the end and then gently dropped it over the side, feeding out the rope until there was none left, then they returned to the cabin and the vessel moved away, heading out to sea again. In a few minutes, they were a distant object, just the light foam from their propeller visible behind them as they slowly disappeared from sight.

Franks looked at his watch – fourteen forty hours – and then across at Kenny. He saw him looking and pointed to the cottage and began walking down the slope. He met him on the small circular wall.

"What do you reckon?" said Kenny.

"Could be a lobster pot or something similar, but I suppose it could be a drop. No ID on the vessel. Right time," replied Franks.

"Can you use a RHIB?"

"Nope."

One of the local guys, who had some nautical knowledge, volunteered, and they pushed Tompkins' RHIB down onto the beach and out against the incoming waves. They collected the outboard motor, carried it down to the beach and clamped it onto the boat's stern. Kenny jumped in and they fired up the engine and headed out to the red buoy, the front of the boat slamming against the swell as they left the protection of the bay and went out into the open sea. It took them about ten minutes to reach it and manoeuvred up against the buoy. Kenny hauled in the rope that they had seen the men drop overboard, bringing a small bale onboard. They then unhooked the rope, flung it back in the water and returned to the cove, slamming the front of the RHIB up against the only sandy section.

Kenny carried the package away from the vessel and they then manhandled the RHIB back to its original position and removed the outboard engine. Without unwrapping the package, they examined it and estimated its weight as about five kilos. It was vacuum-wrapped in a green outer casing and appeared to be slightly weighted to ensure it sank below the surface.

"And?" Kenny shouted above the incoming waves.

"At a guess, about four kilos, probably coke, but maybe 'H'. Just as the note suggested. '17th 1430 Red 4'."

"A planned drop at about fourteen thirty hours on the seventeenth at the red buoy of four kilos. Probably a Spanish, French or perhaps Dutch vessel doing drops to order, well on its way back home now, I reckon. No name, no serial number," said Franks.

When they had beached the craft, Kenny and Franks lifted the package up to the cottage and placed it just inside the front door. Tompkins was in the same chair. He leant forward to look at it, then looked at them. He'd taken his decision; he knew then that the game was up.

"There's nothing in the house, you're wasting your time." His voice was deep and resonant and as he spoke he looked directly at Franks and Kenny.

"But you know we're going to look anyway."

"It's in the barn across the way; you've got the key."

"What's there?"

"I'll show you." He stood up and the dog stirred, eager to stay with his master.

"Why?" asked Kenny. "Why are you telling us this?"

"Because I have nothing to lose now. You'll find it eventually, so let's get it over and done with, eh?"

Standing up, he removed a key from the property they had gathered.

"That's the key," and handed it to Kenny.

One of the local officers held onto the bar linking the two cuffs that still held Tompkins hands together and the group made their way up the path to the outhouse. Kenny unlocked the wooden door and entered. They followed. It was roomy but was full of clutter, boxes, wood, old buoys and netting. He told them to clear the debris to one side and pointed to a space roughly in the middle.

"If you clear away the sail there and brush the earth to one side you'll find a slab of ply – move that," he explained. As they gently moved the dried sail and cleared the soil, the dust rose and they exposed a section of ply, about two feet square.

"Lift that," Tompkins instructed.

They removed the piece of wood and leant it against the

wall. Beneath was the upper face of a metal box, presumably a safe, that was embedded in concrete. In the middle was a keyhole covered by an escutcheon.

"Now, feel with your fingers over there," he pointed with both his handcuffed hands, "and you'll find a jam jar. The key for the safe is inside that." They scrabbled around trying to find the lid of the jar and eventually pulled it out. Undoing the lid, they removed a key from a polythene bag and tried it in the lock.

Two turns and the door of the safe was lifted on hinges. It was so jammed with polythene bags containing money and other unmarked paper bags that the contents lifted the lid slightly as it was opened.

"No-one touch anything," said Kenny. "Forensics please, photos and lifts!" he said with a voice of authority, looking at the local team.

He re-locked the safe, put the key in his pocket and then locked the main door and returned to the cottage with Tompkins and the rest of the team to complete the search.

An hour later, two forensic officers arrived, manhandling their kit down the path from the main road.

Kenny pointed them towards the outhouse and told them what he wanted – photos of the scene at each stage of the examination and a fingerprint search.

Light was starting to fade but they'd brought illumination; it was important to finish the forensic search and take Tompkins into safe custody before dark.

After returning from the outhouse, Tompkins had been returned to his chair and settled into an incommunicative, disinterested and morose state. His dog remained beside him, attentive and alert to any movement.

Sometime later, the house search was completed. Nothing further of interest was discovered but a large box of exhibits, mainly papers and documents, had been collected. The forensic team were halfway through the painstaking examination of the safe and its contents, and it was decided to take Tompkins to the nearest police station – Launceston – to book him in and formalise the procedure. The local team had one car in the lane above the cottage that was already partially loaded with exhibits, and a second round at Poundscombe. They had two choices: to walk or take the RHIB. They decided to walk, leaving the forensics team, who had their own transport, to finish at the address, and the exhibits officer to lumber up, with the exhibits, to the car parked on the upper road.

Tompkins, his coat draped over his shoulders, left the cottage. One of the local team held his handcuffs, whilst the other brought the dog up at the rear of the group.

Kenny and Franks carried nothing and walked ahead of the other three up the slope to Bullhead Point. Darkness began to cloak the area as they reached the top and although there was very little breeze, it was cold, and dusk drew in the icy tentacles of winter. The dog, still in familiar territory, sniffed, snortled, tugged and wee'd his way to the top, where they all paused.

Tompkins' head was bowed. He half turned and looked down at the cottage, his home for so many years, and then out to the sea with the sun melting behind the horizon. The dog came up and nestled against his calf. He crouched down and stroked him, and then brought one hand beneath the animal's chin, bringing his head up so that they looked eye to eye. The officer holding him stretched downwards in unison and, at that moment, Tompkins broke loose. From a hunched position he raced for the cliff, his shoulders rolling as he ran, his two arms tethered together. He gathered momentum as he reached the cliff edge, there was no hesitation, no second thoughts, no locking of the legs or backward movement – he launched himself into the vacant space beyond and disappeared from view, his coat wafting away to the right and becoming entangled on some heather. The dog immediately stood on all fours and tugged on his lead, the hold loosened and then worked free, sensing the freedom he ran forward, dragging the lead behind him to where Tompkins had been lost from view. As he reached the edge, as if he sensed the height of the drop, he hesitated and used his legs to slow his forward momentum. But his front legs lost traction at the very edge of the cliff where it was slippery and slimy from the wet weather. He looked back in desperation but slid sideways from view and out of sight.

The officers ran to the edge and peered over. Thirty metres down they saw Tompkins, his broken body lying face down on the jumble of rocks at the bottom at the water's edge, his hands clasped above his head. His dog lay beside him, his body slumped across a large, angular rock. The sea washed and lapped around their bodies, and gently moved Tompkins' legs and feet with the ebb and flow of the waves.

The officers were in shock for a few seconds. The local lads immediately contacted their control and then the RNLI, whilst Kenny and Franks ran back down the slope towards the cottage and then turned right along the bottom of the cliffs and scrabbled along the rocky shoreline, the tide was going out and it took some time to reach the two bodies. Kenny checked for signs of life – there were none. Tompkins' head had been smashed on the rock and was leaning at an awkward angle. They surmised that he had broken his neck. The dog's body was badly twisted, his back probably broken. Kenny undid the handcuffs from Tompkins' lacerated hands as the lifeboat loomed around the corner from the direction of Moorworthy.

It took several hours to remove the limp bodies from the foot of the cliffs, made easier by the receding tide. Tompkins' body was taken to Launceston mortuary, whilst the dog was recovered by the RSPCA.

Kenny, Franks and the other officers knew the consequences of a death in custody – an internal investigation by the IPCC, followed by an inquest that would determine the cause of death and the circumstances leading up to it.

They phoned their relevant line managers, updated them with the circumstances and then returned to the cottage. There was nothing more they could do; there was no obvious next of kin, no outside party involved, and no criminal culpability.

The forensic team finished their investigation and, after securing the property, they and the detectives left the cove. Kenny and Franks went with the local team to Launceston and then returned to The Anchor pub where they stayed for a final night.

In the morning they left their digs, avoiding questions from the Landlord, and drove across country to Launceston to tidy up that end of the investigation. Following a meeting with Pete Lee and the team that had accompanied them to Poundscombe, they went down to the forensic team in an annex away from the main building.

They told them that the package attached to the buoy that they dragged from the sea was four kilos of cocaine, and that the safe contained, she looked at her sheet, "One hundred and sixty-seven thousand, six hundred and seventy pounds in sterling; thirty-one thousand, one hundred in euros; about four hundred and fifty grams of crack and two kilos of cocaine. There was cocaine residue inside the safe and Tompkins' prints covered the interior and exterior. There were no other outstanding prints." This indicated, they both concluded, that Tompkins was the only person who had access to the safe. There was no third party.

After several months the internal investigation determined

that the officers were not culpable and that Tompkins had taken his own life.

Warden and Purves received lengthy prison terms. Purves never uttered a word.

The inquest was held at Launceston into Tompkins' death after the trial and the coroner recorded a verdict of suicide.

Some of Tompkins' assets were deemed the proceeds of drug trafficking and were forfeited, including the cash found in the safe. Following the sentencing the drugs were destroyed on the orders of the judge. His house and the surrounding land, in the absence of any relatives, were handed to the Crown, *bona vacantia*.

Kenny and Franks are false names. The officers continue to work at the forefront of drug enforcement.

# GLOSSARY

| | |
|---|---|
| Acid | Lysergic Acid Diethylamide 25/LSD |
| All about himself | Very aware, on edge, always looking around |
| Alpha | Surveillance person on foot |
| ATS | Automatic Traffic Signal |
| Bang to rights | Strong evidence against an individual |
| Billy Whizz | Amphetamine/Speed |
| Bins | Binoculars |
| Brief | Lawyer/Solicitor |
| Brown | Heroin |
| Clock/clocked | Seen/be seen |
| Cloud Base Alpha | Police Station/Office |
| Comms | Communication system |
| Cover | The type and number of obstacles or vehicles between the eyeball and the subject being followed |
| Crack | Cocaine without hydrochloride, in rock form |
| Cross system | Surveillance system – an easy method of establishing the location of units around a target located at the apex of the cross |

| | |
|---|---|
| Custody Officer | Police officer in charge of detainees whilst at a police station |
| DC | Detective Constable |
| DI | Detective Inspector |
| DS | Detective Sergeant |
| DLB/Dead Letter Box | A safe point of communication between two parties avoiding direct contact |
| Dollar Dealer | Street Dealer |
| Dope | Generally cannabis |
| Dope head | Long-term cannabis user |
| Drive past | Driving past a suspect, a vehicle or premises to establish the situation |
| Dry Cleaning | Method used to ensure that a person is not being followed or watched, by sterilising the area around them |
| Exhibits Officer | A person in charge of exhibits, normally in large or serious cases |
| Eyeball | In surveillance, the person who has sight of the suspect or their vehicle and is therefore in control of events |
| Gander | To look or glance at something |
| Go-be | A go-between, a person who acts as an intermediary between others |
| HA | Home address |
| Handler | A person who manages a source |
| Heads-up | Be alert |
| HUMINT | Intelligence from a human source |
| IC1 | White Male |
| I/D'd | Identified |
| In 1, 2 or 3 | Identifies the lane the subject vehicle is in on a dual carriageway or motorway |

| | |
|---|---|
| IO | Intelligence officer |
| Jobsworth | A deliberately obstructive person |
| Julie | Operation Julie – a police operation in the seventies that effectively removed LSD from the streets |
| Keyed in | Aware, locked in place |
| Kit | Equipment |
| Lay Gear On | Supply drugs without receiving payment, on the understanding that payment will be made later |
| Legit (*Lejit*) | Legitimate |
| Lifted | Arrested |
| MIR | Major Incident Room, set-up for a major incident such as a murder |
| MO | *Modus Operandi*/method/system |
| Monkey | False, not what it seems |
| Narky | Bad tempered or irritable person |
| Nick | Police station or prison |
| Ninja | Uniformed officers in protective equipment |
| Non-Desript | (in this context) A vehicle that doesn't stand out by colour, type or model |
| NSY | New Scotland Yard |
| Obs | Observation |
| On Original | During surveillance, following an interruption or stop, to confirm that the subject has moved off in the same direction he was going prior to the stop and that there has therefore been no change in direction |
| On Remand | In custody, awaiting trial |
| OP | Observation Point |
| Op Order | Operational order – details the |

| | |
|---|---|
| | operation, the information, intention, method to achieve the aim and the roles within it |
| Personal (in this context) | Drugs for 'personal use' only |
| PDX | Pedestrian Crossing |
| PH | Public house |
| Plotting | Placing Vehicles or People on a surveillance |
| PM | Post-Mortem |
| PNC | Police National Computer |
| Potting | Arresting |
| Pre-Cons | Previous Convictions |
| Propped up | Brought to notice |
| Punter | A person buying drugs |
| RA | Roundabout |
| Recip/Reciprocal | When a subject being followed in a vehicle or on foot has turned around and is re-tracing their steps, travelling back the way they have come |
| Relay | Method of enhancing communication between units by using a relay at a midway point |
| Remand | Suspect who is remanded in custody |
| Resto | Restaurant |
| RHIB | Rigid-Hulled Inflatable Boat |
| Roach End | The filter end of a spliff or joint that contained cannabis |
| Scam | A trick designed to deceive |
| Series of clicks | Used when the officer can't transmit verbally and wants to show that the subject he is watching is moving off |
| Shiv/shivved | Stab/stabbed |
| Shrapnel | Shell splinters but in this case, it |

| | |
|---|---|
| | relates to loose change |
| Sitrep | Situation Report, generally a verbal report on the current situation |
| Smoke | Cannabis |
| Snide | Underhand, not to be trusted, not what it appears to be |
| So Far | Inserted in the middle of a long transmission, confirming that the recipient has received the content up to that point |
| Source | Confidential origin of intelligence |
| Speed | Amphetamine |
| Stash | Hiding place |
| Subject | Suspect, during surveillance – given consecutive numbers when more than one person |
| Temporary loss | When the eyeball has temporarily lost sight of the subject |
| Time (doing time) | Serving a prison sentence |
| TFA | Tactical Firearms Adviser |
| TFT | Tactical Firearms Team |
| Third Eye | A covert officer acting as lookout/observer to cover a meeting between a police officer and someone else |
| Three Clicks | Yes. When a surveillance officer is unable to transmit verbally and wants to confirm a positive response to a question |
| TK | Telephone Box/Kiosk |
| Total loss | When the 'eyeball' has lost the Subject completely |
| Turned over | Two meanings: being the subject of a search by the police, or being robbed |

| | |
|---|---|
| | or deceived out of possession of something |
| Two Clicks | No. When a surveillance officer is unable to transmit and wants to confirm a negative response to a question |
| UC | Undercover Officer |
| U/K | Unknown |
| Unident | Unidentified person or object |
| Walk past | A walk past a suspect, vehicle or premises to confirm or establish a situation |
| Watcher | One who observes another |
| Wheels | Vehicle |
| White | Crack cocaine |
| Willocky | Unreliable, very nervous or timid |
| Windows and Doors | Working left to right, i.e. 1/1, 1/2 etc – ground floor, 2/1, 2/2 etc – first floor etc |
| (House Colours) | Positioning for containment or observation on a building using the colour clock code; clock dial – 6 at front, 12 at rear, colour; white – front, black – rear, green – left, red – right |

This book is printed on paper from sustainable sources managed under the Forest Stewardship Council (FSC) scheme.

It has been printed in the UK to reduce transportation miles and their impact upon the environment.

For every new title that Troubador publishes, we plant a tree to offset $CO_2$, partnering with the More Trees scheme.

**MORE TREES**
LET'S PLANT A BILLION TREES

For more about how Troubador offsets its environmental impact, see www.troubador.co.uk/sustainability-and-community